I0598109

Schopenhauer's Maxim

Joe Formichella

for Laura, who first asked, "if you have the guts…"

and,

for Ruby Pearl, who's *always* had them

Joe Formichella

"What is truth?"
Pontius Pilate

"To the living we owe respect,
but to the dead we owe only the truth."
Voltaire

"Convictions are a greater enemy
of truth than a lie."
Nietzsche

"All Truth passes through Three Stages:
First, it is Ridiculed…
Second, it is Violently Opposed…
Third, it is Accepted as Being Self-Evident."
Arthur Schopenhauer

"In a time of universal deceit,
telling the truth becomes a revolutionary act."
George Orwell

Typesetting and page layout: Joe Taylor
Proofreading: Maggie Slimp, Tricia Taylor
Cover design and layout: Amanda Nolin

This is a work of fiction.
Surely you know the rest: any resemblance
to persons living or dead is coincidental.

Livingston Press is part of The University of West Alabama,
and thereby has non-profit status.
Donations are tax-deductible:
brothers and sisters, we need 'em.

Part I

Joe Formichella

1.

THIS time the recorded message was different. "I know you've been getting these messages. If you're not interested in my proposal, that's fine. I would have preferred we had a chance to talk about it, but will stop bothering you if that is your wish. I'll call back one last time to get an answer, one way or another."

Jerry Weaver didn't know how to react. He hated games, was *not* good with ultimatums, and loathed waiting. Because of the message change, he no longer felt like he was in control, and that bothered him, more than a little. The calls had started at 7 that morning, a Sunday morning in April of 2005. Every hour on the hour his cell phone had rung, the view screen announced "WITH-HELD" by way of ID, he let the voice mail pick up and the same female caller said, "I have a very important project I'd like to discuss with you, a project uniquely suited to your skills. I will call you again in exactly one hour." That's it. No name, no number, just a promise to call back.

He'd spent the first few calls trying to attach a name or a face to the voice, though had been unable to discern any distinctive qualities, no immigrant accent, ESL formality, Southern drawl, Midwestern twang; no Creole lyricism, big city attitude or West Coast altitude. That didn't mean much, he knew. In his life, in both his fame and his infamy, there were doubtless scores more people who knew him, or thought they knew him, than he'd ever recognize.

No one who *really* knew Jerry though would have been surprised by his behavior. He was famous for not answering his phone. Famous. The peculiarity, in fact – something too many castigated as a weakness – was part of a body of evidence amassed in a campaign to malign and silence him a decade ago. One of his former co-workers was actually quoted saying, "He never answered his phone: he just checked messages." Seriously.

Thing is, it worked, the campaign. He was maligned, and for all practical purposes, silenced. Who's to say what part that particular charge, about not answering his phone, played in its success? Jerry wouldn't discount anything, at this point.

So why didn't he answer? His response would have been, "Didn't have to." And in the calculus of didn't have to if he didn't want to, Jerry's learned – something he considered one of his few strengths – that he avoided more risks if he didn't. Truth was, he had a weakness for those risks. Jerry Weaver was an unmitigated sucker for a good story or a fetching woman. He knew that at least. And this instance threatened both.

That being the case, the caller had to give him cause—any little thing, a name, something more specific, anything—to answer. He didn't need whoever it was. They were looking for him. If they wanted him that bad, or had any chance of getting to him, they'd figure out how, one way or another. That's how Jerry Weaver tried to work: calculated, determined, unflinching, with purpose. He would not resign nor would he be deterred. At least that's how he *used* to work. Maybe that's what the caller meant by his "unique" skill set: he didn't know when to quit, even with his entire existence being shredded around him. Jerry Weaver never learned to let it go and walk away. Back in Ohio, as a cub reporter, chasing down a black-market gasoline racket run out of city hall, that belligerence had almost gotten him killed, and eventually got him arrested, but he also got the story, busted the city manager.

"I was young," he said to the phone. Right.

Some years ago—what, six, seven, a seasoned professional by then, not quite as young, who still hadn't learned the lesson—a source told him, "You'll be killed one day if you continue to pursue this." The man then *suggested* it wouldn't happen anytime soon—"Not for five, ten years, maybe," he said—and it wouldn't be anything obvious. "Say you're driving in the mountains, coming down a steep slope," he shrugged, "and your brakes fail…"

What he was pursuing at the time was the redemption of his reputation against the campaign being waged against him. He lost that battle, but nothing worse has happened, yet. Freaked his wife out when he told her about the warning. His response didn't help. "You can't go around worrying about that kind of thing," he told her. "It might happen, it might not."

Not much of a reassurance, admittedly, but he didn't have to worry about *that* any more, at least. She'd kicked him out not long afterwards, though not because of the death promise. "Because of a female voice on the phone," he said, staring at his, finding that humorous somehow.

Well, not really, though it had been a phone conversation that led to the affair that led to the intercepted call to their home that led to the estrangement that led to the divorce. She never believed he could end the matter and find fidelity. She was right.

So here he was, another female voice on the phone, promising to call one last time. Yes, the last message had been different. But what did it mean? "I know you've been getting these messages," she'd said.

"How does she know that?" he asked.

He looked instinctively toward the windows of his Cupertino digs, as if the only way she could know such a thing was if she were spying on him. But his practice had long been to shutter and shade all the windows of his place, an attempt to insulate himself as much as possible, which was a shame. It robbed him of the lone last fondness he held for California, Bay area sunsets. He'd seen sunrises over Manhattan, Miami, Havana, and San Salvador, even sunsets over Key West. They were no match. He had always welcomed each and every one he witnessed as a glorious absolution to the day, no matter what kind of day it had been, one full of success or failure, accolade or attack. He was tempted to open the blinds and catch this day's benediction, fast approaching, but didn't.

"Why not?" he had to ask himself. And, if he couldn't, what reason did he have to remain in California? Fact was, he had none.

There hadn't really been a reason to move to the coast from Ohio fifteen years earlier, at least not a positive one. There was the job offer, sure, but mostly it was an attempt to get away from something—another female voice on the phone, now that he thought about it, another affair.

"Quite a pattern, Weave," he said. He'd never considered himself a ladies' man, but there it was.

At this point, what *could* be considered a crossroads in his life—most days it felt like anything but—he had to question whether there remained any possibility for altering those patterns, of getting on a track he wasn't consistently derailing, of really and truly starting over. Nearing fifty-five years of age, he still held on to the hope for such a thing—that is, he could still mathematically justify hoping—but it was becoming an increasingly insular effort.

Not that he minded having to work independently. Far from it. For the first few decades of his life *that* had been one of his few strengths. It was only recently that it had been wielded as a damning cudgel. No, his difficultly lay in the resulting paralysis of not knowing whether to trust instinct or *ad hominem*. Alone with that inertia, in the dusking gloom of his apartment, he waited.

"Do I know you?" he asked when that last call finally came.

"I'm glad you answered."

"Would you really have quit?"

"Sure."

"How did you know?"

"About the messages? Part hunch, part bluff, that and the fact that your mailbox didn't fill up."

"You're good."

"Thank you," she said. "Would you like to hear my proposal?"

He hesitated. As a journalist, he'd been at this juncture countless number of times, most of them a waste. And yet, every fiber of his training beckoned him to reach, because as every reporter knows, this is where the brass ring is, in the innocuous phone call that comes out of the blue. He'd had a friend back in Cleveland who'd say, "The big one," every single time his phone rang, every single time, "The big one," the story that would render every other word they wrote anecdotal. And Jerry laughed, every single time.

"Would you?" she repeated.

"Why me?"

"I think that will become self-evident."

She went on to say that if he had the guts, there were a couple of threads he could pull that would unravel not just the current administration, but the entire dynasty.

"Why would I want to do that?" he asked, out of skepticism more than anything else.

"I understand your reluctance," she answered evenly. "But I think we both know the answer to that."

"Really? What's yours?"

"I've got my reasons."

"Care to divulge?"

"No, not yet. But I know how you work. I doubt you'll have much trouble answering any questions you have."

"You seem to think you know a lot about me."

"Does that bother you?"

His sparring with her wasn't working. Normally, if you let the nutcases who called into the newsroom prattle along on their own for enough time they eventually revealed themselves as the cranks they were. The trick was stringing them out *without* really engaging, probing solely for the purpose of exposing their particular theory, giving them a chance to air it out which is mostly what motivated them in the first place. This woman was different. If nothing else, he'd learned over the years to discern and appreciate such differences.

"Why don't you tell me about these threads."

"I won't waste your time. Let me give you one question to probe and you can decide however much you want to continue."

"Fair enough."

"Sister Helen Prejean—you know who she is?"

"Of course."

"She wrote a piece for *The New York Review of Books* in January, called 'Death in Texas.' Look it up and then ask yourself, why was Henry Lee Lucas never brought up in the Governor's presidential campaign."

"That's it?"

"You'll be surprised, and disgusted, I expect. You look into it and I'll call you back in exactly a week."

"You got a name?"

"If you answer your phone next Sunday, we'll discuss that."

He stared at the disconnected phone for a moment. Clever, giving the appearance that he'd dictate his level of commitment all the while controlling all other aspects of the process. As many next steps as he might have preferred, she'd only really left him with one, or none. He couldn't help but think of a movie line, something like, "you're either very good or *very* stupid."

Typically, his immediate next move would've been to investigate whatever information he could gather about the source. She must have known that, leaving him in the dark, which was curious enough, but it was a place he did not like. He had a week to try to figure out a way to shed a little light on the situation and had all but already decided he'd go another round with this woman as he powered up his computer.

He logged onto the Dialog database, a most reliable archive of millions of newspaper and magazine articles. "If you've ever been written about," he'd been known to tell people, "it'll be in the Dialog." Sure enough, there was Sister Prejean's piece, January 13, 2005. In it she wrote about the Karla Faye Tucker case—a teen-aged drug induced revenge robbery turned to murder—and execution, an execution in which she famously—along with thousands of others, including everyone from Jesse Jackson, Pat Robertson, Jerry Falwell, to Pope John Paul and one of the Governor's own daughters—tried to intercede. She presented an argument that despite his autobiographical claim to have employed a "fail safe" method for reviewing death penalty cases and ensuring "due process" and certainty of guilt, in actuality he proved to be the deadliest executive in the deadliest state in modern American history, signing off on executions at the rate of one every two weeks over the course of his six-year tenure. She highlighted a 1997 case, of a thirty-three-year-old mentally retarded man with the communication skills of a seven-year-old. After a thirty-minute summation of the case delivered by his malfeasant legal counsel, the "compassionate conservative" denied clemency. Never mind that the jury had never heard of the man's handicap, or that the "fail safe" review omitted it as well.

When the Pope weighed in on Karla Faye's case, hizzonor responded, "Ms. Tucker's sentence can only be commuted by the Governor if the Texas Board of Pardons and Paroles recommends a commutation of sentence," disingenuously absolving himself. Publicly he was fond of telling people his decision was guided through prayer, burnishing an appearance of a law-and-order, holy rolling, good ole boy. Karla Faye was executed on February 3, 1998.

In his 1999 autobiography, he claimed the pending execution "felt like a huge piece of concrete was crushing me as we waited." But as a presidential candidate out on the campaign trail that same year he dismissed, even mocked the hubbub over the case. He contemptuously rebuffed the mere question of whether he met with any of the dignitaries or protestors who'd gravitated to Austin for audience and then proudly volunteered that he'd even refused to meet with Larry King when he'd come to Texas to interview Tucker, deriding the interview for such "difficult questions" as, "What would you say to the Governor?"

"What was her answer?" the interviewer asked.

"Please," he whimpered in response, pursing his lips in mock desperation, "please don't kill me." So much for compassion. And so much for truth. Karla Faye never uttered the phrase.

Jerry wasn't surprised by any of it. And whatever disgust he could summon for the man—or, as a friend back in Ohio referred to him, "That little man you elected president." Jerry always answered, "*I* didn't vote for him," to no avail. "No, jackass, you didn't vote at all!" which, he understood, was worse—had been used up a long time ago. And then Sister Helen brought up Henry Lee. Jerry vaguely remembered the name, something about a confessed serial killer back when he was beginning to get his journalistic chops twenty years ago. She cited the Lucas case as an example of the *actual* power a governor possessed in the death penalty process. On that instance the otherwise recalcitrant—some say blood-lusting—governor, a mere four months after the Tucker execution, intervened himself with the Texas pardons board *before* they had a chance to make a recommendation, which in turn delivered a 17-1 vote—precisely matching his number of appointees to the board—for commutation of Lucas's death sentence. The rationale? Jurors at his trial "did not know" certain facts that later came to light, such as evidence suggesting Lucas wasn't even in Texas at the time of the murder he was convicted for. No great loss, though, if Jerry read Sister Helen's comments correctly, since Henry was already serving six life sentences for other murders, "which he may or may not have committed, since on a fairly regular basis he confessed falsely to hundreds of murders." Odd, granted, and completely inconsistent with other executive behavior both before and after, but at first blush it sounded to Jerry like judicious, even—dare he say it—ethical behavior. At the very least, he didn't see anything there that would have constituted a significant campaign issue. Sister Helen was no help, as she dropped the topic as quickly as it had arisen. He was having a little difficulty, in fact, figuring out both the relevancy of the article to this woman's "proposal," and the reason for the article at all. What importance would *The Review* see in the piece so many years after the fact? The only potentially "new" information he could detect was her mention of Alan Berlow's work uncovering the clemency memos. He looked into that story.

Berlow first reported on the memos, which he obtained through a Public Information Act, in the *Atlantic Monthly* during the summer of 2003. In his reporting he painted the same cursory treatment of the "fail safe" review process as Sister Helen. The memos, Berlow wrote, assumed that if, in the appellate process, one or another of the defendant's claims was rejected there was no reason for the governor to revisit the issue, completely ignoring the fact that the justice system—the Texas justice system, espe-cially—made mistakes. Of the lone instance where the governor intervened, Berlow wrote that Lucas had been "wrongly convict-ed" for the murder that brought his death sentence, and repeated the governor's explanation for the singular deviation that the jury didn't know certain facts of the case, a claim, Berlow suggested, which could have been made in any number of other cases. The piece was repeated in 2004 and then picked up by *The Washington Post* one week before Prejean's article appeared.

"Why?"

The only reason Jerry could delve was that the gover-nor-now-president's counsel was at the time his nominee for Attorney General and whispered to be destined for the Supreme Court. Okay, but what, if any, connection did that have to the mys-terious phone calls he'd received?

"What the fuck?" Jerry said to the glowing screen, frustrated, then entered a search string on Henry. He got over eight million hits, or four times as many for Karla Faye. "Whoa."

A quick perusal of some of the items evidenced the story of Henry Lee Lucas was all over the map. He was either the most monstrous serial killer the country had ever seen, victim of government mind-control experiments, or had perpetrated the single greatest hoax on the vaunted Texas law enforcement establishment, the Texas Rangers in particular. In short, it stunk, like a moldy festering conspiracy theory, and Jerry was super sensitive where conspiracy *theories* were involved. He believed in conspiracies, all right, but knew too well the booby-traps connected to them. That was the principle smoke and mirrors used to discredit him way back when. He was attacked as a tin foil loon and no one bothered to look into his actual allegations, preferring to focus on what they thought he was suggesting. Never mind that the basic facts of his story were later substantiated. His career was already ruined. The CIA itself admitted to turning a blind eye to the drug trafficking conducted by their right-wing Latin American guerillas and that the tons of cocaine distributed in the States funded the armament *for* their insurgency. Were they also responsible for the crack epidemic that blighted urban communities across the country and decimated a whole generation of young inner-city poor as many have *always* believed? He never said that, though he doubts it was merely coincidental.

There was one niggling little piece to the Lucas story, though. Henry's commutation had been the only one doled out by the governor—who otherwise rubber-stamped over 150 other death sentences. That was a puzzle. It was reported that there were sufficient doubts about the trial evidence, and yet no re-trial was ordered. There were further disputations about the sheer magnitude of murders Lucas confessed to, but no effort to extradite him to any of those other jurisdictions. There were allegations that the governor was protecting his own involvement in a Satanic cult Lucas confessed to have contract killed for.

"Protected by keeping the man alive?" Jerry said, incredulous.

And there was the hypothesis that the move was pure politics, the governor displaying his "compassionate conservatism." But it was never played up or even mentioned in the campaign? Didn't make any sense.

He found a June 25, 1998, *Corpus Christi Caller-Times* article, "Board voting on Lucas clemency." Curiously, toward the end of the article in which two Texas district attorneys argued for and against clemency, he found this quote from the latter. "A jury of 12 citizens heard all the evidence relating to the confession and heard all the alibi evidence cited." What, then, to make of the governor's later claim that information had surfaced that the jury previously had not known? Twenty-three *different* judges over the course of a decade and a half had reviewed the case and every single one of them upheld the conviction.

Clearly, given the politically sensitive timing of the decision—readying to launch a national campaign—if the issue *didn't* come up in the course of that campaign that would indeed be odd to the point of suspicious. And yet, after trying various permutations of data searches, Jerry couldn't summon a single item where anyone probed the candidate about Henry Lee Lucas. Why not, indeed, was a very good question. Odder still, was the fact that the issue itself did come up, just not concerning Henry Lee Lucas. A June 1, 2000, *New York Times* article said the governor "Expects to Grant His First Reprieve to Killer-Rapist on Texas' Death Row." And then the second sentence of the piece reiterated that it "would be the first such stay" the governor had granted. That caught his eye. The point was technically true, but not entirely honest—surprise, surprise—for reasons Jerry couldn't begin to fathom. But his peculiar radar picked up the fine line they were dancing on. There was certainly no love lost between Jerry and the *Times*, which *may* have accounted for the signal, but he doubted it. And it proved to be irrelevant as the man was indeed executed that fall to seemingly no one's notice. This story was starting to take on a different character.

He kept probing for campaign specific examples, staying with the "one question" his caller had given him, moving onto the web in general. Astonishingly, he didn't have any success there, either, no bloggers hollering, "Why won't he answer the Henry Lee Lucas question?"

"That's what I would have wanted to know," Jerry said.

The closest he got was this: "Brownsville Satanic Cult Member?" a Sunnyvale, California dispatch after a 2000 campaign stop there.

Jerry looked toward his north-facing windows and smirked. Sunnyvale sat just a handful of miles beyond. Had he still had a beat he might have been at that event, might have gotten a chance to ask his question. Instead, he had this story, and it was all over the place, at both decidedly kooky sites and legitimate looking news portals. "Telling reporters and critics to 'stick to the issues that matter', the Republican presidential candidate declined to answer questions Monday concerning his alleged involvement in a 1984 Brownsville, TX, mass murder, in which 17 people were ritualistically murdered and skinned."

"Jesus," Jerry said. "Hell of a lead."

Further down he read that the future governor was living "near-by to and also inside the headquarters of a Satanic Cult of which he was a member." Wait a minute? 1984? In the midst of Reagan's reelection? This son of a billionaire was living in *Brownsville*? He "disappeared for three days during which all of the other of his fellow Cult Members were slaughtered." After he surfaced, the piece said, "he could not explain where he had been."

"What?"

Discussing a similar cult ranch in Matamoros, Mexico, the reporter said it was "involved in snuffing out dozens and dozens of primarily Latinos useful as 'mules' in the drug trade and controlled through sexual satanic rituals and mind-control." He then linked the operation to the Texas Commerce Bank, already implicated in drug trafficking, owned and operated by the governor's family. And then he dropped this bombshell. "One of those convicted of the satanic cult mass murders in the Brownsville/Matamoros region and elsewhere was a fellow named Henry Lee Lucas," writing that there was "no basis in law or fact for the Governor to so favor Lucas," other than a purported business connection "in respect to the drug trafficking and satanic cult operations of the Brownsville/Matamoros region."

Now she had his interest, and he understood better why she'd called him. As a former investigative reporter, keenly attuned to the nexus between covert government initiatives, black-ops intelligence and the drug trade, he quickly started seeing the outlines of a seismic story. And he wasn't necessarily happy about it, how little resistance it seemed to be offering. If he'd learned nothing else, it's that truth was a damn stubborn thing, almost an impossible thing to gain full and unblinking purchase of. Hell, even non-truth was ever more equivocating these days. Used to be truth mattered, and as such, when you saw a lie, knew a lie, you could call it a lie and people would pay attention. Not so any more. No, the lies are shoveled so fast and so furiously, truth gets buried so damn deep people don't know what to believe. So they don't believe anything, they believe people. They choose sides. And those sides just keep telling lies about each other but it doesn't matter, because once those people are believed, they can say anything they want. And if the other side doesn't like what someone's saying—if they're getting too close to the actual truth, say—they attack the person, not the thing that he's saying. That's what happened to Jerry. So he instinctively suspected any story that served "facts" up so easily. To Jerry's way of thinking, that wasn't a story so much as a whore.

For Jerry, stories had personalities, and the really and truly good ones made you work for it, teased you, tested you, strung you out, so that by the time you might be wondering just what in the hell you'd gotten yourself into, it was already too late. They captured your attention and then rebuffed you; tested your worthiness, and then tested you again. They were fetching, much like a woman. Ergo, Jerry's weaknesses. They could be bitches, but never whores. It was axiomatic, and absolutely necessary: bitches, often; never whores. And this one was giving him all the wrong vibes.

What did he know, for certain, what facts did he have? Henry Lee Lucas was the only death row inmate whose sentence was commuted by the governor, for dubious, not yet substantiated reasons, and with absolutely no follow-up action. Curious, certainly, but not yet a story. It didn't appear as though anyone ever answered for that adequately, least of all a presidential candidate in a tight election who should have been the *first* person to reconcile the story. What else? The crazy story about some Brownsville cult massacre and the rumored association of both principles with the cult.

He decided he'd ask one of those principles. Since there was probably zero chance he'd get an audience in the White House, he went looking for Henry Lee's whereabouts. He still had friends, presumably, in the Texas penal system he could call on to get him access, from his time interviewing crack dealers back in the 90s.

"Well, damn," he said, discovering, without too much trouble, that Henry died in prison from a heart attack four years earlier. But he hadn't been quiet over the years. There were at least two books and one movie about Henry's life.

Finding the books was a bit of a chore, but within a couple of days and the help of some second-hand and rare outlets, he had his hands on them. Neither of the books mentioned the governor, though both were written before he'd risen to that office—the first in 1985, in the midst of the investigations into all the murders Henry confessed to, and the other six years later when Henry's death sentence was winding its way through its motions. Neither of the books mentioned Brownsville, either, but there was considerable discussion of a Satanic cult, the "Hand of Death," and talk of a cult death ranch in Mexico, but near Juarez, not Matamoros. The first book opened with a foreword by the Texas sheriff conducting the Henry Lucas Homicide Task Force and the second one ended detailing an investigation *of* that task force, resulting from the backlash to the media frenzy surrounding Henry's encyclopedic confessions, the "Lucas Report," conducted by the state's Attorney General.

That man, Jim Mattox, opened his report by stating that his office "sought funding for a full-scale investigation" of the Task

Force "but that funding was not forthcoming." With such "limited resources and staff", though, the office produced a 231 page document detailing as best they could Henry's activities from the time he was released from the Michigan State Penitentiary on August 22, 1975, to his last arrest in Montague County, Texas, on June 11, 1983. Jerry cross-referenced the dates from the report to the books, and they checked out. What the report didn't say was that parole from Michigan came only ten years into a 20-40 sentence for killing his own mother—and then violating her corpse, as one report had it. At that parole hearing Henry was asked would he kill again if he were released. "Yes sir," Henry answered. "If you release me now I will kill again." Jerry wondered how often *that* happened, and why. He made a note to check on possible answers to those questions.

The report's introduction stated that the Attorney General's office "first learned of potential conflicts between Lucas' confessions and available evidence from Hugh Aynesworth on October 18, 1984." Hugh Aynesworth? Jerry knew that name. Most every investigative journalist alive knew that name, and would disavow *any* connection to the man. He's a man who made his name and his career on the Kennedy assassination by reportedly manufacturing his proximity to the events in November, 1963, and then deliberately obstructing or castigating anyone investigating what might have really happened that morning in Dallas, presumably motivated by the crassest need to preserve his claim to fame—he was the first to interview Marina Oswald after the president's death—and protect his government contacts. He once said on PBS as late as 1979, after so much of the official version of what had happened had been seriously challenged, "I'm not saying there wasn't a conspiracy. I know most people in this country believe there was a conspiracy. I just refuse to accept it and that's my life's work." Jerry had absolutely no use for the man or his "life's work,"—he ended up a "reporter" for the *Washington Times*, which was pretty much all anyone needed to know—and if he was the precipitating operative for the Lucas Report, whatever followed was at best, dubious. If anything, Jerry might be interested in figuring out why Aynesworth vehemently insisted Oswald, a "hard-driven, politically radical Leftist," was singularly responsible before anyone had investigated the events; why he worked so hard to influence the Warren Commission; and why he attacked Jim Garrison so viciously during his investigation. Such behavior, to Jerry, was the antithesis of investigative journalism. It reminded him of Judith Miller, and *that* disgusted him. Another time, perhaps.

It was Aynesworth who reported in the *Dallas Times-Herald* that Lucas told him he "never killed anybody but his mother," a claim that had already been proven palpably false but which, nonetheless, led to the firestorm that ignited the investigation of the investigation by the Attorney General. Why would he do that? Interestingly, Henry Lee Lucas gave probably the best clue for the answer to that question. Throughout all the furious doubts and charges of hoax swirling about during that time Henry maintained that it was the story of the supposed cult he worked for, the Hand of Death, that gave everyone the biggest problem. "Nobody wants to know about a cult," he said. "They don't want to know it exists, because if they do know it exists, they don't feel they have the power to stop it. This is what law enforcement's afraid of. I've sent them back, and they found a lot of stuff, but they never found a cult. I told the FBI whereabouts to look for a cult, and they found four to five million dollars worth of opium. But they didn't find the cult," his biographer attributed. It certainly seemed to be true.

Joe Formichella

There was not one mention of any cult in the entirety of the 231 page "Lucas Report."

Henry told the biographer that he'd been recruited for the Hand by his partner in crime, Ottis Toole, the "Cannibal Kid." Ottis was a *bad* man, and crazy. "Too crazy for execution," he once told an interviewer. And true, his death sentence was commuted and he lived out his life in a Florida pen. He did talk about his days with Henry, admitting to hundreds of murders together, the work they did for the Hand—kidnapping children for human sacrifices, young women for snuff movies, contract killings and assassinations—and the death ranches down along the Texas/Mexican border. When just such a ranch was located in Matamoros in March of 1989, the excavation revealed the remains of over a dozen ritual sacrifice victims. The discovery mirrored almost exactly the ranch near Juarez Henry had described for his first biographer in 1985, the story, he said, no one wanted to touch, throughout the hundreds upon hundreds of interviews he gave to law enforcement and media. Henry also talked about the cult's operation in Texas, trafficking in children and drugs, but never said where, exactly. Brownsville, Jerry saw, consulting a map, was less than two miles from Matamoros. Mean anything? Tough to say. But Aynesworth's "expose" came late in 1984, the same year as the Brownsville thing. He went back to that story.

But every time he accessed a link about the story he got the same copy from the same source, a guy named Sherman Skolnick. Looking into that guy was a trip. Labeled many places as one of those dreaded "conspiracy theorists," he didn't seem to shun the tag, judging from his dispatches. Jerry found waxings on everything from "Wal-Mart and the Red Chinese" to "Coca-Cola, the CIA, and The Courts." But for all his postings—easily a hundred or more—he found nothing about Brownsville. So he went looking anew, and sure enough, within a few minutes he found this, "'Refuses to dignify' mass-murder allegations," with the sub-head, "'That's not what this election is about,' he says" posted by *The Onion* on March 8, 2000, with the word for word article that was showing up in all the other places under Skolnick's by-line.

"Well, shit," Jerrry said, and closed down the screen to his laptop.

2.

HE probably should have dropped it right then. And had the phone call come soon enough after the discovery, he certainly would have. As it was, he had enough of a time lag to build up a volcanic sized sense of indignation and relished the opportunity to vent. He was a goddamn Pulitzer winner! An Ohio Investigative Journalist of the Year! He didn't slug through this kind of crap, he recalled over and over again as he paced the apartment, phone in hand, waiting for the call. This is Drudge territory, *not* Jerry Weaver.

"Who the fuck are you?" he yelled into the phone when it came.

"Call me Coyote," she answered.

He lowered the phone from his ear and stared at it. "Shit." When he raised it again, she said to him, "You found the Brownsville piece?" as if on cue.

He noticed that but did not process it, snapping instead, "You're goddamned right I did! The *Onion*?"

"Curious, don't you think."

"The fucking *Onion*? What curious? It's bullshit."

"That's what you're supposed to think."

"What the hell does that mean?"

"It means you're supposed to react to the sensationalized parody and ignore potentially damning facts of the story."

"What *potentially* damning facts?"

"From the original *Brownsville Herald* stories on the ranch."

"I didn't find anything like that."

"Of course you didn't. They've disappeared."

"Well, *Coyote*, I'm not at all interested in any cult story."

"Did you read Henry's books?"

"Yeah."

"And the 'Lucas Report'?"

"Yes."

"And you know what 4 to 5 million dollars of opium, in 1983, suggests?"

"A shit-ton of dope."

She chuckled. "At least."

"What's your point?"

"Didn't come from Kansas, Dorothy."

"*What*?"

"How does that much tar get across the border?" she asked.

"Not without sponsors."

"And you know both how that happens and what was going on at the time."

"What the fuck does that have to do with the president? At best he was a user."

"Yeah, except he says he can't *remember* whether he ever tried it or not."

"You're nuts. Don't call me again."

As Jerry was moving to close the conversation he heard her say, "His father."

"What about him?"

"You know what he was doing in 83."

"The South Florida Drug Task Force."

"Right. Yet a ton of opium is found in Texas."

There was an explosion of drug trafficking into the southern United States—stuff was airlifted into Miami, dropped into Louisiana and smuggled into Texas—in the early 80s, at precisely the time of the administration's formation of the Drug Task Force, headed up by the vice president, and its sponsorship of the Contra insurgency in Latin America, facilitated in many ways—training, arming, informing and coordinating—by the CIA, his former agency. Weave had focused most of his reporting for how that infusion was directly related to the crack epidemic in South Central LA, but his research had led him to a direct relationship between weapons bought with the proceeds of the drug trade shipped to the guerillas with the acquiescence if not the management of the agency and those planes then loaded with more cocaine to haul back stateside. And he noted a seemingly damning correlation—what should have been damning, anyway, or at least the fuel for further investigation—between the political upheavals in Jamaica and Nicaragua, both of which the CIA had an active role in, and the subsequent cocaine, then crack, epidemics hustled, primarily, by exiles *from* those countries in Miami and LA, respectively. It was well known that the agency was at least complicit in how it back-door supported the right-wing militias. Other writers had traced the genealogy, written stories about it. But they'd all been marginalized, refuted, or removed on trumped up charges. Jerry had even contacted one of them for his story, asking if they knew anything about the contras dealing drugs on the West Coast. That person hadn't, since they focused solely on the "external drug dealing activities of the contras," versus what happened internally once the drugs hit the streets. He was impressed, asked if Weave had any idea of what he was getting himself into. "You will be facing a serious counter-attack," Weave was told. Because that's what had happened to everyone who had written about the story. Still battered by the experience, it was not something he'd wish on anyone else.

"I still don't get the Henry Lee connection."

"No, you're still being cautious. I don't blame you."

"I'm inclined to walk."

"Wouldn't blame you for that either. But you got to wonder about that family penchant for conveniently not remembering things."

"Such as?"

"Such as daddy saying he can't remember where he was on November 22, 1963, when everyone alive at the time knows where they were that day, and most folks acknowledge he was in Dallas."

"You got proof?"

"Look it up."

"Another *Onion* piece?"

"I'll call you in a week, but do me a favor, get yourself a disposable phone by then."

"Are you kidd—" he started to say but she was gone.

He was *so* not interested in any cloak-and-dagger shit. Funny thing about "the big one," he knew, they didn't come in neon.

Although, he had to admit, what he considered his "big one," the South Central story, had come much the same way this one had. It had come in the form of a pink While You Were Out slip left on his desk in July 1995. He'd written a series of articles about California's "drug war," and what the state's law enforcement was *actually* doing to alleged traffickers and their possessions, a series so illuminating that the legislature abolished part of the program some weeks later. A woman was calling to tell him about her boyfriend's—a very successful "businessman," she said—experiences with the law. She thought it would be a nice follow-up story.

"We've done that story already," he told her.

There was something different about her story, she insisted. "One of the government's witnesses is a guy who used to work with the CIA selling drugs. Tons of it."

"What?"

"The CIA. He used to work for them or something. He's a Nicaraguan too."

Jerry spent the next thirteen months researching the story, it was that big. A year after that, having been reassigned to Cupertino to write about traffic accidents rather than drug traffickers, lost dogs rather than smuggling mules instead of landing a gig as an expert commentator on any one of the burgeoning cable news networks as he might have expected, he quit, ending a 20-year journalism career, so severe was the blow-back.

He trusted "Coyote" knew all that. Why then did she have any faith in him, and what made her think anyone would listen to him again? There were only two answers. She was either profoundly naïve and was wasting his time. Or there was something to the dribs and drabs she was doling him. He instinctively dismissed the former. But why? Because he desperately wanted to recapture the limelight that had been stolen from him? He couldn't answer no. "But," he said, "I don't have to answer that one at all."

Jerry'd always heard the Dallas story, of course, but never thought much of it, by itself, not even after a similar story surfaced about one of his other sons who'd insisted he couldn't remember where he'd been on 9/11, when, the story goes, he was pretty clearly in Manhattan. Again, fun shit to dig around in, but not much point to it. He couldn't say he thought any differently now, nor why he might, but he had a week to kill, so he started poking.

For the myriad versions of what happened that day in Dallas, anyone looking to forge some kind of consensus about the events had been well-warned off the story, it was that radioactive. You couldn't even mention JFK without being labeled a CTW—insider shorthand for "conspiracy theory wacko." Oliver Stone had tried in 1992, picking up the sabotaged Garrison investigation, and everyone knew how roundly he was castigated. Hasn't stopped the dozen or so since. That's not to say there hadn't been some residual effect. For all the new theories, the new evidence, the newly declassified documents, the official version never altered nor was there any irrefutable disclaimer offered to knock down the story. The smear had always been enough, somehow, based on not much more than the catch-all "plausible deniability." That tactic had thinned over the decades, so that all subsequent "rogue assassin" explanations had been greeted with ever increasing skepticism. And, predictably, but unconvincingly, such skepticism was met with the same invective. But, Jerry had to wonder, how much longer would that diminutive, "CTW," continue to pack the same punch, or would it become as eroded as "socialist" or "communist" had in their day?

Funny that the issue had surfaced again as late as less than a year earlier. Kitty Kelley had asked him about that fateful day in Dallas for her biography, *The Family*, and he'd told her he was "somewhere in Texas." Well, that was a given, seeing as how he was launching his unsuccessful campaign for senator. Jerry remembered a brief brouhaha about the "apparent evasiveness," when a sixteen year old story by Joseph McBride in the *Nation* circulated, in which the author had unearthed a November 29, 1963, memo from J. Edgar Hoover outlining an oral briefing the bureau had given two individuals the day after Kennedy's assassination on their intelligence estimate about anti-Castro Cuban activity in the wake of the tragedy, one of those being "Mr. George Bush of the Central Intelligence Agency." The story had legs because up until that moment the proffered public resume had denied any involvement of his with the agency until his appointment to the DNI by President Ford in 1976. McBride tried to follow up on the story on the eve of the 1988 election, but was told by a White House spokesman, quoting his boss, "I was in Houston, Texas, at the time," and then suggesting, "Must be another George Bush."

Not long afterward, during the party convention that summer, the *Nation* ran a follow-up op-ed furnishing further investigative evidence and calling the denial "a lie." Be that as it may, a pertinent question, for Weave, was when he said "I was in Houston" did that mean in Houston on the day of the briefing, the day after the assassination, or at the time of the memo, a week later? That question was left unanswered until, curiously, his wife's memoir came out a half-dozen years later, where she seemed to go to great lengths—quoting from a letter she was writing that very day from a beauty parlor—to situate the couple in Tyler, Texas, not Houston, a hundred and forty miles closer to Dallas. The book, as uninteresting as it was, was savaged by critics and seen as not much more than a whitewash in the aftermath of the Iran/Contra scandal, a failed presidency, and the Stone movie, and so not much ink was given to the seemingly concocted correspondence. Houston? Tyler? Who cared, seemed to be the consensus, which only prompted Jerry to wonder why he'd been steered in this direction. He dug a little deeper.

He found another FBI memo, declassified in 1993, in-between Stone and the memoir, detailing a tip called into the Houston bureau at 1:45 the afternoon of the shooting from the chairman of the Harris County Republican Party fingering a politically active student who'd been overheard "talking of killing the president when he comes to Houston." The call, the memo said, had come by "long distance . . . from Tyler, Texas." The caller then gave the names of two party staffers who might know more about the suspect, and told the agent "that he was proceeding to Dallas, Texas, would remain in the Sheraton-Dallas Hotel and return to his residence on 11-23-63," in Houston. The memo—some allege conveniently—supported the claim that he was in Tyler. But it also begged an awful lot of questions. Why did he identify a suspect who supposedly talked about killing the president while in Houston, a day earlier, and then reportedly send a campaign staffer to go to the suspect's house to pick him up and effectively provide an alibi at nearly the exact time he was making the call? Nothing became of the investigation of course, and the lamb he tried to deliver ended up instead working on his re-election campaign thirty years later. It got even weirder. The Tyler story was corroborated years later by the woman who'd been vice president of the local Kiwanis Club at the time, where, she said, the candidate was scheduled to speak. Feeling the need to admit to being a Republican herself—and pointing out that Kennedy "represented extremely opposite views" from her—she detailed what transpired that afternoon, how the featured speaker was supposed to go on at 12:30, about the same time as the shooting, but was interrupted with the news of the fallen leader, and cut his speech short. She thought that was "rather magnanimous of him," and then described his demeanor "at the time of the news as matter-of-fact and supremely well composed." Odd, granted, but surely more proof than anyone should ever need for where he was at the time of the assassination.

Still, the central question, the screaming, glaring question, of how, in the midst of everything that was going on and his own, documented activity so closely entwined with the events, how could he possibly not remember where he was that day, remained. It was reinforced, obviously.

Then Jerry got a little lucky, which scared him. In the lifespan of any investigation, there were those moments of serendipity, or luck, that both validated the project and pushed it along. Jerry was still looking for a reason to abandon this story, any reason to dismiss the crank phone calls, when he found an obscure document dump itemizing the senatorial candidate's itinerary from entering the race in late 1963 until his defeat in November, 1964. In it he found information that, to his knowledge, had never been noticed, never been reported, never been asked about before. The evening before the assassination, he indeed had been in Dallas, speaking to the gathering of the American Association of Oil Drilling Contractors at the Sheraton Hotel. He didn't leave Dallas, presumably for Tyler, until sometime the next day. He'd *already* been registered at the Sheraton-Dallas, a fact at variance enough with what the bureau agent recorded about his next day's phone call it should have sent reporters and investigators and conspiracy theorists clamoring to find exactly when he left Dallas, if he left Dallas, and what he did that morning.

"Incredible," Jerry said. "There's no *fucking* way you don't remember all that," he hollered at his computer, and then naturally wondered what could possibly be behind the equivocation—when even the attempt, for *any* public official, to suggest they didn't know where they were that day would guarantee scrutiny, what could the truth necessitating such obfuscation be? But before he could entertain exactly where that information might lead him, Jerry vowed himself off *that* story. The industry built up over the decades protecting the official JFK assassination story could run a developing country. "Suicide," he said, to any thoughts of entering that arena.

But what did it mean in Coyote's scheme? He remembered Aynesworth, and figured there had to be some connection there. He tried, over the course of the next few days, to find that connection, politically, ideologically, through Ruby, Oswald, the CIA, or equivocating news reports. His business with the bogus Warren Commission and its absolution for all the usual suspects was damning enough, but he found nothing that would lead directly back to the father, the son, or Henry Lee Lucas. He *did* find plenty of interesting information he hadn't previously known about the episode—particularly stories about the involvement of Bay of Pigs operatives that would turn up again and again in subsequent agency shenanigans, the extremely intriguing story of a Frenchman who served as kind of foster parent to Oswald, though when he appealed to the agency director for protection a decade later to call off the dogs wound up "suicided" in a Miami hotel room, the intricate and documented intersections between the dynastic family and the accused, the interference, the benefactors—but nothing that would tie it all up with the strange tale of Henry Lee Lucas. As Jerry pondered the ramifications of that information, what kind of story it might yield, he kept coming back to what it all meant to Coyote, how it all fit with her questions concerning Lucas, why, given the potentially indicting information he'd stumbled upon, she'd maneuvered this inquiry through the death row inmate? What, exactly, was her angle? It bothered him, professionally, that he couldn't begin to answer that question.

Joe Formichella

"Still believe in the lone gunman theory?" she asked, a far simpler question, when she called again.

"Hah," he answered. "Did you ever?"

"Yeah," she said. "I did. I believed, wanted to believe in our government."

"What changed that?"

"Florida. 2000."

"Really," he said. "You had a dog in that fight?"

"Didn't we all?"

"I suppose. What was yours?"

"The same as anyone's. When the highest court in the land gets involved and fucks the rest of us, we're all involved, aren't we?" she asked, setting him back on his heels.

"Yeah, but you sound like you got a personal beef."

"Some other time," she said. "What do you think?"

"Look," he said, dismissively, "the Oswald story has never really stood up."

"Nor should it."

"But I don't see what that has to do with Henry Lee."

"They did the same thing to him."

"How so?"

"All the confessions the local guys were getting, giving them info only an insider would have—weird stuff like the color of a seatbelt used to tie a victim to a tree in Alabama, the kind of socks another was wearing in Texas. And then the state shows up and the whole thing gets berserk. Henry's confessing to six different murders in six different states at the same time. They tip off a local reporter—"

"Aynesworth."

"Right. And the whole investigation goes down the tubes,

right about the time they were discovering Brownsville."

"Here we go again."

"Did you wonder about all that opium?"

"Sure, but…"

"Where does most of the world's opium come from?"

"Asia."

"Afghanistan, to be precise. Remember a little war going on over there at the time?"

"The Mujahedeen?"

"Exactly. And the CIA's cocaine running hadn't come out yet. They were working their asses off keeping a lid on all that stuff."

"How do you know all this?"

"It's all out there."

"No, I mean how do *you* know all this, why would you be compiling all this information just to channel it to someone else?"

"There's a good reason for that. If you don't know this shit, you lose. Trust me."

"I hate it when people tell me that."

"Yeah, well, tough."

"Look—"

"Yeah, yeah, I know. You don't need me. But isn't there one question you're just dying to get the answer to?"

"About Henry?"

"Yeah."

"The same question we started with, I guess: why didn't he ever come up?"

"Oh, come on. You and I both know how the news is put together."

"Still…"

"You remember the *Fortunate Son* debacle?"

"Yes, yes," he said tiredly. A 1999 biography of the governor that exposed a decades old arrest for cocaine possession that was expunged from his files. Everyone denied it and the press savaged the author after the *Dallas Morning News* broke a story about *his* criminal history, effectively killing the story. Weave remembered it sickeningly well. "Whatever became of that guy, anyway?"

"The author?"

"Yeah."

"You probably don't want to know that just yet," she said, with what Weave took for a touch of vulnerability. "Don't you have some question *you* want answered?"

"Well, sure. Why the hell didn't he kill Henry Lee when he had the chance?"

"Good question. And *that's* why you."

"What the fuck does that mean?"

"I used to think the answer to that question was because he wasn't supposed to be the one who became president."

"He wasn't?"

"No. Little brother had already been tagged, for good reason. He's smarter, smoother, nastier."

"I thought those plans changed after he lost Florida the first time?"

"Oh, hell no. They could have put in anyone they wanted to."

"Except he had Henry Lee."

"Right, who died of a heart attack not long after inauguration."

"Case closed then, right?"

"Not exactly. That's not the answer Henry Lee gave."

"What?" Jerry stammered. "The answer Henry Lee gave?"

"Yeah. A writer got in to see him between the election and his death."

"What writer?"

"You think you're the first one set on this story?"

That set Jerry back. Who was this chick? "What's his name?"

"You don't want to know what his name was."

"Was?"

"Correct. You don't want to know."

"I might."

"I don't think so. But as I say, I don't doubt you have the skills to find that out for yourself."

"Good enough. What'd he find out?"

"He didn't find out jack, but Henry smuggled a letter out to him afterward."

"No shit? What'd it say?"

"I'll send it to you."

She was starting to scare him. He couldn't say he didn't like it though. "What else?" he said.

"You need more?"

"I'll take more."

"Ah, testing me. That's good. I was wondering when you'd get around to that."

"What else?" he repeated, getting a little perturbed now.

"Hmm, what else. You want big or little?"

"I want anything you got."

"No, no. I get to play my games too. Big or little?"

"Big," he said.

"Good answer. Here's the little, and I'll even give you part of the answer: Why did he pick the running mate that he did?"

"I thought he picked himself?"

"No, not him. The father."

"Ah. To make himself look smarter was the conventional wisdom."

"Conventional wisdom is not nearly as smart as he is. No. The answer is Eli Lilly."

"The drug company?"

"No, the Civil War union officer."

"Why don't you go—"

"Give me your new phone number before you hang up."

Bitch.

3.

HIS annoyance resulted not so much from her tone—though that hardly helped—as it did from this process she was walking him through. Why bother looking into Eli Lilly? The whole world knew their sins by now. Their culpability was certainly not a "little" aspect of however they might fit into her overall scheme. But because they'd been so publicly dragged in and out of courts and slapped with settlements it seemed to him a *tiny* investigative task. Looking into Eli Lilly disinterested him as a reporter and held little or no promise of further defining that scheme, was his guess.

The giant pharmaceutical started over a century ago had been accused of everything from fraudulent research, using impoverished or incarcerated human guinea pigs, even criminal disinformation—all pretty much proven true—to price-fixing, inventing diseases, and poisoning children. One commentator he found called them, "The company that killed babies." He didn't need to go wallowing around in that stuff. He knew the stories: that they created the vaccines that caused brain damage, autism, behavioral problems; that they then manufactured the anti-depressants and ADHD medications to treat those. When one of those medicines was linked to *increased* suicide ideation—conveniently about the time it came off patent protection—they developed the next generation. When that drug was suspected of increasing the rate of diabetes, they came out with a recombinant insulin. Yeah, he'd heard all those, how they lobbied for tax breaks when they dumped unapproved drugs on third-world markets, for extending patent rights, forbidding price competition with Canada, and snuck a rider into the Homeland Security Act blocking all future litigation—with former company execs planted all throughout the administration having their fingerprints all over the bill, though no author was ever positively identified.

He knew that the inbreeding between Republican politicians and the company went back decades, specifically, when the father left his post as CIA director in the late 70's he was appointed to the board of Eli Lilly without any previous pharmaceutical experience by the company's principal stock holder, the man whose son would be tagged as *his* vice-presidential running mate a decade later. He even knew that the two orbits, if not intersecting directly, closely paralleled each for decades before that, with Eli Lilly being the primary LSD provider for the CIA's super-secret MK-ULTRA program in the 50's. A dark, sinister legacy, sure. He just didn't see how all that involved Henry Lee and why her "proposal" rested on gathering these particular, seemingly incongruent dots.

That's what was both problematic and different about this. There was no destination, no focal point, no target, no goal, just the most general of intentions to "unravel" something, whatever that might mean, however one would measure it. He couldn't even say she was giving him information, so much as vague areas of interest. For that reason, he'd have to say his training, his "skills," were completely *unsuited* to the task, so far at least. He was used to receiving a tip—by whatever means—and then using the tools of his trade to flesh the leak out toward a legitimate story or, more often than not, a waste of time. The leak itself was not the story. It wasn't even, really, a leak. It was only information given by a source that they wanted you to have. It told you nothing about the story, less about the source. It merely revealed a path to pursue, to find the truth, separate from what someone might *tell* you is true, of a story. That's where the investigative work began. He had none of that. He could either hope the next tidbit provided something more definitive, workable, or he could forget the entire enterprise.

Two days later it arrived, the bootleg letter from Henry Lee Lucas. It didn't have a return address, but it did have a postmark, from LA. He'd try to figure the significance—if any—of that later, and tore open the envelope.

February 20, 2001
Jim,

   Sorry to have taken so long to answer you. I have been very sick these last few months, very sick. I am in the hospital now, the infirmry they call it. I don't think I will be getting any better. I wanted to answer you while I could.

   It had been so long since any body asked me to talk, I needed time to think. If you still want me to talk, I will.

   At first I was mad at you for saying I hadn't found God. At first I was insult. You don't know me. If you think you know me, you don't. But God has not been nice to me, so I will talk. Maybe you are right. Maybe it was drugs, coming down, or a bad trip. I remembered there was never no drugs. Always there was drugs.

   But you asked the question no one else ever has, the only thing I want to know. Why won't he kill me? The only answer I can come to is he is a sick bastard. Now that he is Pres there is no telling what he will do. They want-

ed Carter killed. I had chances, but no excape. So I will talk. I will tell you about Texas ranch, about drugs, about Hand, any thing you want.

Henry

ps You can bring you're book if you want. They won't let me have it but maybe I can see it.

Well, that was interesting. "Who's Jim," Jerry wondered, one of several immediate questions. "What book?" was another. Most pressing, though, was, "Why would anyone have wanted Jimmy Carter killed?" And when?

It would have to had been sometime after 1975 and before 1983. "When did Henry and his partner hook up?" Varied, though most folks put it around 1979. Afghan war, Tehran hostages: killed for how he was handling those? "Unlikely," Weave thought. He couldn't think of many assassinations for ineffectiveness. Something else. "Department of Education?"

Salt II, the Panama Canal, the Camp David accords: Jerry remembered from his work that the Canal treaty had been something of a tightrope act for Carter. When it was all said and done it came out that while Panama waited for US congressional ratification, Torrijos had planned to sabotage the canal if it failed; while at home, Congressman Charlie Wilson—the same Charlie Wilson who would later funnel funds and munitions through the CIA to the Mujahedeen—threatened to sabotage ratification if Carter didn't offer more support for Somoza's failing government in Nicaragua. He'd always thought it was a rather deft handling, not cause for an assassination plot. "Besides," he said, recalling Coyote's latest directive, "how did any of that involve Eli Lilly?" Had to be something else, something deeper in that dark revolving door between the Agency, the Indianapolis drug giant and the White House.

The most identifiable marker within the nexus that he knew of was the CIA's MK-Ultra program. It was an extension of wartime intelligence efforts to find the elusive "truth serum" spooks the world over having been looking for ever since there have been spies, prisoners of war, and moles. Nothing much became of the search through the OSS's—predicate to the Agency—efforts to wrangle info out of captured U-boat mariners during World War II. When the first American took an acid trip in 1949, the brand new agency turned its attention toward the potential of the psychedelic for mind control and chemical warfare. Early experiments on mental patients, drug addicts, prison inmates and unwitting colleagues didn't dampen their expectations. The original medical literature documented users losing all their inhibitions and/ or their worst fears and phobias accentuated. What's more, the effects could be sustained for hours, even days, with a relatively small amount of the drug. Initially thought of as a possible cure for schizophrenia, they quickly discovered something of the opposite, that the drug tended to induce dissociative personality disorder: as close as they'd yet come to mind control. Perfect.

In fact, the only real obstacle they faced was getting the LSD in sufficiently reliable—and secret—quantities. At first their source was the European pharmaceutical Sandoz, which produced the drug through a slow and expensive process using an obscure fungus for the base lysergic acid. Uncomfortable with that on several levels, Eli Lilly was approached. Could LSD be produced synthetically? In 1954 they got their answer, as Lilly researchers worked an elaborate process whereby LSD could be manufactured in the laboratory utilizing common chemicals available on the open market, providing, as one agency memo put it, "tonnage quantities" for the program. Operatives started talking about being able to trip entire cities through drinking water and enveloping whole battlefields in an acid fog. Eli Lilly, for its exclusive federal funding, kept a tight track on the distribution of the drug as the agency, safely from the shadows, sponsored and funded human experimentation at scores of universities, hospitals, mental facilities and prisons around the country, often without the institutions knowing who was behind the grants, or why.

Horror stories of zombie assassins and Manchurian candidates percolated about the project for years until they bubbled to the national surface in the early 70's. The agency conducted a massive paper dump in 1973, and the program was ceremoniously shut down in 1974, without anyone *really* discovering exactly what they'd been up to. It wasn't until a single post-Watergate Freedom of Information Act request and a 1977 select Senate Intelligence Committee hearing testimony from new director Turner and other agency witnesses approved by the Carter administration—much to the dismay of one Donald Rumsfeld and other Ford-Nixon thugs—that anyone got anywhere near the truth. Was Carter and Turner's subsequent campaign to clean up the agency enough to take out the president? Jerry couldn't say no, especially since so many of the "old boys" swept up in the housecleaning ended up working in the next administration and were deeply involved in the never explained "October surprise" of 1980. There was plenty of evidence that they'd work to overthrow Carter. Would they have been plotting to take him out at the same time? Good question. And then Jerry looked to remind himself when Henry was pardoned from prison: 1975, at least ten years early, despite insisting that he would definitely kill again. A year after MK-ULTRA was shut down.

"Isn't *that* interesting," he said, and got up to mix himself a whiskey. "Convenient," he thought—the closure truncating Henry's training, say, and his being loosed on the world without precedent, without explanation, "almost, *almost*, to the point of believability."

But that was the crux, after all, what he could and couldn't believe. When he read Henry's biographic comments about following the president around for months affording him plenty of opportunities to follow through, he didn't want to believe. It didn't make sense at the time, especially when they started picking apart so many other parts of Henry's story. Everything he told authorities couldn't *possibly* be true, which called into question anything he said. But Jerry'd been around enough powerful people who did bad things for ill will to know that that's a particularly popular and effective tactic of theirs—provide enough "plausible deniability," something this family seemed congenitally prone to and skilled at, about any one aspect of a damaging story, and you could knock down the whole story. Oh, he'd seen that, as when the original Iran/Contra story broke, the downing of Hasenfus' CIA plane in Nicaragua which none other than CIA covert, Bay of Pigs conspirator, Watergate burglar Felix Rodriguez received the first notification of and reported that his very next move was to call his boss at the White House, who said he knew nothing of the operation despite documentation that he was there at the first planning meeting of the smugglers, but whose "official" log later surfaced placing him somewhere else. Oh yeah, Weave had seen that movie—and he'd seen enough psychotics like Henry Lee Lucas to know that they live in a world of delusion and fantasy, where distinctions between true and false, good and bad, real and fantasy didn't at

Joe Formichella

all have the same meaning as most of the world. Those types took a little bit of truth, mixed it with a pinch of fantasy and a heaping helping of what they thought you wanted to hear and came up with a finished version that not only defied verification, but quite likely would change from moment to moment. There was even a name for it: confabulation. Still, though, what he always tried to remember, to remind himself of, was that "little bit of truth." What, exactly, was the little bit of truth to Henry's story?

Sometimes, Jerry learned, questions had to be pursued. And sometimes they had to be allowed their own course, whether or not they came back to you. At all times, he remembered, from better times, gazing through a parted curtain of his apartment window out at the lights of Cupertino, it was not his conscious choice. He had to leave it alone, let it decide, and the best way he knew to let go of a question to see which way it went was to grasp onto something else, often a cold, wet whiskey sour.

When she called the next day Coyote asked, "What do you think?"

"I don't know if I'm buying all this CIA, MK-Ultra, Carter shit."

"Oh, honey, that's just the beginning of the shit."

That amused him, some, and settled him down, a little. "Who's Jim?" he asked.

"I'd rather not say just yet."

"Why not?"

"I don't want you to get spooked."

He thought about that, uneasily. "Then what's this book Henry was interested in?"

"He wasn't interested, really. Jim had offered it to show that he was fair-handed, wasn't a hatchet man."

"What's the name of it?" She had to know she couldn't fend him off forever.

"You really want to know?"

"If you want me on this thing, yeah, I think I need to know."

Her silence lasted several moments before she told him, "*Fortunate Son.*"

"Oh shit," he said, and reflexively threw the cheap phone against the wall, shattering it.

He'd done a little research on James—Jim—Hatfield in the interim. When his record was splashed across the nation's headlines in the blowback to his book, his publisher, St. Martin's, recalled and burned all copies of *Fortunate Son*. Several weeks later a small underground imprint, Soft Skull Press, the self-styled "punk of publishing" announced that they were going to re-publish it. On the way to the presses, though, Hatfield was still being warned off the story, even though the process had dragged on through 2000, past the election, and on into 2001. On May 31, 2001, he told an interviewer, "Not one single statement in *Fortunate Son* has been disproved during the past year and a half. What truly worries me and wakes me up in a cold sweat during the middle of the night, is what one of my confidential sources for the cocaine arrest told me when it was announced that Soft Skull press was going to re-publish the book less than 3 months after St. Martin's Press recalled it: 'Jim, we're not done discrediting you. The wheels are already in motion for more of the same.' Then he went on to say if I 'valued the lives' of my wife and baby daughter, 'then you'll cancel this publishing deal right now, today.'" Four days later Hatfield revealed the name of one of those sources, an operative very high up in the new administration and already infamous for his no-holds-barred approach to politics, life, and any opposition whatsoever. Two weeks later Hatfield was dead, found in an Arkansas hotel room. Official cause of death? Suicide.

She called him back on his primary phone. "You still got the guts for this?"

"I'm going to need to know more about you."

"I'll think about that, but too much overlap is dangerous for both of us."

"Well, if I wind up dead," he told her, "it won't be suicide."

"Good," she said, laughing softly. "So you're in?"

"Still in, yes."

"Fair enough, because the pharmaceuticals weren't done."

"Ask your doctor."

"Seriously. They're a lynch pin."

"To what?"

"Check out a certain Texas congressman's July 1969 intelligence committee investigating the scourge of 'black babies,' and then a Pentagon budget request for $10M a month later to R&D a synthetic infectious agent, and then a 1974 State Department 'National Security' memo on the 'political consequences of current population factors in LDCs'—that's 'Less Developed Countries' for you civilian types."

Weave was scribbling notes as fast as he could. "Why don't you just tell me what I'm looking for."

"That depends on whether you believe HIV was a natural occurrence."

"Versus what, man-made?"

"Exactly."

"Come on, Coyote—that's not *really* your name, is it?"

"Tell you what, you figure out that riddle and I'll tell you anything you want."

He laughed. "What kind of credibility could I hope to have by going there?"

"Don't mean to be cruel, but how much do you think you have going in?"

That stung, and angered him. He hadn't lost his credibility, it had been taken from him, without any substantiation. He'd broken the biggest story of the 90's, and rather than follow his lead—a lead that was later confirmed—his colleagues—his *colleagues*—had ravaged his personal life, digging into past improprieties, past newsroom confrontations, past infidelities, all of it completely irrelevant to the story, just like Hatfield, and just like anyone else that's tried to investigate the agency. You get put through what's known in the business as the buzz saw.

"Do you know the epidemiology of AIDS?"

"The what?"

"The epidemiology, where it first showed up, how it spread."

"I've heard varying histories, from the 80s in humans to back in the 50s in chimps."

"All lies. And the history of AIDS is unlike any other infectious disease. The first ever reported cases were in a New York City homosexual population, every one of whom had received a Hepatitis B vaccination. Next, a year later, it blew up in sub-Saharan Africa a year after a widespread UN small-pox vaccination program."

"Wait a minute," Weave stopped her. "Do you know what you're saying?"

"I sure fucking do," she snapped. "Do you know what you're hearing?"

"How the hell do you prove something like that, get people to believe it, or even consider it?"

"Only matters if you believe it."

"All right, how do you get me to believe it?"

"I don't think that's the question. If you think it's possible, you'll find the evidence, or you'll disprove it."

"Then what is the question?"

"Why *don't* you think it's possible?"

"And I guess you've got an answer for me or something else to 'look into.'"

There was another long pause on the line. "You don't think they're capable of flat-out lying about being complicit in an event where people die?"

"I wouldn't have much of a job if I thought that," he said, and immediately regretted it, since he didn't need to give her an opportunity to remind him that he didn't have any kind of job.

But she let it slide. "An event like TWA 800?"

"You seriously think that was intentional?"

"Nobody ever *said* that. And it may very well be that HIV wasn't either. The point is, they *lied*!"

Jerry was quiet this time. "I get your point," he finally said.

"Get another phone," she said and hung up.

When TWA Flight 800 blew up in the sky over Long Island on the evening of July 18, 1996, killing all of the 200 some people on board, every single one of the scores of eyewitnesses—pedestrians, professionals, military and law enforcement—said they saw a surface to air streak hone in on the plane and blow it out of the sky, a streak and an occurrence that could only be explained by a missile. The NTSB, however, first speculated that an explosive device had been planted on board. When no evidence of that was found they floated their mechanical malfunction—a mysterious electrical short igniting an empty forward fuel tank, that caused the mid-air explosion, without any explanation for the aft impact point, the missing rows of seats at that point, and the incendiary damage to the recovered bodies in those seats. They then set about squelching any other investigators, withheld evidence not supporting their theory, and prosecuted journalists poking holes in the theory. They lied about FAA radar logs, lied about missile propulsion residue found on the wreckage—first that it was there, then what it was composed of—and lied about any military presence in the area at the time. And when that didn't stick, they lied about the number, nature, and mission of that military presence. They lied, and held to their story. To this day they hadn't told the truth. Hundreds of innocents perished; a handful of journalists had their careers ruined or irrevocably altered, all because the military couldn't admit to a horrible mistake, which, with each passing day, looked less and less like a mistake.

Much, *plenty* had been written about TWA 800, by reputable people in the business, people Jerry knew, to no avail. Not so, he found, on Coyote's allegations about HIV, which, *prima fascia*, fit perfectly with the characters involved. They were *very* good at burying paper trails, creating distractions, and, their favorite, manufacturing plausible deniability. They'd elevated it to an art form. Some salient facts, though, couldn't be disappeared. The congressman who campaigned in 1964 against Civil Rights chaired a "Republican Task Force on Earth Resources and Population," examining, especially, how allegedly runaway birth-rates of African-Americans were "down-breeding" the American population. That same summer Pentagon official Donald MacArthur went before a Congressional committee asking for $10M to develop, "over the next 5 to 10 years, a new, contagious micro-organism which would destroy the human immune system." Five years later a State Department "National Security Study Memorandum 200," which wasn't declassified until sixteen years later, said, in part, "The political consequences of current population factors in the LDCs [Less Developed Countries]—rapid growth, internal migration, high percentages of young people, slow improvement in living standards, urban concentrations, and pressures for foreign migration—are damaging to the internal stability and international relations of countries in whose advancement the US is interested, thus creating political or even national security problems for the US." They saw this as not in the country's "best interests," and sought to "achieve a replacement level of fertility." And almost exactly ten years after his budget request, McArthur told a group of international bankers, "We can begin with the most critical problem of all, population growth. As I have pointed out elsewhere, short of nuclear war itself, it is the gravest issue that the world faces over the decades immediately ahead," he said. "If current trends continue, the world as a whole will not reach replacement-level fertility—in effect, an average of two children per family—until about the year 2020," which is not a world McArthur wanted to live in, with its "poverty, hunger, stress, crowding and frustration" rampant in the developing nations—"which by then would contain 9 out of every 10 human beings on earth." There were only two mechanisms by which such a catastrophe could be averted, according to McArthur. "Either the current birth rates must come down more quickly. Or the current death rates must go up." Enter AIDS, that very same year, 1979.

"Jesus," Jerry said, rubbing the ache around his eye sockets. He was both compelled to dig further, and nauseated by what likely awaited him.

When Coyote next called, she asked, "What's the number?"

He told her.

When that phone rang, he said into it, "What do you want me to do with all this?"

"Write the story."

"That the Pentagon manufactured HIV?"

"You refuse to see the bigger picture."

"What bigger picture?"

"Let's just say HIV was a happy accident. Did you look at everything else they've been into? Is diabetes an accident? Autism?"

"But why?

"De-population."

"You can't prove that."

"No? Take a look around: who's getting sick, who's fighting their wars, who're the refugees, who suffers the natural disasters and famines, who's in the prisons, who got out of the World Trade Center and managed to take their money with them? You need more proof?"

"Yeah, you need proof-proof."

"Ever heard of Occam's razor?"

"*Yes*, I've heard of Occam's razor," he said, not hiding his disdain. "But if it's so obvious, how come nobody else is blowing that whistle?"

"Who's that journalist you like to quote, George Seldes? Remember what he said: 'it *is* possible to fool all the people all the time—when government and press cooperate.'"

She stunned him yet again.

"They've been at it for almost a hundred years. They're getting very good at what they do, Florida 2000, Alabama 2002, Ohio last year. And they're sure as hell not going to stop now."

"Unless someone speaks up."

"That's right."

"And says what, exactly?"

"That it's evil, for one."

"That always works."

"And they're wrong, as usual. It's not overpopulation that causes poverty. It's the other way around."

"Good luck selling that one."

"You want easy, go back to the city council meetings. We're talking about the whole damn system."

"Why me? Why not you?"

"Because of who you are, your past."

"I should think that'd be an indicator of why *not* me."

"That thing they accused you of, the accusation you never made, why do you think they went there?"

"What, the inner-city thing? Maxine went there, not me."

"Not before they did."

"Doesn't matter. They buried me with it."

"Exactly. But did they bury you because you were wrong or too close to right?"

"I'm telling you, it doesn't matter. Nobody cares."

"She cared. You care."

"So what? Nobody's interested in what I have to say."

"You don't really believe that."

"Oh, I don't?" he said, all but fed up with her presumptuousness.

"It's too big for you to see," she said, mysteriously, and a little deflated.

"Your de-population theory?"

"That's only half of it."

"What's the other half?"

"What did you tell your mother last year?"

"My what?"

"Your mother. You were upset, depressed, didn't know what you were going to do with your life. Your bike had been stolen, you'd lost your house. What did you tell her?"

He stood there in stony, bewildered silence.

"You said, 'All I want to do is write.' That's all I'm asking."

"Who are you?" he said. "How the hell do you know all this? I don't want to talk to you anymore," and hung up.

But it was true. He had nothing at the time, the previous holiday season. He'd been beaten down to a shell—the self-assured, tireless workaholic who'd *never* failed to elicit some kind of reaction from anyone and everyone who crossed his path, had gone begging for a job—he'd sent out almost a hundred resumes to dailies across the country but didn't get a single response. And then he wound up at his mother's, a middle-aged, drop-out, pariah to the only profession he ever loved, tucking his tail and going home. It had been humiliating, and nearly crushed him. The only thing that kept him going was he *knew* he could write. In fact, having been reduced to such a minimally acceptable existence, he rebounded on that one piece of knowledge. The only thing he was left with was the only thing he wanted, his writing. He took the cheap apartment and vowed to pen his own path back to relevancy.

But it hadn't been going well. The story was so old at that point no one was much interested. His only gig had been an essay for a collection of first-hand accounts from other likewise marginalized journalists, *The Myth of the Free Press*, but that had hard-

Joe Formichella

ly been satisfying, though the title, "The Mighty Wurlitzer Plays On," tickled him, as always. In the piece, though, he recounted his disillusion with the profession. "If we had met five years ago, you wouldn't have found a more staunch defender of the newspaper industry than me," he told readers. "And then I wrote some stories that made me realize how sadly misplaced my bliss had been." The reason, he admitted, that he'd avoided the buzz saw for so long, was not because he'd been so careful and diligent, had been so *good*. "The truth was that, in all those years, I hadn't written anything important enough to suppress."

"*That's* where she found the Seldes quote," he remembered suddenly, and decided it was past time he tried to find out what he could about Ms Coyote.

"Mom, it's Jerr."

"Hi, honey. How are you?"

"I'm fine. Listen, do you know anyone goes by the name Coyote?"

"I don't think so," she said slowly.

"Anybody calling there asking about me, a woman?"

"Yes, yes there was. A few weeks back, as I recall."

"You get a name?"

"Well," she thought, "no, I don't guess I did. She said she wanted to talk to you about a writing job, I got so excited I forgot to ask. I'm sorry."

"That's all right."

"Then she called you?

"Yeah, a few times."

"And?"

"We're still working out the details."

"Good. I'm so happy for you."

"Thanks mom. I'll talk to you later."

So that's how she got that other info. He'd check his mother's phone bill next chance he had, but didn't expect it to reveal anything. Then he wondered how easily caller id could be blocked and how. He called an old friend at the phone company for answers to those.

"Oh, yeah, piece of cake," he said. "They got apps that can do that, knock-offs of the apps, and knock-offs of the knock-offs, SpoofCard, FoneFaker, you name it."

"And you can't get around them?"

"No way. In fact, it's pissing the man off so much there's talk of amending the 1934 communications act making the things illegal."

"No shit?"

"No shit."

"Thanks Pete."

No help there. What else did he have? "Occam's Razor," he answered, and went searching the obvious, just in case.

Coyote. *Canis latrans*. Predominantly North American, "Which is good," considering his budget. Popular figure in Native American folklore, variously depicted as a trickster or a cultural hero, usually a male figure, paired against the female bear. "Great," he said. If ever more information was less help, this was it. What was he dealing with, a "nativist" hero or a meddling jackal?

What else? Not much, that he could think of. Was that because she'd covered her tracks so well? Or had he lost his edge? He'd never before wandered into a situation so defenseless, and so exposed. "How's that working out for you, Weave?"

And, he had to wonder, what did he have to fear from that?

"Nothing," was the obvious answer, the Occam's razor. He had no real vulnerabilities. He looked around the apartment, bed/bath, living room masquerading as an office, kitchen nook. He had nothing on the walls, boxes still packed, a coffee maker and the computer. He had nothing but his writing. He thought back to the "Wurlitzer" piece, his confession, and Coyote's question, "Did they bury you because you were wrong or too close to right?"

It had been a most unusual phenomenon, that summer of '96. The series broke in between the Republican and Democratic national conventions, into a political black hole. None of the big players paid it any attention, for weeks, while it exploded in inner cities, across the AM radio dial, television talk shows, ultimately the Congressional Black Caucus—all of whom believed that the reporting proved what they'd suspected for years, that the crack cocaine epidemic and its attendant "war on drugs" was at the very least government complicity in the decimation of a whole generation of African-Americans, if not deliberate genocide. One DJ particularly rabid about the story, repeatedly pointed out that every single black person in the country was either on crack, had a family member on crack, was selling crack, imprisoned, or had been felled by the violence surrounding the trade. "Every single one!" He then asked his audience, "Where did all that cocaine come from? We don't grow it here? How does that much cocaine cross the border *without* government knowledge?" Jerry always thought it a fair question.

His defense, and that of his editors, until they abandoned him, had been that he never said that. And the attack, when it did come, in early October, seized upon that particular point. Rather than pick up the story and try to advance it—as everyone involved fully expected—the big news organizations, in an unprecedented manner, ravaged *him*, for irresponsibly inflaming the black community with unproven and unsupportable allegations, for relying on convicted criminals as sources, for not providing enough of a rebuttal platform to those he accused, completely, it seemed to him, missing the story. He never even hinted the CIA was dealing crack in South Central, but that was pretty much the entry point for the deconstruction of his story and he was left with trying to disprove a negative, find saints in a sinners' game, standing alone against a colossus with a history of being able to bring down anyone in the world any time it wanted to for whatever reason. He'd never spent much time considering how close he'd cut to the bone. He'd been obsessed with substantiating his original thesis—which, most everyone thought, even, later, the CIA itself, he had, not that it mattered. The damage was done. And yet here he was again. He had nothing left to lose, he thought, giving another quick survey of his surroundings, "Just my life," he said, smiling, settling his gaze on the twin cell phones next to his computer.

"What's the worst that could happen?" he said—a threshold he's relied on for much of his life, with few regrets—sat and powered up the laptop.

4.

ONE answer to the Black Eagle's radio rant was that cocaine
had been marketed in the country for decades upon decades. If
you picked up an 1890s era Sears & Roebuck catalogue you'd
see a syringe and dose of cocaine offered for $1.50. What's more,
even after it was outlawed for recreational use in 1914, it was
still distributed and consumed as the stealth secret ingredient rumored to be responsible for Coca-Cola's "kick," until 1989, at
least in its domestic product. While the circumstances regarding
that Harrison Act of 1914 were interesting, but not surprising, they
weren't much use. In 1900 the *Journal of the American Medical
Association* published an editorial claiming that, "Negroes in the
South are reported as being addicted to a new form of vice—that
of 'cocaine sniffing' or the 'coke habit.'" Newspapers and pros-
elytizers picked up the "revelation" and began circulating stories
that "cocaine use caused blacks to rape white women and was
improving their pistol marksmanship," two bogeymen certain to
bring swift congressional action.

"Can't have sharp-shooting black rapists running around,"
Jerry said.

Although, he saw, in one of the earliest congressional commit-
tees investigating cocaine use, hardly any of the expert witnesses
thought the habit was addictive to anyone, much less gun-toting
randy southern "Negroes." Few gathered in the hearing room of

the Rayburn House Office Building shared the concerns of the committee's chair, congressman Tennyson Guyer of Ohio, that, "This is a drug which, for the most part, has been ignored, and its increased use in our society has caught us unprepared to cope effectively with this menace." Quite the opposite, the consensus was rather that cocaine snorting was no more menacing than a couple of martinis. It didn't give you a hangover or alter your consciousness. Doctors noted a conspicuous lack of dependency on the drug. Their testimony suggested only that cocaine use merely made you feel great while it helped you keep the pounds off. Besides, it was so chic, which was maybe the principal beef for Mr. Guyer, an ultraconservative aghast that references to the drug's use were showing up in movies, songs, and newspaper stories, mostly in a positive light.

"Recent developments concerning the state of cocaine have come to my attention, which call for decisive and immediate action!" he bellowed as he opened the Cocaine Task Force of the House Select Committee on Narcotics Abuse and Control in July of 1979. "The availability, abuse, and popularity of cocaine in the United States has reached pandemic proportions," he said. Not necessarily so, witness after witness retorted. At best, they told him, if the drug magically became much, much cheaper—than $2,500 an ounce—it could pose a threat. Otherwise it was just a "naughty pleasure" for an exceedingly tiny segment of society.

"The so-called elites and intellectual classes," the chairman sneered.

There was one witness in the gallery who shared congressman Guyer's sense of alarm, though, but not for the same reasons. When Dr. Robert Byck, a professor and drug researcher from Yale, stepped to the witness table, after being welcomed by Guyer

Joe Formichella

and complimented for his "very, very impressive" credentials, he said, "What I would like to talk to you about for the most part is the importance of telling the truth." That truth was not what Guyer wanted to hear, however. "Cocaine," Byck said, "doesn't have the kind of health consequences that one sees with drugs such as alcohol and cigarettes." As it was commonly used in America, cocaine, in his estimation, "is a very safe drug."

"I think we make a mistake when we say that snorting cocaine every once in a while is a dangerous habit and is going to kill people, because it does not," he told the committee. "There are a great many people around who have been snorting cocaine and know that their friends haven't gotten into trouble. If you tell those people that cocaine is very dangerous, they won't believe it. Then, when you get to the next step—when you are talking about something that is really dangerous—they are not going to believe you the second time." That next step, the reason he consented to testify, was a veritable cocaine "epidemic" first documented in Peru five years earlier.

For most of a year a police psychiatrist in Lima, Dr. Raul Jeri, had been screaming that drug users there were being driven insane by cocaine. Dr. Nils Noya, a psychiatrist in Bolivia, started making the same claims in short order. Jeri said the epidemic swept through Lima's fashionable neighborhoods in 1974, spread to other Peruvian cities and then to Ecuador and Bolivia. Their siren calls garnered scant credence. After all, natives had been chewing on coca leaves for thousands of years. But this was an entirely new and unheard of application of the drug. Instead of munching the raw leaves for their medicinal effects, and instead of snorting the processed powder as America's sophisticates were, these users were smoking a cocaine paste, the gummy residue left over in the process from the former to the latter. They were drying the goop, crumbling it into cigarettes and smoking it. The high was four times as potent, instantaneous, but short-lived. No other drug in existence was as pleasurable as this *basuco*, according to users. But the bliss only lasted a few minutes and unless it was regained through another hit of the stuff, quickly, a suffocating depression would set in. Jeri likened these users to sufferers of a malignant disease. "It is hard to believe to what extremes of social degradation these men may fall, especially those who were brilliant students, efficient professionals, or successful businessmen," he wrote. "Those individuals became so dependent on the drug that they had practically no other interest in life."

Byck, among others, was skeptical of the reports. But then in 1978 he sent one of his med students, David Paly, down to Peru to study the leaf-chewing natives. Once in country, Paly was quickly hooked up with Dr. Jeri, who arranged tours of the neighborhoods, middle-class neighborhoods, where the stench of cocaine hung heavily in the air and thousands of otherwise bright young men who had abandoned their lives to smoking cocaine were exhibiting all the behavior of heroin addicts. Shocked by what he saw, Paly called back to his mentor at Yale and warned him, "If this shit ever hits the U.S., we're in deep trouble."

The alarm bells from South America were sounding up and down the continent as the practice spread northward. That's why Byck was speaking before congress a year later. He was adamant. "Here is a chance for the federal government to engage in an educational campaign to prevent a drug abuse epidemic," but only if they acted "as rapidly as possible."

But the feds had another idea. The DEA planned to ask the Peruvians and Bolivians to please quit growing coca plants.

"I don't think you can eliminate the growing of coca in Peru and countries which have had it for thousands of years," Byck laughed.

Guyer asked if crop substitution might work.

"I don't think so."

Guyer persisted.

"It *can't* work," Byck finally snapped.

Guyer promised they'd get back to the issue as the committee hurriedly scattered for a break, but they never did. Instead, members wanted witnesses to speak to whether Hollywood cocaine use was contributing to the degradation of what was passing for television.

In effect, Congress listened to Byck's dire warnings and responded, "Yeah? So?" and embarked on their foolish and impotent "Andean strategy" to wipe out the coca plant. Thirty-six months later the earliest references to "ready-rock" cocaine showed up in LAPD files—which means it had already hit the street a good year, year-and-a-half before that—and inner cities across the nation were on the way to ruination, if not through crippling addiction, then death at the hands of the competing dealers or incarceration courtesy of Reagan's "war on drugs" which levied sentences ten times as harsh for crack users and pushers than their powder counterparts.

"Jesus Christ," Jerry said, leaning back from the monitor. When he overlapped the time-lines of all of this shit—Eli Lilly, the agency, HIV, crack—it's no damn wonder his story caused the stink it did. He didn't yet know how interconnected it all was, and seriously doubted how much could ever be proven, but one thing was certain. They knew. They damn sure knew and any protestation to the contrary was nothing but a fucking lie. "Jesus," he said again.

The most important next questions were what did they do with that knowledge, and why? As to the former, Reagan's response to the crack epidemic was his infamous "war on drugs." The results of which were achingly evident. His successor's response to AIDS was to call for "behavioral changes"—tone-deaf, wrong-headed, and heartless, as usual. As to the question of why, the most obvious answer was nothing less than chilling. It was documented that population control of the Third World was an official objective of the United States State Department by 1974—abetted, funded, and egged on by many of the cast of characters dabbling in eugenics under one rubric or another all the way back to the 1920s, and before—the same year, 1974, *basuco* was discovered decimating young Peruvians and five years into the Pentagon's program to manufacture an "infective microorganism which could differ in certain important aspects from any known disease causing organism," most importantly, one that "might be refractory to the immunological and therapeutic processes upon which we depend to maintain our relative freedom from infectious disease."

"Did you talk to your mother?"

"I'm glad you called."

"Did you think I wouldn't?"

"All I know is it was out of my hands, which sometimes makes me skittish."

"Well, you're forgiven."

"You don't vary the formula much, do you?"

"Not when it's this important."

"Agreed," he said, ready to relax into Coyote's structuring. "But I have to ask, why is all this so important to you?"

"What do you think the answer to that could be?"

"They've got, or gotten to, someone you care about."

"Good," she said.

"You sure you want *me* on this?"

"You just proved you're the one."

"Don't know if I agree with that."

"Why not?"

"I just don't know how comfortable I am with making some of these crazy allegations; don't know how the hell you can prove some of this stuff. I'm a journalist, right, and that's not generally how it's done. And, I found out, remember, once they smell any unsubstantiated charge, that's when the pile-up starts."

"What do you mean that's not generally how it's done? Plenty of folks do it all the time."

"Yeah, I know, I know. But the question is always, what's the profit of stooping to that level?"

"Sacrificing integrity?"

"It's not a bad thing."

"You sure about that?"

He'd never been asked that before.

"Here's the difference," she said before he had to answer. "They *know* they're lying. We don't. We don't have any idea of what might be true or any way of finding out until we put it out there and it gets shot down, or not. All we've got are some scary suspicions, plenty of questions, and a lot of hideous looking circumstantial evidence. Does it add up to truth? I don't know. I do know it doesn't add up to nothing."

"Still, we can't just say *anything* we want."

"Isn't that exactly what passes for journalism these days? A bullshit claim or talking point is concocted by some opposition operative or in somebody's communications bunker and passed around between the focus groups and talkers and bloggers and shills. The media sniffs around for the latest stink or bends its ear for the loudest ill wind, and forwards the story as somehow legit by reporting 'some say' blah, blah, blah, giving a spokesperson in the target camp a chance to call the bullshit actual bullshit and it becomes news without anyone having to do any investigating, without having to source anything. And if there's a poll available to put numbers to how the 'American people' feel about the 'controversy', all the better. That's enough to land you in at least one cable green room."

"What if I told you I don't know how to do that?"

"I'd say bully for you, but it's about time you learn."

"How am I supposed to go about that at this stage?"

"Same way you always learn something new. Go back to the beginning."

"She said."

"Fine, if you feel that way. You've seen the info. What *should* be done with it?"

"Good question," he said. "Just for kicks, what kind of writing did you have in mind?"

"You're the better person to answer that, aren't you? Newspapers are probably out."

"They won't touch me even *with* proof."

"You've got an agent, though, right?"

He did, or used to, and wasn't, for the first time, taken aback by how thoroughly she'd set about her task. Actually, he found himself wanting to meet this Coyote more than he needed to find out who the hell she was. It made him smile.

"I'll put out a feeler."

"Now you're talking."

At least he was on more comfortable turf, taking such initiative. He could write a query, or memo. Every important story he'd ever worked on began with such a memo—designed to pique interest, foremost, but also garner enough time and space to ferret out the story he'd thought he'd stumbled onto. Once the initial interest was there, he knew, it was only a matter of doing the research and grunt work necessary to bring the promise to fruition, something else he was very good at. Maybe that's what Coyote meant by his "unique skills"?

Al,

 Thirty years ago it became official US policy and concern to address worldwide overpopulation, especially in developing countries, especially developing countries rich in those natural resources dwindling in other, industrialized parts of the world. Poverty in those regions of the world was viewed as the source of the problem. According to their calculation, the higher the poverty rate, the denser the population. At no point did these policy makers consider the elimination of poverty as an answer. Greed and altruism never cohabit. These were, after all, the same men who had risen to power in opposition to Johnson's "Great Society." No, their solution to this threat was simple, Manichean: depopulation had to be pursued, urgently, through either decreased birth rates or increased death rates. What followed then, were bloody coups in Brazil, Indonesia, Chile and Nicaragua—with the imposition of ruthless, CIA-backed dictators, ruinous economic policies, hyper-inflation, unemployment, starvation and staggering poverty—HIV/AIDS, the crack cocaine epidemic, and super-power wars of aggression in some of the poorest countries in the world, hundreds of thousands of people diseased, arrested, disappeared, tortured and killed, strengthening economies across the Southern Cone and Asia deliberately destroyed, social safety nets eliminated and vast swaths of public functioning and public commons auctioned off wholesale to multinational corporations. What if there's a causal connection?

Many of the men responsible for these policies back then are once again in seats of power—the only difference being now they're in the foreground—being "led" by a man whose dynastic strain and attendant lust for power— at whatever costs—dates back generations. What if I told you that the state of the world was no accident, Al, from the constant warring to the explosion of predatory capitalism, the obscene wealth divide to the crushing poverty? And what if I could show that dynasty, with a handful of enablers and stooges rotating in and out of their ranks, has been deeply involved in it all clear on back to the earliest of eugenics societies of the Jazz Age? Would you be interested?

You know how to reach me, Al. All the best,
JW

Now all he had to do was wait; like fishing: choosing the best spot, appropriate bait, and putting it into play. It didn't take long.

"I'd say you're fucking *crazy!*"

"Hi Al. Nice to hear from you, too. How've you been?"

"You got a death wish?"

"Al."

"You trying to kill me?"

"Al."

"Do you *know* who you're fucking with, Jerr?"

"But what if it's all true?"

"True? Since when did that matter? They'll kill you."

"Al."

"They'll kill me!"

"Al."

"They'll kill anyone that publishes this, not that that's ever going to happen."

"Why not?"

"Because it's *you*."

"So?"

"Jerr, are you serious? Look, you got a history. And even if by some miracle I could sell this on spec—which I can't—you know as well as I do that as soon as they figure out what they're sitting on, they'd privish this thing so goddamn fast no one would *ever* read it—which is a good thing. They'd be saving lives."

"So you're interested?"

"Don't do this to me Jerry."

"I got an idea."

"Jerry, I got kids."

"What's the date?"

"The date? Jesus. It's May 20th."

"Good. Give me a couple of months. I'll send you a package."

"I'll update my will."

In what way would truth *not* matter, Jerry wondered, peering through the cracked blinds of his apartment window. He wasn't naïve. He knew what a slippery notion it was and how cavalier people—people pursuing or preserving power, especially—used and abused facts to shade truth to their advantage. In principle, though, in *principle*, what kind of world could we hope for if we didn't acknowledge that there is, in most cases, *a* truth to be discovered and that it very much *does* matter? It is still preferable to operate through facts toward truth, isn't it?

He backed away from the window, felt almost pushed backwards from the reverberations of just how tenable that stance might actually be. What if, he wondered, the axiom he'd *always* lived by—that the truth would eventually win out—wasn't true? It was a crushing, suffocating thought. Never one to be bullied long, Jerry suddenly realized his larger task, examining those questions.

"Yeah, great, but how do you do that?" he said out loud as he commenced the pacing that in years' past had almost always been the first gestational step toward an idea.

What seemed like hours upon hours later, he checked the locks on the door, turned off his phones, and sat down to write.

5.

January Nineteenth
by Anonymous

LIKE most other houses large or small—like most everyone everywhere, really—Salt City Publishing lived off their back-list. Other people called it their laurels, their fame, their "glory days"; for publishers it was their backlist. Nothing wrong with that, so long as you've got one. Salt City did. They were one of the first to publish Raymond Carver when he was at Syracuse University for one. But just as lucrative was their hefty collection of calendars and bookmarks and political cartoon books that sold a couple of thousand copies year in and year out. Enough to make their nut. Otherwise, they were down to just two or three new titles each catalogue.

"And that's shrinking," Settle had told him. Times were tough.

"But the good news is," Bentley added, "we can devote our full resources to each book."

And so they did. It took a while for Squat Montgomery to convince them his was worthy—even if they were eager for something sniffing like a blockbuster—but they did. And in Montgomery's case, like no other case in their experience, full resources meant full resources.

When he first showed up at their offices on West Fayette

Street in downtown Syracuse, Bentley Morse and James Settle thought he was just another suburbanite misled by the shingle suspended over the entranceway that said SALT CITY PUB., was looking for a bar and had started to direct him to the nearest watering hole, like they always did. But Montgomery didn't look lost, or thirsty. He looked scared, which they couldn't fathom, and it left them momentarily and unaccustomedly speechless.

Montgomery closed the office door, locked it, pulled down the window shade, turned around and braced himself against the thing like he was going to fend off a marauding horde and asked, "Is there anyone else in here?"

Bentley and Settle looked at each other across the open space between their respective desks, said, "Nope, just us."

"Good," he said, pulled a chair fronting Settle's desk to a spot equidistant between the two of them, sat down, reached for a handkerchief from the back pocket of his khaki pants and mopped his forehead. "It's safe."

Safe from what, exactly, they couldn't fathom either. Montgomery didn't look at all like someone who'd be mixed up with dangerous crowds or situations in any way. He was short, round, prematurely balding, pale and soft. He looked, for all the world, like the Pillsbury doughboy grown up, any and all cuteness long since surrendered to life and responsibility, dressed to look like any preppie off any Ivy League campus.

And there was very little arbitrary danger in downtown Syracuse. There was very little arbitrary anything. The urban flight that had affected so many northeastern cities back in the 80s had never reversed in Syracuse as it had in most. They were still waiting for their renaissance. Salt City Publishing was the only occupant of the four-story Bentley-Settle building, for instance. The only reason they held on was because the building and the business had been in their families for a century.

It took him a moment or two, probably because the demeanor he was studying was not what he was used to seeing from the man, but Settle said, "Wait, don't I know you?"

Bentley looked over at him with a frown on his face as if to say stop teasing the poor man. "That's Squat Montgomery," Settle told him. "The press secretary."

"Former," Montgomery added.

"Former presidential press secretary."

"As in the president?" Bentley asked.

Then it was Settle's turn to frown at his partner. He was something of a political junkie, especially in an election year. Bentley, on the other hand, in Settle's opinion, was what a more cynical person might call blissfully ignorant, oblivious. In Bentley's defense, it saved a lot of arguments—not that they were remotely politically incompatible, just that Settle loved to argue.

"It's an honor, Mr. Secretary," he recited, deferring to his office more than orientation: Settle struggled with civility sometimes, but recognized its value, something he found altogether lacking in the administration Montgomery formerly represented, civility as well as recognition. "Is there something we can do for you Squat?"

"Is that really his name?" Bentley asked.

"It's the only name I ever heard him called."

Montgomery stared at them, eyes twitching from one to

the other, said, "It's a nickname!"

The sharp tone in Montgomery's voice gave Settle pause. In the three years he'd watched the man's press briefings he'd never once seen him exhibit anything other than bland equanimity, despite whatever provocations the corps served up. This was a man who could stand behind the lectern under a barrage of klieg lights and accusations, with the rest of the world fairly certain his boss had at least bent the truth if not completely torn it to shreds and blithely answer, "No, David, I wouldn't say that's entirely accurate," famously offering the administration's ten-thousandth non-denial denial. "Next? Yes, Chandra." Bentley noticed Settle's pause, followed suit.

"I want to write a book," Montgomery said.

They looked at each other, back. "And?"

"And?" Montgomery repeated, sprang from his chair and careened about the room, checking other doors, to closets, adjoining offices, surveying the scene from the three sets of windows facing north, and east.

They watched him ping-pong about, and when he was at the final window Bentley said, "From there you can almost see where the Vanderbilt House was, at the corner of Salina and Water, where Charles Dickens stayed in March of 1868, when he came to town to give a reading of 'A Christmas Carol' at Wieting Hall across the street, alas, also now gone."

Settle sighed.

Bentley's thing was history. Between the two, they could pretty safely evaluate most non-fiction manuscripts that came over the transom—almost all of them wading into either politics or history to some extent. Fiction, of course, was a matter of taste over style.

Settle looked over at him like he'd lost his mind. When Montgomery looked across the room at Bentley with the same expression on his face, Settle explained, "He's a book nerd."

"But you guys do books, don't you?" Montgomery asked, coming back around their desks and facing them again.

"Of course."

"I want you to do my book."

"What's it about?"

"I can't tell you yet."

Settle thought on that. Bentley asked, "Do you have a manuscript?" not seeing any.

"It isn't written yet."

They both pondered that one. "I don't want to seem hesitant," Bentley told him.

"We're used to more traditional queries," Settle said.

"Proposals."

"Or email pitches."

"Phone calls, even," Bentley said.

"Couldn't do it that way," Montgomery told them. "It isn't secure."

"I told you so," Settle said. For years he'd been railing on and on about the Patriot Act, how nothing was private any more, everything was under surveillance, Big Brother had arrived!

"You didn't read that book very closely, did you?" Bentley might answer, more to distract than provoke, hopelessly.

"Did you hear that?" Settle would say anyway, any time there was the slightest crackle on a conference call.

"That's from the lightning," Bentley would answer, gesturing out the window to that day's thunderstorm.

Didn't matter. Settle was convinced.

"Well what can you tell us about it?" Bentley asked Squat.

Montgomery leaned over his desk pointing to his forehead, said, "I can tell you that when they found out I was researching it they tortured me!"

"Really?" Bentley said, leaning back in his chair from the man.

"No kidding," Settle said, getting up from his desk to come over and take a look. All he saw was what looked like a slight thumb-sized indentation in the middle of Montgomery's brow. Could have been an unusually large pockmark.

"Chinese water torture," Montgomery told them.

"Tortured by whom?"

"Whom do you think?"

"I thought you said the United States government doesn't torture?" Settle challenged.

"I lied," Montgomery said. "The whole damn world knows I lied. What is the matter with you guys?"

"Why would they torture you?" Settle asked, derisively.

"Because I asked the wrong question."

They waited. Finally, Settle had had enough. "Look," he said, turning back to his desk, "this conversation is going nowhere, mostly because you won't let it. If this is some kind of joke…"

"Joke?" Montgomery jumped on the word, leaping from one desk to the other. "This is no goddamn joke!"

"Fine," Settle said, not backing down. "If it's not a joke, what is it?"

"It's an expose."

"About the administration?"

"About him."

"The president?" Settle asked. "What more is there to be written about him? We've read about him on the couch, his wit, wisdom, tragedy, his brain, at war, his impeachment, his prosecution, his legacy, his greatest hits, for crying out loud."

"Not by an inside source."

"Actually," Bentley said. "There was Clarke, and Frum, Suskind…"

"And Draper," Settle added.

"Was he an insider?"

"Might as well have been. Point is, nobody wants to read about him now."

"Yeah, and that's working out just great isn't it," Montgomery said.

"What's that supposed to mean?" Bentley asked, losing a little bit of patience, which was unusual. Generally, he was the good cop of the operation.

"I mean even in the White House, as these successive stories broke, the absence of weapons, the CIA leak, the judges, the wiretapping, the detention centers, even we thought there'd be a gigantic shit-storm to deal with, but one after the other they blew over or he ignored them outright."

"Thanks to guys like you," Settle said.

"Yes, thanks to guys like me."

"So what changed your mind?"

"I got a call, and asked the wrong questions, and they came after me."

"I hope you're not looking for sympathy here."

Montgomery stared back at Settle, his right eye noticeably twitching.

Bentley asked, "Questions about what he was doing?"

"What he did," Montgomery said, looking ever more nervously around the room.

"Everybody knows all that stuff," Settle said. "It's like you said, nobody seems to care."

"They don't know all of it," Montgomery snapped.

"All right, all right," Settle said. "Let's say there is something new, something awful. Something egregious. Why come out now? You were there. You could have made a difference when it mattered. Why wait until now, if not for the money."

"If this is about money," Bentley said to Settle, "he's come to the wrong place."

"If this isn't about money," Settle corrected, "how do we know he can be trusted."

"You think I wanted to be tortured? This doesn't have anything to do with money."

"Then maybe you have come to the right place," Bentley told him.

"Everything you guys do is about money!" Settle said.

"Yeah, that's what most of us thought," Montgomery confessed.

"Until?" Bentley asked.

"The wrong question," Montgomery told him.

"Doesn't matter," Settle said. "He's all but gone."

"It very much does matter," Montgomery said, settling back in his seat.

"Why?"

Montgomery leaned over, rested his elbows on his knees, whispered, "Because there are more of them."

"Them?" Settle asked.

"He has brothers."

That was what the voice had said to him, "He has brothers." He hadn't cared in the least at the time. "So?" He'd been working on an entirely different book, a My Years in the White House kind of thing, a light, gossipy, name-dropping thing meant only to get him a seven-figure advance. He didn't care if it was good or if it sold. And then she called, said, "He has brothers."

"So?"

"They won't stop, and you know it."

"Stop what?"

"You know what."

"Doesn't matter. There's no way another one of them would be elected, not after..."

"You don't really believe that."

"You should see the polls."

"Forget the polls. What if there's no election?" she had asked.

"This is America."

"What about PD 51?"

"PD what?"

"You don't have to play stupid anymore."

"You're right. Sorry."

"If you really believed they couldn't pull it off, how do you explain his getting elected in the first place?"

"What do you mean?"

"Look, I know why you quit. I shouldn't be calling you, but if somewhere deep down you really do care, you have to ask yourself this: why is it no one brought up Henry Lee?"

"Who?"

"See what I mean?"

So he did ask, and researched, and wondered—only briefly, but out loud—about expanding the scope of his tome. He mentioned it to his Manhattan editors, and the next thing he knew he was being whisked away to rural New Jersey in a jet black Suburban, sitting in the back seat, hooded, between two suited and shaded thugs who wouldn't answer questions, wouldn't tell him anything. He was brought into an old farmhouse, seated in a chair with a single bald light bulb dangling over his head, and a vaguely familiar voice asking, "What are you looking for, Squat?"

"Looking for? I'm not looking for anything."

"What are you looking for, Squat?"

"I'm not looking for anything," he screamed, as his wrists were strapped to the arms of the chair, his head pinioned, the seat tilted back, a cistern appearing out of the rafters above his face, intermittent drops of water falling ten feet and splattering, plop, in the middle of his forehead. He could see them coming, could see the next one forming, waiting while it glistened toward critical mass, letting go, falling, plop. It drove him nuts, the watching, the waiting, the knowing. He couldn't look, couldn't not look, and through it all he hollered, "I'm not looking for anything," willing to say anything to make them stop, just not knowing what it was they wanted to hear.

"It's the worst kind of pain," he said. "The worst."

"In what way?" Bentley asked.

"All ways, mentally, psychologically, physically. You can't possibly know."

"Just from dripping water?" Settle asked.

"You wouldn't last thirty seconds."

"Try me."

"Whoa," Bentley said. "That's not what we're here for."

"And then they put the Page-Russell on me."

"The what?" Settle asked.

"Page-Russell."

"Electro-shock," Bentley told him.

"Multiple shocks, at the same time."

"Jesus," Settle said. They both looked on Montgomery with a renewed pity, bordering on willingness.

For Montgomery, finally, after an interminable number of minutes, of the dropping, the splattering, the waiting and screaming, they stopped. And then the jolts of electricity meant to scramble his brain function to reintroduce a new pattern of thinking. They tilted his seat back upright, hooded him again, and told him, "You're asking the wrong questions, Squat."

"What'd they say in Manhattan about that?" Settle asked.

"I didn't think there was any such thing as a wrong question," Bentley mused.

"Good Lord," Settle told him. "That's a 'bad' question, there's no such thing as a bad question."

"Oh, that's right."

"What are you guys," Montgomery yelled, "fucking morons?"

"Excuse me?"

"I couldn't go back to New York. You think I'm out of my goddamn mind?"

"Ah," Bentley said. "That's true."

"Kind of," Settle added.

"Why us?" Bentley asked.

"You fit the profile."

"Profile?"

Montgomery had done some further research, once he had moved out of his Arlington townhouse, moved to Scranton, where he hoped no one would recognize him, took on an assumed name and spent hours on the internet in the Scranton Public Library. He found two houses in the entire country that fit his profile: no one involved with the business had gone to Yale, was from Texas, Wyoming, or Connecticut, voted Republican, attended a fundamentalist church, listened to talk radio, worked or lived with anyone connected to the CIA, or married their sister.

"Married their sister?" Bentley asked.

"I threw that one in there for good measure," Montgomery told him, laughing demonically.

Settle looked on warily.

"Some pretty impressive research," Bentley tried to console him.

"All right, fine!" Montgomery shouted, springing from his chair yet again, circling their desks, challenging, "There's another house, don't forget. I got their address right here," he said, pulling a crumpled slip of paper out of his pocket. "Maybe they'll be interested in the mass murder in Brownsville twenty-five years ago, or his father's coup attempt three years before that—of the United States fucking government—but that's no big deal, his father botched a coup himself fifty years earlier, no big deal, except they both fucked it up, they're a family of fuck-ups, they couldn't storm the Bastille, they probably can't even spell Bastille, and I know he couldn't begin to pronounce Bastille, what's the big deal, why should you care, why should anyone care!" he said.

"Exactly," Settle agreed. "Daddy's doddering and grandpa's dead."

"Tell that to Spiderman."

"Who?"

"Spiderman," he said. "He was a journalist."

"Was?"

"That's right, was. Was a journalist working on this story a dozen years ago connecting Poppy to the Columbian drug trade, running bah-say into Miami, LA, the CIA giving them a pass in exchange for shuttling weapons to the Contras. Story blows up, he gets fired, is run out of town. But he's got a memo, an old memo everyone's forgotten about, so Spiderman turns up dead two years ago."

"Dead by…" Bentley prompted him.

"Two gunshot wounds to the head," Montgomery told him, pointing to his temple. "It was ruled a suicide."

"Two?" Settle asked.

Montgomery just smiled.

"Jesus," Bentley said, turning over his shoulder and glancing out the window.

"And you can prove this?" Settle asked.

"All of it."

"The coups?"

"Brownsville?"

"Yes!" Montgomery said, slamming his hands on Bentley's desk.

"Really?" Settle asked.

"Look it up," Montgomery told him, sitting back in the

chair, folding his arms across his chest.

Settle said, unkindly, "On the Google?"

"Jim," Bentley tried, even as he was doing that very thing.

"Sorry," Settle told Montgomery. "Couldn't resist."

Montgomery sat shaking his head, suspecting that would be their legacy, that would be the thing that would haunt him to his grave, the thing he'd do anything to get off his backlist.

"Here it is," Bentley said. "Governor deflects questions about Brownsville, Sunnyvale, California, April, 2000."

Both Settle and Montgomery moved to look over Bentley's shoulder.

"At a campaign stop here yesterday, when asked to account for his whereabouts while seventeen of his cohorts were slaughtered in a Brownsville, Texas, ranch house in 1984, the Republican candidate responded, 'I'm not going to discuss that.'"

Settle read the page address. "Conspiracy Planet?"

Bentley backed the page to his search list. "Here it is again."

"Konformist?" Settle said of the page. "Cute." Then, after reading a little, said, "It's the same story."

"So?" Montgomery said. "That's good, right?"

"No," Bentley told him. "That's bad."

"It's viral," Settle said.

"What's that mean?"

"You really don't know much about how 'the internets' work, do you?"

"Jim!"

"Sorry."

"Means somebody posted something, in this case something pretty incendiary, and legions of like-minded bloggers posted it all over the web, verbatim."

"So?" Montgomery said again.

"Verbatim is not the same thing as true," Settle told him, wanting to add it was a tactic right out of their playbook: repeat a talking point, no matter how outlandish, enough times and volume begets veracity. "There's no primary source."

"Here's another one," Bentley said. "Portland indymedia dot org."

"Same story," Settle said. "They got a link?"

Bentley scrolled down, said, "Here's one," clicking on it.

"The anti-Christ?" Settle said. "Now we're getting somewhere."

"There, how about that one," Montgomery said, pointing to another portal.

Bentley followed it, to an article by Sherman Skolnick: "Brownsville Satanic Cult Member?"

"Nice," Settle said, reading out loud, "...declined to answer questions Monday concerning his alleged involvement in a 1984 Brownsville, TX, mass murder, in which 17 people were ritualistically murdered and skinned."

Bentley picked up the story, "I will not stoop to discussing that."

"Naturally," Settle mumbled.

"We've got people across this country without health care, a broken educational system, taxes that are way too high, and all you want to talk about is something that may or may not have happened 16 years ago? I'm sorry, but I find that offensive."

"Satisfied?" Montgomery asked.

"Not nearly." Settle asked Bentley, "This guy got a source?"

"Right here," he said, accessing it.

"Shit," Settle said when he saw the page, spinning away from the huddle.

"What?"

"It's the Onion," Bentley told him, seeing the exact same copy that'd been on all the other pages. "Fake news."

"It's a goddamn parody site," Settle said. "Not just fake news, ridiculous shit."

"It's actually pretty funny some times," Bentley said.

"I'm sure you guys sourced them, but the rest of the civilized world knows bald-faced lies when they see them."

Bentley didn't scold him that time. Montgomery collapsed in his chair, cradling his head in his hands. "Wait a minute," he said, raising his head again. "You said parody, right?"

"Complete fantasy," Settle said, rolling his eyes.

"Doesn't there have to be some antecedent for parody?"

"Some what?"

"An antecedent, an original story that they're mocking?"

"I'm not sure these guys know that rule," Settle said, waving toward Bentley's computer.

But Bentley was busy clicking away. Deep into the web, he said, "Here it is," looking up. "Brownsville Herald, April, 1984."

Montgomery and Settle returned to their perches behind him. "Community horrified by ritual slayings," Bentley read the tease.

"Click on it," Settle said.

He did. "Page has been removed," he read.

Bentley looked up. Montgomery and Settle studied each

other. Bentley turned from his partner to their client, asked, "What's the title of this book?"

"The Hands of Death," Montgomery told him.

"By?" Settle asked.

"Coyote."

"Coyote?"

"That's what she called herself."

6.

"So where do I set up?" Montgomery asked.

They'd finished the negotiations, such as they were. "We really don't have any money to give you," Bentley had told him.

"I don't need any money," Montgomery said. "I don't *want* any money."

"There goes your credibility."

"You're going to have to believe me. Look, I got nothing, nowhere to go; I just want to get this story out. All I need is coffee and a computer."

"Why?" Settle asked.

"Why does he need coffee?"

"No, damnitt. Why does he need to get this story out?"

"Because you guys haven't heard anything yet," Montgomery told them. "That Brownsville thing is just the tip of the iceberg."

"Hell of a tip," Bentley said, "Seventeen ritualized murders and skinning."

"Trust me."

"If you say so."

"Trust me," Montgomery said again. "So," he said, standing in the middle of the office looking around him, "where do we set up?"

"We?"

"The computer."

"And coffee," Bentley said.

"Right. Got to have coffee."

"You mean here?"

Montgomery looked at him blankly. "Well, yeah."

He meant, it turned out, that he intended not to leave the building again until the manuscript was completed, which presented a bit of a logistical dilemma. Not the space. They had plenty of space, two other smaller offices off the main, one of them entirely unused.

"Where will you sleep?" Settle asked, a vague foreboding determining him, even as Bentley said, "We'll roll in a cot."

There was a second restroom in the suite, even a break room complete with microwave, refrigerator and toaster.

"That's all I need," Montgomery said.

Which was not quite true. He needed food, on occasion, needed hygiene accessories.

"He needs a goddamn change of clothes," Settle said after a few days.

It became an issue of management. Not that they were swamped otherwise, though Bentley and Settle did have a business to run, day-to-day upkeep that couldn't be abandoned on a whim whenever Montgomery needed a notebook, a reference book, colored pencils and a spare desk to be drug into his "space" so he could doodle and draw on what he called his "map" of the book.

"We'll get Lisa to work as his assistant," Bentley finally suggested.

"Who?"

"Lisa, your daughter, my niece. She's wanted more hours anyway."

"No," Settle said. "And she's only your niece-in-law."

"What are you talking about? There's no such thing."

"You're my brother-in-law, she's my daughter. She's your niece-in-law."

"She's my sister's child."

"She's no child at all. And your *sister* left, forfeiting any claim she might have had, including yours."

"Fine," Bentley said, more frustrated with himself for hazarding any kind of argument with him. That was how arguments went with Settle.

But he was right about one thing, Lisa was no child. She was a stunning young woman of twenty-four, with a degree in accounting, her whole life before her, her pick of any man she wanted. She was tall, slim, with a shocking mane of auburn hair and Uma Thurman good looks. She could have walked off of any Tarantino set, which is what worried Settle the most. Because she had at least one bad habit. She tended to fall for writers.

"She's our line-editor anyway," Bentley reasoned.

"No," Settle insisted. "I won't have her fawning over *him*," he said, motioning to the spare office where Montgomery labored.

"You don't *really* think that'll happen, do you?"

"Happens every time."

"Hey, you guys," Montgomery called. "Is diabolical capitalized?"

"No!" they both hollered back.

"She's a *really* good line-editor," Bentley reminded him.

"Lord, help me," Settle said, and Lisa was brought in.

The first thing Montgomery said to her was, "I don't know where to start."

"Most folks think you should start at the beginning," she told

Joe Formichella

him.

"He just stared at me," she told Bentley and Settle later. "Like he has absolutely no sense of humor at all."

"How could he," Settle said, "considering the company he keeps."

Bentley just said, "Certainly no fawning there."

"What?" Lisa asked.

"Shut up," Settle told him.

To be fair to Montgomery, he wasn't at all certain what the beginning was. It could go back seventy-five years, it could go back ninety years, or more. He was still in the process of discovering that. He only knew his entry point: the phone call.

She'd prefaced all of her remarks with, "You know, if you're writing a book, and you have the stomach, there are a few threads that could be pulled that would unravel this whole sick dynasty."

"Why would I want to do that?"

"It's not a question of you, Mr. Montgomery. It's a question of when *anyone* is going to finally tell the truth about these people."

"If there's truth, as you say, it's bound to come out, isn't it?"

"I'm not going to debate whether there's truth with you, Mr. Montgomery."

"Then what makes you think I *won't* tell the truth?"

"Loyalty."

"And that's a bad thing?"

"It is when it's only one-sided. Then it's called fear. Do you honestly believe you can count on their loyalty to you?"

He didn't answer, directly. "What do *I* have to fear?"

"You know how powerful they are, and how ruthless."

Silence.

"There's an easy enough way to measure it, you now. Answer

this question: Why is it no one has *ever* taken a shot at one of them?"

"How the hell am I supposed to answer that?"

"Start with Alyssa Peterson."

It was back in the fall of 2003, the war in Iraq turning sickeningly sour. The first female death in theater had occurred that September. But it wasn't a combat death. It was a suicide. Army interpreter Alyssa Peterson complained about interrogation techniques in country and was relieved of that duty and sent to suicide prevention classes where, she said, she "learned how to kill herself." Her suicide note spoke to the irony of that.

There was one particular day, though, that the news wasn't about Alyssa Peterson—if she ever was given much airtime—and it wasn't about the dreadful things going on over there. It was about John Hinkley. The alleged would-be assassin, who'd been locked up in the St. Elizabeth's mental ward for 22 years was petitioning for longer home visits to his parents in Virginia. People were outraged. If Hinkley got his way, one journalist noted, he'd be home in time for Thanksgiving turkey and pumpkin pie. Never mind that he'd been granted unsupervised family visits years earlier. The petition hoped to extend those from three days to five. That's all. Why was this a story at all, much less a prominent subject for *Newsweek* and the cable shows?

A little digging into that question resulted the already known similarities between Hinkley and Mark David Chapman, the very much assassin of John Lennon—the facts that they shared an eerie resemblance to one another, were both fanatic about Lennon, and both found with copies of *Catcher in the Rye* on their persons. But then there was a theory that attempted to explain the *Catcher* connection: that the book was a trigger mechanism used by a super-secret mind-control Manchurian assassin program coordinated by the CIA, the British psychological warfare unit called the Tavistock Institute, the Scottish Rite Masons, and the beneficent contributions of the pharmaceutical giant Eli Lilly back in the 50s known as MK-Ultra. They were notorious for their brainwashing by drugs, hypnosis, electroshock, and other sundry techniques. A partial list of their "research subjects" is truly a rogue's gallery, including Charles Manson, David Berkowitz, Lynette Fromme, Sarah Jane Moore, Theodore Kaczynski, Sirhan Sirhan, Mehmet Ali Agca, Mark David Chapman and John Hinkley Jr. Interestingly, Sallinger had served with Henry Kissinger in World War II in counter intelligence.

The project was exposed in the 1970s, prompting Gerald Ford to appoint a commission to examine the CIA's—directed by Poppy, who was also otherwise on Eli Lilly's board—misconduct, which explains, for some, the two assassination attempts on his life—Ford's, that is. Hard to imagine, though, such an operation would then pack up all its spook toys and go home. Many investigators believe they just moved it all overseas to obscure little countries under the radar, like Guyana, which is how Henry Lee's name came up.

Jonestown, Guyana, is where Jim Jones moved his People's Temple in the summer of 1977. Jonestown is also the location of the "revolutionary suicide" massacre in November of 1978, when nine-hundred plus cult members reportedly poisoned themselves. Henry Lee told his biographer in 1985 that he was a close friend of Jim Jones and the cult, and that it was he who had delivered the cyanide to Jonestown.

Except there is considerable disagreement over what happened at Jonestown. The Guyanese coroner, Dr. C. Leslie Mootoo, concluded that only three of the 913 victims died by means of suicide. All of the rest were executed, some by means of lethal injection, some by strangulation, and some simply shot through the head. If Lucas was indeed in the country that day, he was probably there as more than a delivery boy. By his own admission, his self-ascribed talents would have been uniquely useful in the clean-up operation that was Jonestown. And what was being cleaned up? Speculation posits that it was another MK-Ultra project, with its vast stockpiles of drugs, sensory deprivation equipment, and a band of zombie-like assassins who'd gunned down Congress-man Leo Ryan's—the first and only Congressman murdered in the line of duty in the history of the United States—investigative entourage just prior to the massacre—necessitating, of course, the cleanup. But Henry Lee's rap sheet and special qualifications had been well established by then.

"And it just keeps get weirder and weirder," she told him.

"You're not kidding."

"So, you got the guts?"

"Why me?"

"Why not?"

"Exactly," Montgomery said. "Why not you?"

"Has to be someone close."

"Close?"

"Close enough, that if you disappear, someone might notice."

And then the line went dead.

Joe Formichella

End

FROM *The Onion*, January 19, 2009: "Navy at a loss to explain simultaneous submarine hi-jackings"

Yesterday six fully operational US Navy nuclear subs were hijacked by South American terrorists who launched missiles armed with conventional warheads partially destroying Langley Field, the Pentagon, SAC headquarters, NORAD, the White House, and the Bentley-Settle building in Syracuse, New York. Miraculously, all facilities happened to be exercising what officials refer to as Kool-Aide drills—for different levels of alert there's a different color designation, a different flavor, if you will: this one happened to be code Orangey-Porngey, which calls for a complete evacuation of the building or buildings—so casualties were kept to a minimum, except for the Bentley-Settle, from which no survivors have yet to be found. Aboard Air Force One, the president has declared martial law, and he has suspended all other branches of government in accordance with 2007's Executive Directive 51. Asked about the extreme nature of the administration's response, the president said, "I always told you this would be a heckofa lot easier if I was a dictator. Now we're going to find out."

Meanwhile, at an undisclosed bunker somewhere in Delaware, the president's press secretary, when asked about the possible target value of the Bentley-Settle building in Syracuse, said,

"We wondered about that too. We don't have all the facts just yet, of course, and would rather not respond to inquiries until the investigation is complete."

"Could you speculate as to what possible motive there was for that strike?"

"No."

"If I may, Dwayna, it's just that the pattern of the other targets suggest that they were striking at military and intelligence facilities around the country. Why Syracuse? Is there a secret facility there perhaps?"

"As it happens—and you may know this, David—I went to Syracuse University for a whole semester. I *know* Syracuse. Trust me, there's *nothing* in Syracuse."

Another administration official, speaking on condition of anonymity, suggested that the Syracuse hit may have been a case of mistaken identity, or what they like to call, a "miss." When pressed to identify what the intended target *may* have been, the source added, "If I'm a terrorist, and *I've* got my finger on that trigger, I'm aiming for Niagara Falls."

7.

JERRY wasn't entirely happy with the copy, but assumed that was more because of the process than the product. The ontogenesis from journalist to novelist hadn't been smooth, or easy. He'd devoted weeks to the effort, repeatedly bushwhacked by ingrained habits—from the lead to the tease, and trying to craft dialogue that didn't read like a scripted interview.

He wasn't entirely unhappy with it either. And when he reached the pivotal point where he welcomed the challenge of fiction rather than dread the work as some kind of punitive penance, he bundled up the pages and mailed them off, fairly certain it was enough for Al to glean the scope and direction of the book. Or, he had to admit, when he had finally managed to write something that amused him—a necessity he'd decided pretty early on would be the only saving grace for the subject, humor—it dawned on him how much fun this writing could be, and wanted to share it. Or, if he was going to be completely honest, he wanted validation, wanted someone else to think it was funny, too.

"You're going to hurt yourself if you keep thinking that way, Weave," he said, and poured himself a stiff whiskey to blunt the regression.

Two days later, still tipsy, he remembered to turn his phones back on and saw he had multiple voice mails and dozens of missed calls. "Holy shit," he said, even as one of them started vibrating.

"Where the hell have you been?" Al screamed at him. "Whatever else you do, you keep in touch with your agent! Don't you know that? I was afraid they'd already gotten to you."

"Then you got the package?"

"Why don't you ever answer my questions?"

Fair point, Jerry conceded. "What do you mean where have I been? I've been writing."

"For three months?"

"Kind of lost track of time."

"Jesus."

"Then you got it?"

"Yeah, I got it. Fiction?"

"Figured that was the best way."

"But you don't know anything about writing fiction."

"Well, that's what took so long. Did you like it?"

"I've only scanned it. We need to talk before this goes much farther."

"Talk about what?"

"Why Anonymous?"

"That was a no brainer."

"Because it's fiction, or is it fiction so it can be Anonymous?"

"It's Anonymous because it has to be about the story."

"What about your readers?"

"It's not about me, *can't* be about me." In fact, Jerry thought, if that other thing—he hadn't been able to refer to it by name in more than a while—had been "anonymous," it might have all worked out quite differently. If there hadn't been anyone to attack, his theory went, they might have actually looked harder at the story.

"My point is, that never works, Jerr."

"Never? What about *Colors*?"

"All right, it worked once. But that was fiction."

"So is this!"

"I know, I know; but why?"

"Why fiction? Actually, that's the biggest no brainer of all."

"Humor me."

"You know the libel laws, Al. First, there can't be any charge of 'false light.'"

"Because they're public figures…"

"Exactly. Which leaves only a claim of 'falsity.'"

By declaring it as a work of fiction in the first place, the only way a claim could be brought against him was if they admitted that what he wrote might actually be *true*, which was precisely the best thing that *could* happen.

"So you *want* to get sued?"

"In a perfect world."

"Let's go back to the beginning: you're fucking *crazy*!"

"Then you'll do it?"

"Gonna be a real hard sell with the lawyers."

"But you'll try?"

"Yes, yes, I'll try. But they're business people, Jerr. How am I supposed to convince them getting sued is the right thing to do?"

"Tell them to put it all on me. Let them raise their concerns, I'll swear I can cover any and all challenges and take full responsibility, that I've got to protect my sources, blah, blah, blah. You know the lingo, Al."

"What about me?"

"Al, what would you be worried about? Write up any agreement you're comfortable with, and I'll sign it. Promise."

What Jerry actually wanted to say was, Are you kidding?

You're worried about getting sued? You think you'll survive long enough to ever see a courtroom? But he didn't want to scare him off. And he wished the cynicism hadn't occurred to him, either. It was not a comfortable thought. It was a damn frightening one, one that only whiskey could soften.

It was Friday evening. Nothing much could develop over the weekend. Jerry decided to shut out the world again, indulge himself in a good long bender, and when he sobered up again sometime Monday or Tuesday, really, really ask himself if he wanted to do this thing.

But when he plugged back in seventy-two hours later, before he had time to think, before he had time for coffee, even, he got a call.

"Are you watching this?" Coyote asked.

"Watching what?" he said, looking around aimlessly for something supposedly showing.

"The *television*," she said.

"Oh," he said. "Which channel?"

"*Any* channel!"

He saw people on rooftops, flooded streets, waders in the floodwaters towing makeshift vessels piled with earthly belongings past submerged cars and bloated bodies. Hordes of angry, screaming people on dry islands of sidewalks and storefronts, old people in wheelchairs, mothers holding squalling babies, snarled at the camera.

"Where is this?"

"Jesus, where have you been, in a coma? It's New Orleans."

"New Orleans? Louisiana?"

"Yeah, as in the United fucking States of America!"

"What happened?"

"Hurricane, the levees broke, flooded the whole city."

"But," he said, checking the muted images again, clicking from one cable outlet to another, all of them variations of the same theme, all of them live feeds.

"Does that look like a 'crazy allegation' to you?"

"But," he said again, like the thought he was trying to utter was so foreign he might as well have been attempting to translate it into Swahili. "There're TV crews in there filming it all."

"Round the dial, round the clock."

"And no one's helping these people?"

"Hardly even trying."

"What the hell is going on?" he said, even as he sat transfixed by the images, which, honestly, should have been answer enough.

"Shock and awe, baby, shock and awe," she said, reviving the hideously failed intention of Operation Iraqi Freedom.

"What are you saying?"

"You watch, this is the introduction of 'crisis capitalism' stateside. Look for them to start talking about the 'opportunity' this presents, lobbyists and developers flooding the place once the water recedes. They'll bust the unions, the public school system, they'll tear down public housing, probably put up high-rise fucking casinos. Look for Uncle Miltie penning op-eds calling for the privatization of everything, laying waste to the wasted city with profiteers and carpetbaggers, driving those people of color not killed in the storm out of the way and into the shadows."

"Uncle Miltie?"

"Milton Friedman."

"Are you serious? I didn't even know he was still alive. He's got to be like a hundred and fifty or something."

"You watch," she said, and hung up.

So he did. Sure enough, within days there were rumors floating around that some Republican congressman from the city had told a bunch of lobbyists, "We finally cleaned up public housing in New Orleans. We couldn't do it, but God did." And then there was a *Times* article quoting a wealthy developer, "I think we have a clean sheet to start again. And with that clean sheet we have some very big opportunities." The Louisiana State Legislature was reportedly crawling with those corporate lobbyists pushing for lower taxes, fewer regulations, cheaper workers, a "smaller, safer city," code for, level all those public housing units—sturdy brick buildings that actually withstood the storm and its flood—replace them with condos. And, by what Jerry could gauge, they mostly got their way. Private security—the same corrupted, fundamentalist outfit poisoning the atmosphere in Iraq—was brought in alongside the 82nd Airborne. No-bid contracts went out to the usual suspects and local labor protections were suspended so those contractors could pay whatever they wanted—in many cases what amounted to nothing at all—which meant much of the work went to hordes of day laborers bused in from the border states.

Still, though, in spite of his marginalized position within the profession, Jerry instinctively leaned toward advocating against the presumption of so-called evil. There were already too many folks willing to board that train. He'd covered disaster stories, from the *Loma Linda* earthquake to Midwestern floods. He'd investigated corruption at every level, even once joking with another reporter in the aftermath of some California political shenanigans, "These guys are amateurs compared to the old boys back in Ohio." This kind of stuff goes on everywhere, happens all the time. Did it necessarily add up to a pogrom? He couldn't quite bring himself to go as far as Coyote predicted, even as much as he might have wanted to.

But then not long into the tragedy she proved to be every bit as prescient as promised, almost scary prescient. Uncle Miltie did indeed scribble a missive for the *Wall Street Journal*. "Most New Orleans schools are in ruins," he observed, "as are the homes of the children who have attended them. The children are now scattered all over the country. This is a tragedy. It is also an opportunity to radically reform the educational system."

His idea? Rather than spending any portion of the billions of reconstruction dollars on the crippled public school system, Louisiana should instead bury it all and channel that money to private educators, convert New Orleans schools into "charter schools," not as a stopgap measure but a means toward "permanent reform," effectively erasing as much of the progress that had been achieved since *Brown v. Board of Education* in the process. Why? Well, the reasons proffered were the old bogeymen: State-run schools smacked of "socialism" in Friedman's worldview. All states were *supposed* to do was "protect our freedom both from the enemies outside our gates and from our fellow-citizens"—from the huddled masses outside the gates, the serfs beyond the mote, presumably—"to preserve law and order, to enforce private contracts, to foster competitive markets." He wanted New Orleans to become "the nation's preeminent laboratory for the widespread use of charter schools," which necessitated, surprise, surprise, the firing of every single one of the forty-seven hundred members of its teachers' union. And with most of those directly concerned or affected by this Friedmanstein experiment "evacuated" and dumped in far-flung corners of the country, it worked. Long before the levees were repaired or even the electrical grid, New Orleans schools were auctioned off with the urgency of a fire sale. His cheerleaders were ecstatic. "Katrina accomplished in a day," they chanted, "what Louisiana school reformers couldn't do after years of trying."

Why no one thought to or was able to stop that madness, despite Miltie's abominable record for meddling in such practical matters and policy advice, couldn't possibly be the mystery it presented, and therefore might be reduced to something as simple as, the motherfuckers just didn't care. We'd seen such machinations before, after all.

The single greatest—or most heinous—example of Friedman and his Chicago-style "disaster capitalism" put to work had occurred in Chile thirty years earlier. His formula for instituting his brand of fundamentalist capitalism was simple and on the record. He wrote that "only a crisis—actual or perceived—produces real change. When that crisis occurs, the actions that are taken depend on the ideas that are lying around. That, I believe, is our basic function: to develop alternatives to existing policies, to keep them alive and available until the politically impossible becomes politically inevitable." Following the CIA—and Ford, and ITT—backed military coup of democratically elected and defenseless president Allende, Friedman advised Chile's new dictator, General Augusto Pinochet, to impose his textbook rapid transformation of what had been a thriving economy with a rising middle class and standard of living—but also manufacturing protections, trade restrictions and price controls, everything Friedman and his multinational moneymen *hated* and had failed to curb even with their constant refrain of "Communism! Communism! Communism!"—by slashing taxes and social spending, deregulating, privatizing and throwing open the borders to free trade. Oh, and for good measure, the General should also replace his public schools with voucher-funded private ones. He could do all that, Friedman assured him, even though the general didn't know diddly about economics, because so many of the professor's acolytes, the "Chicago boys," had been planted in country over the preceding decade. The catastrophe became known as a "Chicago School" revolution, the most extreme capitalist makeover ever attempted.

Lost in the furor was the fact that those same "Chicago boys" had been trying for years to introduce their radical ideas in a more democratic manner and were rejected time and again. The people didn't want that shit. Not a worry after the coup. In as little as twenty-four hours the free-marketers had achieved their holy trinity: privatization, deregulations and cuts to social spending. The results? Well, not so good. Inflation shot up to 375 percent—something as basic as bread was impossible to purchase for most—unemployment, starvation and poverty went through the roof, not to mention the hundreds of thousands of citizens who had to be disappeared and tortured in order to keep the general population terrorized and in crisis mode. Within a year even Chile's business elite had wearied of the adventure, as only foreign manufacturers and piranhic financiers were profiting—and profiting handsomely. The president of Chile's National Association of Manufacturers called the experiment "one of the greatest failures of our economic history."

You'd have thought that would have been the end of Chicago style economics. Guess again. Argentina was next, with similar, if not worse results. Thatcher swallowed the bait, as did Reagan. It was the only post-war plan for Iraq, and we've seen how that worked out. And then they were still being listened to in the wake of Katrina. All of which could only lend credence to Coyote's claim, and should have created enough doubt in anyone's mind to ask whether the disastrous outcomes were really all that unintended.

It also, for Jerry, afforded her a lifetime of "I told you so's." He was finally, firmly, completely on board. He even, in an unexpected instance of epiphany following orientation, thought he understood suddenly what she meant by "going back to the beginning," as a means of unlearning his journalistic instincts. For him, that meant going back to the Brownsville story, though not the story itself, its originator, *The Onion*. He knew some folks with the outfit, as it turned out, and hoped—on hope alone—that they might be able to steer him to the authors of that story.

Turned out, if you disregarded their disregard for facts, they acted in pretty much every way like a news operation. They had rolodexes, kept archives, even vetted their reporters, for reasons Jerry couldn't begin to comprehend, though he was glad they did.

"We were just starting to crank it up, going national, back then," he was told, at the time of the Brownsville story. The outfit had started a dozen years earlier as a campus alternative in Madison. "We were using a lot of stringers." And after numerous transfers and much searching, he was provided a number only, no names. "Company policy," he was told.

"They disappeared not long after we ran that piece," his informant told him, "so there's no telling how current the number is. But good luck."

"Disappeared?" he asked, momentarily over-sensitized to the term.

"Yeah, they were regulars at the beginning, but about a year afterward we quit hearing from them."

Not nearly relieved, Jerry muted the celebrity charity benefit for Katrina victims on the screen, dialed the number, listened to it ring. Voice mail picked up after the first ring, which was as good a sign as any. "Hi, this is Scarlot, or Marilyn," the message began, in the same voice. "We can't answer the phone right now. Leave a message." Jerry didn't, preferring, for the moment, to keep his cards close, resolving to call back in a few minutes.

He un-muted the television—seeing Mike Myers standing there like a deer in the crosshairs as if something was going horribly wrong—just in time to hear Kanye West say the president, "doesn't care about black people." Jerry nearly spit back his drink.

Joe Formichella

Part II

Joe Formichella

8.

SCARLOT and Marilyn Serolfino had disappeared voluntarily that summer of 2000, driven by equal parts paranoia, a sense of mission, and habit. Their Texas source, Peter Pardew had gone *incommunicado* right after the Republican National Convention in July. Marilyn was instantly anxious. Scarlot was dubious.

"He's probably proselytizing in Africa, or the Amazon," she said.

"He's quit all that," Marilyn reminded her.

"He said."

"I'm worried it's just the opposite. He said he was working on a big story for us."

"He's done this before, you know."

"Done what?"

"Disappeared."

Twenty years earlier he'd found God, closed his St. Louis law practice and moved to Port Arthur, Texas, and joined a mega-church. He told everyone, at the time, that he'd been bathed by Jesus' blood during his morning shower, instantly repented his sins, and was going to devote his life to battling wickedness and preparing the way for the Lord's second coming.

"And he's only been back a couple of years, don't forget."

He'd called them out of the blue late in 1998, breathlessly telling Scarlot, "These people are *crazy*!"

"You're just now figuring that out?"

"It's been building," he admitted.

All year long the congregation had been alternately cheering and praying for Clinton's impeachment and/or his bombing of Iraq before being thrown out of office. Then they prayed for the accused in the lynching of James Byrd in nearby Jasper, Texas. The tipping point came, oddly enough, when they celebrated the savage beating and death of Matthew Shepard in Wyoming.

"I mean, Lord knows I've got nothing good to say about queers, but he was just a kid. And they were partying, like it was a righteous sacrifice, this *human* being!"

Marilyn wanted to answer, "Tell that to your brother," but didn't.

And then, when the millennium came and went without the rapture, without Armageddon, or anything remotely close, he lost all faith.

"Which was a *bonanza* for us," Scarlot fairly sang.

He went on something of an anti-crusade.

"Converts are *always* the most zealous."

"So what happened to him?" Marilyn asked.

"What is it you think happened, that he was nabbed by the God-cops?"

"They've been known to do worse."

"Who?"

"Those crazy end-timers."

Which was true enough. No less than Prime Minister Yitzhak Rabin had been assassinated for meddling with their prophesy. "If someone believes God told him to do something," Rabin's security advisor said of those fanatics, "you cannot stop him. Religion," he added, "is the most powerful gun in the world." They wouldn't even hesitate to off a show-me-state Texas snooper if they thought he was interfering with their schemes.

Thing was, she didn't know, and that worried her, almost to death.

"And a worried Marilyn is a pretty useless Marilyn," Scarlot said to one of Peter's younger brothers, tying to enlist his help in finding out what might have happened.

"Me, go to Texas?" he answered. "Honey, are you out of your mind? Do you know the lengths I've gone to avoid setting one single foot in that state over the years? Why don't *you* go?"

"Right, Johnny, like getting Marilyn out of the house is going to happen."

"What about Paul, have you tried him?"

"You know how he feels about me. Besides, he's *your* brother."

"As if," Jack said, not on the best of terms with Paul himself. "He's probably out campaigning somewhere anyway. Let me think about it," he said, but didn't.

"Bunch of damned drama queens," Scarlot hissed at the vacated phone. "I tried," she said to Marilyn, who took no solace from the effort.

Instead, she worried herself with what clues she could recall from their last conversations, clues which might—though only in Marilyn's mind—yield a potential location for Peter *without* necessitating her leaving the house. Marilyn was a rabid agoraphobic, and Scarlot had given up all attempts toward intervention long, long ago. Once she'd removed whichever interior walls that could be safely removed—so that their "house" amounted to essentially one all-encompassing great room—and then wanted to install latches screwed into the joist struts all around the ceiling so that aliens couldn't peel off the roof and "spirit" her away, it was pretty obvious that only medication, a lot of medication, could crack that nut, and Scarlot let it go.

"Did he tell you what he was looking into?" she asked, to try and get Marilyn to stop pacing, another not-very-good indicator of her temperament.

"Not in so many words."

"In *any* words?" Scarlot asked, trying to keep her patience in check.

"Well, kind of," she said. "He was most alarmed about the 'coupling,' as he called it, of government and religion."

"I mean recently," Scarlot told her. That's what had led him to the Brownsville story, what he saw as a messy mop-up of previous derelictions prior to a miraculous conversion on his way to becoming campaign *attaché* for the Christian crazies. In her current state, chronology became as frazzled as everything else for Marilyn.

"I know, I know, but when it started to look more and more like it might actually happen, he kept saying they could then do anything they wanted to."

"Do anything like what?"

"Well, he said look for them to steal the election, and after that, all hell breaks loose."

"Meaning?"

"End times. He said they were determined to make it happen; they weren't going to wait on God any more."

"That's insane. He's nuttier than you are."

"Maybe so," Marilyn told her, though that didn't comfort her much either.

"Did he happen to say anything slightly more specific than

that?"

"Not really. He thought he was close to puzzling out an important date, though."

"What date?"

"I said he was *close*," Marilyn said. "He mostly babbled about pilgrims, Palestinians, the Antichrist's birthday…"

"Jesus. I give up."

But Marilyn couldn't. She obsessed on the issue, and they missed several weeks' worth of deadlines, prompting Scarlot to start thinking about other possible sources of income. In the years since Marilyn had been so severely shut-in, they'd managed to accomplish most day-to-day functions remotely—from fast food and grocery delivery, ordering books, movies, other necessities, even paying their bills online—but supporting those habits was a bit trickier, trickier still because Marilyn wouldn't abide by just any work. She refused any suggestion of at-home marketing, for instance, said it was, variably, *bourgeois*, or predatory.

"You're impossible," Scarlot said.

"I'm a *writer*," Marilyn insisted.

But as a *writer* unwilling to go out and find stories and with one of the few people she would talk to at all to feed her stories gone silent and off the radar, "*What* do you propose to write?"

"You'll think of something," she said. "You always do."

And so she had. Scarlot got them a tenuous freelancing gig supplying bite-sized "news" copy for various internet home pages—those tabs of enticing headlines and cursory filler meant only to keep browsers on the site, maybe even go to one of the sponsors. It was a minimally workable solution to their dilemma, where Scarlot would snag a headline in the midst of Marilyn's searching and searching for news or insight into Peter's whereabouts and guilt her into generating the 30-50 word article copy. When the H. L. Hunley Confederate submarine was raised that August, for instance, Scarlot wrote, "First U-boat in naval history recovered to tell their tale," and ordered Marilyn to write something about it.

"Write what?"

"I don't know. Make something up. Just give me five good sentences."

That was the extent of attention Scarlot could command from her, but in order to make it all work they needed to post something at least half a dozen times a day, every day. It added tension to the house, to be sure, but it worked. Scarlot kept them in the black, and Marilyn could keep chasing her ghost.

She had fixated on a date, trying to derive a calendar point from Peter's ramblings. Pilgrims and Palestinians got her no-where, or everywhere, from the Mayflower's landing to the Brit-ish Mandate. The Antichrist's birthday seemed, at first glance, the most easily accessible. But there was considerable disagreement about who the Antichrist might be. Candidates ran the gamut from Bill Clinton to Vladimir Putin, predictably. The former's birthday was August 19th—though that passed without incident—and the latter's October 7th. She didn't put much stock in either of those choices and kept looking. Repeatedly—though she didn't want to believe it—she encountered hysterics who insisted the pope was the antichrist, if only because of his literal position in the church—as God's vicar on Earth, he was, etymologically, at least, the anti, "in place of," Christ. But John Paul II the Antichrist? He was such a nice guy. She didn't want to begin to believe that. The farthest she would go was to allow that maybe it wasn't the man, but the office, and as such focused on the date he *became* pope, October 16th. So there were ten days in October she was *not* looking forward to.

"Madness," Scarlot mumbled, but that was life inside their hollowed out, battened down sanctuary.

October passed safely, except for the monsters ringing their doorbell all night long on Halloween, causing Marilyn to jump each and every time they did. And then the elections of 2000.

"You see!" Marilyn cried. "He was right."

"Gee whiz, fraudulent elections, what a shocker."

But then the new administration settled in and nothing much happened, literally. They spent most of their time on vacation, in fact.

"In *Texas*!" Marilyn tried.

"It's a big, big damn state," Scarlot said. "Keep writing," became her constant refrain, while Marilyn wandered off into the internet and studied revelations. She would not be disabused of her quest or suspicions—even with Scarlot repeatedly insisting that with each passing day of Peter's silence it surely meant he'd gone off on his own pilgrimage of one sort or another, "He may be in Tibet for all we know,"—but she could be detoured from time to time, which is all Scarlot needed.

"Look at that," she said that August, of a story about some crazy judge in Alabama being taken down for installing a granite monument of the ten commandments in his courthouse. "Still think the apocalypse is nigh?"

Marilyn had to admit that it didn't look good for the dominionists, and relaxed ever more into their routine as summer gave way to fall.

Scarlot trolled the wires for possible headlines early September, but the pickings were pretty slim. Good Neighbor Day last week in New Jersey. "Humbug." She scanned the blurb: "Thought so," she said, when she saw a local florist was giving out free roses to attendees. "Porn in Peoria," she read. "Who knew?" Someone offering a home correspondence course in miracles.

"What?" Marilyn jumped.

"Good Lord. Ah, here's one," she said, and typed, "Dog with six legs and two penises found." It was a report out of Malaysia.

Staring at the sentence a moment, Scarlot asked, "Should it be peni?"

Marilyn closed her eyes, answered, "I don't think it's ever come up."

"Good one," Scarlot said.

Worrying over implications, Marilyn had missed the pun. Implications be damned, Scarlot loved the play, loved it more than just about anything else. "Good one," she repeated, and cackled.

Marilyn sighed. "Leave it as penises, if you must."

"Needs more zing," Scarlot said. *Six Legs and Two Penises: Master Breed?*

"Must you?"

"It's the only fun I have any more."

"You're despoiling the profession."

"What profession, mutant journalism?"

With a little fudging, they could be called human interest—the off-beat, often absurd pieces they submitted to various ISPs, in this case SwiftNet—which sometimes satisfied Marilyn. Their collaboration was working out better than Scarlot expected: her writing the headlines at the bottom of the list of more reputable sources, like AP, Christian Science Monitor, or Reuters, on various home-pages. Marilyn wrote the attendant filler, a paragraph or two baited browsers would find if they followed the headline link, along with a bevy of ads from site sponsors. Scarlot and Marilyn, whose by-line was TH—for Tender Hookers, LLC, things were going so well—made their money off the curious clicks on the headline, the "hook," two cents a pop, three for any hits over ten thousand. The home page, SwiftNet, in turn, got paid any time someone clicked on an ad banner.

"We sound like prostitutes," Marilyn had complained when Scarlot incorporated the name.

"We *are* prostitutes," Scarlot answered, and then explained, "only now we're not *liable*," which proved dangerously liberating. "How about this," she said: *Sign of the Apocalypse: Dog with Six Legs and Two Penises*.

"Why the recent fascination with animals?"

Just a month or so ago, Scarlot had penned, *North Carolina Couple Trains Pygmy Seeing-Eye Horses*.

"People *love* animal stories. Gets them every time."

"We went to school for this?"

"We went to school to make money," Scarlot reminded her. "You want to win a Pulitzer, do it on your own time."

"When would that be?" Marilyn asked, as much of a challenge as she'd ever offer Scarlot, shifting behind the lap-top.

Scarlot was her life-line, the one who answered their correspondence, the telephone, knocks at their door. Scarlot did the shopping, when they couldn't find what they needed on-line, and deliverable. Scarlot called the repairmen, picked up the mail. Scarlot made the doctor's visits. She was the one who facilitated *any* contact with the outside world. Marilyn would have retreated so far as to disappear years and years ago—way back in those college days—had Scarlot not come along. That was back in the seventies, nearly thirty years ago now, right there at Washington University in St. Louis. Marilyn knew she was in trouble the first time she set foot on campus alone, without her protective parents, without an upperclassman liaison. She felt like she was drowning, swallowed up by the hugeness of it all, the stately buildings, the teeming campus population. It wasn't at all like high school, at Catholic, a small, private school, where she navigated in tight, manageable circles, the newspaper, the yearbook staff, the honor roll. There she was looked upon as smart, and not unattractive, with her long, auburn hair, worn loose, and flowing. She was reserved, quiet enough, an embodiment of the parochial uniform all the co-eds had to wear. She had avoided falling "in love," as so many of her classmates had, though only accidentally, only because she didn't trust her worthiness to pursue any of the typical crushes she'd experienced. She avoided that until she was a sophomore at Washington, won a damn prize for one of the first columns to carry her by-line, then swooned under the attention that notoriety brought, sweeping her over a psychic edge which was always there, just not recognized. Enter Scarlot: bold, brassy, a little butch, even, and unapologetic, who disdained make-up, lingerie, and anyone who couldn't laugh at the world, or laugh at themselves. She turned out to be a newsroom junkie, absorbing events, opinions, debates, always with an acerbic attitude, a sarcastic wit, and a steady diet of hardened cynicism. Marilyn was the hopeful, but fearful optimist. "Naïve," Scarlot called her. Marilyn was shocked by both the criminality of Nixon's administration, and Ford's pardons. She still didn't fully accept the evilness of Reagan's October Surprise, or his VP's culpability in it *or* Iran-Contra. "He seems so *tame*," she had said of HW. "Right," Scarlot had said.

"When would that be?" Scarlot answered her, who would, by contrast, challenge Marilyn at *every* opportunity, which was part of her job. "Any time you get the balls to take it. Start writing."

"What in the world am I supposed to write about that?" Marilyn said, feeling the press of their deadline.

"Write whatever you want, you and I both know it doesn't make a piss-pot of difference. Nobody *studies* this stuff," Scarlot told her, untangling the headphone cord, lining up a row of individual Star Bursts taken from their package, in the proper order, yellow, then pink, then red, and orange, so Marilyn could "settle" into writing, this latest aspect of their routine, the constant supply of candy. Whatever it takes, was Scarlot's attitude.

"It's got to be *some* kind of conspiracy, don't you think?" she teased, bringing up an old argument between them, an argument that usually prodded sufficient response.

"Do you *have* to do that, Scar?" But it was too late.

Marilyn's basic view of the world was one of expectant benevolence, a world she believed tended toward order, fairness, justice. There were hazards in her world, to be sure, but they were arbitrary wrinkles in what she wanted to *believe* was an overall rational system. It was a belief she grappled with nonetheless. She needed to believe it rather than actually believed it. Otherwise the world would unravel, in her mind, all around her. It *had* to remain intact, or all was hopeless, belief or not.

She fretted the wrinkles, and mostly avoided them, by maintaining an order in her tight sphere. She nested, a lot, in their little home. She never went to bed with dirty dishes in the sink, set out her clothes the night before, still brushed her teeth three times a day, dressed and fixed her hair first thing in the morning—even though she very rarely left the house—kept a constant vigilance that there were no crooked pictures on the walls, no lumps in the carpet, and coasters under every drinking vessel: all actions, among many others, designed to defy any outward appearance of chaos. Except when the "arbitrary" chaos could no longer be denied, Marilyn still reached for villains, a reason, a plot—zealous conspirators who couldn't abide by peace and tranquility, normalcy.

"Horseshit!" Scarlot cried. "Reverse projection," she called it. She embraced the chaos. It was her theory that if Marilyn could be a little more accepting of her internal turmoil—didn't struggle so hard to maintain that appearance of stability—she would, de facto, *be* more stable. "It's so fucking simple," Scarlot would insist in her sometimes crude way.

Not for Marilyn. For Marilyn, the logic was twisted, and twisting. Whenever she tried to follow it, she wound up bent into a mental pretzel.

Scarlot tried, harder and harder it seemed. Not long ago, she ran a headline, *Fundamentalists Fight to Overrule Newton's 2nd Law*, the story being that in a biblically rendered world, there was no room for a theory as blasphemous as entropy or randomness. "God does not play dice!" they recited.

"*That's* twisted," she'd hinted, "and ignorant, of course," suggesting Marilyn should distance herself as far as she could from such a platform.

That didn't work, so she kept making subtle and not-so-subtle attempts to illustrate the untenable notion that disorder was the result of malevolent plots to upset the balance, like the six-legged dog story, hoping to push Marilyn off the assumptive stance that it *must* be a conspiracy at work, and onto territory that viewed such behavior as merely deliciously ridiculous. In her sometimes succinct way, Scarlot insisted, *insisted*, "There are *no* plots, anywhere," and even carried that notion into their work, hence the distribution of duties: Scarlot really believed (or wouldn't concern herself to consider otherwise) that nobody cared about the stories, or really read them, certainly didn't "study" them, and so, quit writing the stories behind her headlines long ago, leaving it to Marilyn to come up with something at least a little sensible, or not, depending on the headline.

This current one, the multiply appendaged canine, while vexing Marilyn, was already formulating in her mind, or rather, unfolding, a familiar, recurring tale already embedded there, planted the day the one real, true person—the only person she thought she *could* live with—had abandoned her—planted, and nurtured behind the dead-bolts, behind the curtained, blinded, and foiled windows.

"Abandoned by my whole crazy life," was how she often thought of it, especially now, now that she worked so hard to avoid any contact with that life. Once again: Scarlot.

"Tick, tick, tick," she said, tapping the watch face on her right wrist, which only made Marilyn's task more difficult, and compounded it at the same time, as she slipped the pair of Bose headphones over her ears, to drown out *any* ambient noise: "Best damn headphones in the whole effing world," Scarlot had said when they arrived, yet another *requirement* of Marilyn's.

Inside, though, not having turned on any music, the voices between those ears just swirled. She heard other voices, the crazy millenialists, and their just as crazy counter-millenialists. She remembered Peter's declarations over a year earlier, propounding imminent apocalypse, mass hysteria. One voice said, "Dogs mating with cats!" an old movie line. Didn't matter: *Dogs and cats*, she wrote, the Armageddon beast, the *Scarlet coloured beast*, and the woman who sat upon it, the *mother of harlots and abominations of the earth*, Scarlet, the *woman of the seven hills*, "How many hills in St. Louis?" she asked, the woman, *having a golden cup in her hand full of abominations and filthiness of her fornication* astride the beast, *having seven heads and ten horns*, "That's it!" she said, and started to write, "Bioengineering project designed to birth the Armageddon beast goes horribly awry," and wrote, and wrote, and wrote, talking about the poor puppy, with the six legs and two penises, and attempts by Asian geneticists to clone the biblical monster that was supposed to romp upon the water-turned-blood, the left-behind masses, one of the last signs leading up to the final confrontation and end times.

"Those folks again?" Scarlot asked.

"Don't you think?"

"They're always up to something."

And when she was finished, Marilyn went to SwiftNet's site to upload the story, spotted the headlines already posted there, and said, even with the headphones still in place, in a voice louder than necessary, a voice, though, that wouldn't have ceded to normal restraint anyway, a voice restrained only by the hyper-ventilation overtaking her, "Scarlot, today's the day."

"What day?"

Marilyn held her breath, pointing to a CNN by-line. "Peter's day."

"Son of a bitch," Scarlot said.

"You *still* believe there are no plots?"

WHEN his cell phone went off on the bedside table, Jack Pardew, in his fitful sleep state, first mistook the noise for a cockroach scurrying across the wooden surface, charging, no doubt, for the bag of salted peanuts loosely opened, or his plastic glass of water, or even the remnants of the rum and coke he never finished the night before. He retrieved the copy of *The Globe* he'd fallen asleep to and swatted at the noise, all without opening his eyes—refusing to open them, in fact, refusing any intrusion on his rest—knocking the peanuts to the bare floor, spilling the water after them, barely missing the tumbler, which probably would have shattered and eliminated the possibility of more sleep. As it was, he said only, "Great," to the mess, and pulled the covers up over his head again. And then the phone rang, or vibrated, a second time.

Awake enough to recognize the sound, he reached for the phone, but when he spied the red digital clock numbers glowing 8:20, he stayed his hand from answering. Daylight seeped through the closed curtains, as he rolled away from the table, and "that damn phone," toward the window. Muttering a low curse he then rolled again in the opposite direction, kicking off bed covering tangled around his feet, as another sultry September day in St. Louis was well underway.

Then he groaned into his pillow as the phone started rattling again, a disembodied jitterbug dancing pointlessly. He sat up and draped his legs over the edge of the bed, snatching up the phone in mid-skip, and flipped open the screen even as one of his socked feet found the puddle of water on the floor. "Well, shit," he said, to both his now wet foot and the caller ID he saw. "Who-it?" he said, sounding out the acronym he'd entered into the phone book, which stood for, Which One Is It This Time?, as the vibrating stopped and the phone registered the third missed call in as many minutes.

Jack lifted his foot, felt its dampness, said, "Eyew," and waited. He knew there would be as many such missed connections for however many minutes he resisted answering—regardless of which caller it was—so when the next call came through precisely forty-five seconds later, he answered it, guessing, "Scarlot, my dear?"

There was no response from the other end, just breathing—shallow, staccato half-breaths—evidence enough of who was calling to prompt him to say into the phone, "Relax, Marilyn. Easy, now, relax, honey. You got your bag handy?" he asked, and imagined her nodding her head to him from across town and through the ether, "All right, then, you know what to do. Don't worry, I'll hold," he said, and listened to the rattling of the paper sack, as it expanded and collapsed, until Marilyn controlled her breathing enough to speak.

"Peter was right," she said.

Which cast enough doubt over Jack's assumption for him to repeat, "Scarlot? What are we working on now, deary?"

"No, Jack, it's Marilyn," she corrected him, pausing, in a continual effort to settle her breathing. "I'm serious. This is it. We're under, *attack*! Today's the day. It makes perfect sense. September 11th. This is the day Manhattan was discovered in 1609, so of course they'd attack there. And it's al-Assad's birthday, Jack, the King of Syria, the *King* of Syria!" one, albeit obscure, candidate for the Antichrist.

"Lord, Marilyn, you know you shouldn't be reading that stuff. Let me talk to Scarlot."

"The *hell* with Scarlot," she said. "This is real, Jack. Turn on your television."

"What?"

"You believe in pictures. Turn on your television."

"Which station," he asked, retrieving the remote from the mess of covers.

Joe Formichella

"*Any* station," she screamed.

When the set across the room atop his bureau blinked to life, he saw smoke billowing from each of the twin towers of the World Trade Center, downtown, New York City.

"What the hell happened?" he said into the phone.

"We're under *attack*," she repeated.

"What?" he asked, failing to comprehend the images, the same images he found broadcast by station after station as he scrolled through the channels. "This can't be real," he said, as much to himself as to her. "This has to be some kind of sick *War of the Worlds* thing," not yet turning up the sound of the various commentators.

And then, mutely, they watched the image shift to a gaping, smoldering hole in the side of the Pentagon. "What the..." he started, but didn't continue.

"Jack?'

"What," he said, flatly.

"What's going on?" she asked, counting on him, as she has always counted on him, to be her filter.

"Christ, Marilyn, how would I know?"

"What about," she started, "Him?"

"Paul? What about *him*?"

"He's still in DC, right? You should call Him."

"Not my job," he said, further admitting, "I can't talk, right now." He was in shock, as the whirlwind of realization, the repeated images, engulfed, stunned, even scared him, he allowed, reaching for a pillow. "Call me later," he said, dropping his phone to the bed without disconnecting. He didn't want to call Paul. He didn't want to think about Paul.

He swung his legs back up onto the bed, soggy foot and all,

hugging the pillow to his chest, settling back against the head-board, watching the news, listening to the reports, holding on against a rush of vertigo, or madness, as if the rug of all firmament had been yanked out from under him. Only when he shook his head in an effort to dispel that feeling did he discover that he'd been crying, which was enough of a check for him to admonish himself, "Oh, Lord, honey. Get a grip," reaching for the glass of tepid and diluted rum and coke.

MARILYN was pacing. Not your *job*? she thought. "Whose job *is* it?" she asked, retrieving the bag she'd dropped to the side of the easy chair. He was the one, the one she most wanted to hear about, because if he was all right, if he wasn't panicked, or scared, that was a start, a step she could derive some measure of reassurance, even confidence from. He was the one who always had the an-swers, knew where he was going, knew what he was getting into.

"Forget Him," Scarlot said suddenly. "Did you upload the sto-ry?"

"What? The story?" Marilyn said. "What does the *story* mat-ter now?"

"Nothing's changed, Chickie. Nothing. We still have to make the cycle. You know the nut: six times a day, minimum."

"How can you say that?"

"Watch."

And she did. They watched the reports, the repeating scenes, the latest horrors, as first the South, and then the North tower col-lapsed, Marilyn reaching for the paper bag to settle her breathing, the sights suffocating her as if she too were caught in those narrow Manhattan streets, engulfed by the debris, the smoke, and the silt blasting from the site in great, roiling gray clouds.

She paced some more, wearing a path in the rug nestled up against the threshold to their small home, the front door, back and forth, wondering what was happening outside, fearful of what she might find, but too scared to investigate, back and forth.

"I should call my mother," she tried, searching for an incontrovertible impetus to act, to do *something*, trying to fight her way through the maze of fear, terror, really, which presented resistance enough, on *normal* days, to keep her from venturing outside, to the store, the post office, the movie theater. Scarlot was little help.

"She's in a home," she said. "She's all right. Who's going to bother a bunch of old people? Besides, we call her, we have to hear about her hips, the bad food, the rude aides."

"What about Gail?" a sister.

"At the bank?"

"Right."

"Go ahead, if you want to be put on hold every thirty seconds while she conducts her *business*."

"We should call *some*body."

"Why?'

"Be-*cause*," Marilyn said, waving toward the television.

"That's the difference between you and me, Chickie. You need people more than you can admit, and yet you're scared of them. I don't need anyone, and I'm not that concerned about them, one way or another."

"Even now?"

"Even now."

Marilyn paced, averting her gaze from the door, to the TV, where commentators interviewed experts, military, diplomatic, cabinet members, in between updates from the streets, from policemen, the mayor of New York, all of them searching for answers to Who? and Why?

"You want to go out?" Scarlot asked. She'd been flipping channels, trying to find something different to view. Even her beloved Fox Network was carrying the same repetitive footage. "You want to go down to the church or something?"

"No," Marilyn answered quickly, then, "Yes."

"Thought so."

She *did* want to go out, just not like this, not alone. Or, it was an urge, more than a desire, to connect somehow, with someone, because the outside world, even if it terrified her, could usually be counted on to remain relatively stable, or constant. Now it was more chaotic seeming than her internal territory. And that, if it's possible, was driving her crazy, driving her through any apprehension of mingling, to a *need* to connect, close the gap between those two worlds, if not reconcile them.

"*That's* crazy," Scarlot said.

"No, it's *not*," not if she could find someone she trusted, someone who'd hold her hand, not let her disappear, someone like, Jack…

"You're going to call him again, already?"

"How long has it been?"

"Not long enough."

"Please?"

IT had been forever, or so it seemed to Jack, forever in a timeless way, that he'd been rooted to his unmade bed, interrupting the trance only to freshen his rum and coke, or to pee. He was unmoored in time, and space, unable to say—whenever he thought to think of such things—*exactly* where he was, with any conviction. He could easily mistake the room for any of the countless, nondescript hotel rooms he's occupied over the years.

He could have been in any one of those nameless rooms, with the uniform paint, the requisite prints on the walls, the usual furniture. Never mind that the coloring was of his choosing, most of the framed pictures his work, and the furniture—the four-poster bed, the bedside table, the rocking chair and bureau—his furniture, his family's furniture, his mother's furniture, that he'd carted around the region in move after successive move. It was the context of the setting that was disorienting, a context brought about by the stories on the television, of terrorists, and religious jihads, of judgment, and justice, saber-rattling threats, declarations of vengeance and patriotism, vows, promises, and veiled resolutions. It was all lost on Jack, just as he felt they—all the commentators and reporters, spokesmen, and leaders—were missing the import, the real, *human* import of the scenes, the *pictures* of devastation, vulnerability, sadness, destruction, and death. He was unmoored and immobilized, by a sense that they weren't capturing the true meaning of the event, already looking beyond what had *happened*, were already weaving the tragedy into a new folk tale of might and aggression, missing the *fact* of the attack, the true picture of shock and disbelief that would too soon be buried beneath an already apparent tone of militant retribution and revenge. They weren't seeing, weren't getting, the *pictures*.

Jack knew that collective character flaw, all too well, knew the tendency to mistake the general for the particular, mistake the forest for any given tree, misapprehend a lifestyle for any individual practitioner. Yes, he knew it very well, even in his present condition, numb, from the days' events, and the alcohol, even if not drunk enough, from the alcohol.

"Isn't *that* a bitch," he said, pissed off about it all, though mostly at himself.

His sitting there all morning, partaking in the mass inertia over what had happened—*contributing* to the inertia, he convinced himself—had been the last thing he should have done, the last, last, last thing. He wasn't part of that mass, wasn't party to the consensus, wasn't willing to follow. He'd spent most of his life, over half of his near-fifty years, situating himself beyond the norm, outside of the fascist tyranny of the bell curve, he was one of *them*, the unaccepted them. He had not one, but two brothers tell him as much. "And if you can't believe family," he said, mockingly, getting up from the bed.

"No," he said, deciding. He would not watch any more, would not wait to be told how to feel, how to react. He went into his kitchen and set up a pot of coffee, and then wobbled off toward the shower, intent on gathering his photography equipment, hailing a cab for the airport, and boarding a plane for New York. He would take his own pictures, gather his own impressions, and let them lead him wherever they might, just as he has for the last, "How many?" years. He would freelance.

"It's the *o-only* thing to do," he sang to himself in the shower, water and suds scrolling off him like so much dead skin. It's the only thing he could do, the only thing he's really wanted to do, for as long as he could remember, and beyond, before any explicit memories.

There was one picture, back when he was just a little boy, just in grade school, a *Time* magazine cover, the one of a naked little girl standing in a Vietnamese street, a collateral victim of a napalm attack, the girl's pain and anguish palpable in the image—arms held out wide from her sides, as if her skin were crawling with white-hot licks of fire. The impression didn't crystallize into a life's direction until fifteen years later, until he was almost graduated from college with a business degree, but when it did, he knew it was a right choice, a choice that had been waiting for him all that time. And what's more, it was a choice that came with a model, a model for how to make any subsequent choices in his life, a model that has tended him through plenty of other difficult choices.

Only when he was dried, and dressed, and was pulling the bed coverings into some kind of shape—"Because an unmade bed is so depressing," he reminded himself, just another of his habits, both the act, and the reminder—did he retrieve his phone, and notice the new tally of missed calls, all but one from Scarlot, or Marilyn—what with this new state of things, all of his previously conceived safe assumptions were not without challenge—the other being from his mother. He returned her call.

"Johnny," she answered. "Have you seen the news?"

How could I *not* see it, he thought, how could *anyone* not see it, but said, "Yeah. It's horrible."

That covered, she asked, "Where are you?" and then, the expected follow-up, "Have you heard from your brothers?"

"No, not yet," he answered according to her priorities, her inability to think of any one of her sons without thinking of all three of them—even with one of them disappeared, as if a national catastrophe would bring him out of hiding—a contextual fabric of hers that she'd woven and held to from the moment she'd birthed and named them, first Peter, then a year later the twins, Paul, and John, named them after apostles, binding them together with a common, lasting thread, if only in her mind. "I'm on my way out of town, headed for the airport."

"Airport? To where?"

"New York."

"Why in God's name would you go there, honey?"

"It's what I *do*, honey."

It's what he's done since going to Central America in the mid-eighties, since the 1988 California earthquake, the 1993 flood, Waco, Oklahoma City, EVOS, the millennial hysteria and celebration, the Florida election, rushing into hot spots across the country, around the world, capturing the chaos in digital images, emailing the bundled shots to his agent at McGready Associates, to be shopped to any one of a hundred or so weekly magazines and wire services.

"Please be careful, Johnny."

"I will, Mother," he promised, then as the beeping of a queued call alerted him, said, "I've got another call, sugar. I'll talk to you soon," and answered the other line, "Yes?"

"Where the hell have you been?"

"Scarlot, so nice to hear from you."

"Skip it, fag-boy. Answer my question."

"Now, Scarlot, what have we said about projecting?"

"Oh, Christ. I give up. Talk to her."

"Jack?"

"Hi, honey. You all right?"

"Where have you been?"

"You know, it kind of scares me when you two start to sound alike."

"Jack, be serious."

"All right, all right. I was in a hole for a while, but I'm out, I'm dealing. I'm on the move."

"Dealing? How? And on the move where?"

"New York."

"New York?"

"Yeah. I'm just about at the airport."

"You're going to get on a plane? Oh, Jack, no…"

He heard her drop the phone.

"Perfect. Hey, John-boy, get us some headlines while you're there."

"Scarlot? You asking for my input all of a sudden?"

"Don't let it go to your head, sissy-man. Big, or little."

He laughed at that, first time he could remember laughing in quite a while, and cherished the sound, the sense of it. "Got to go," he said, to whoever was listening. "I'll call you later."

Jack took his first picture almost as soon as he'd paid the cabbie and stepped out onto the departure curb outside the American Airlines door. He swung his overnight bag where it draped over his right shoulder around to the front and took out his Nikon, aiming it along the breezeway where no other passengers, no porters came or went from any of the other carrier entrances. And there were no other automobiles in sight. Strange, for a Tuesday afternoon, or any afternoon.

Inside, the building was just as deserted. He managed to find one sky-cap down near the baggage claim, and when he asked what was going on, was told, "Planes are grounded."

"All of them?"

"Everywhere."

"Everywhere?"

"The whole country's grounded, man."

"Damn."

Only once he was outside again, did he seem to notice that not only were the sidewalks and loading lanes clear, so was the sky. The quiet was complete, and frightening, in its foreignness. He wouldn't have been able to fathom a world without airplanes, and yet there it was, all around him, no droning turbines, no screeching landings, no accelerating take-offs shattering the day. For nearly a hundred years planes have been crisscrossing the sky above St. Louis, but on that afternoon, there was absolutely no trace of a jet trail to be found anywhere in the bright blue dome above him, in any direction he turned.

"Marilyn would *love* this," he said, and thought to call and tell her as much, but didn't. Instead, he called for a cab to return to his apartment and work out what his next step would be.

SHE would have loved it, had she any inkling of the development. She might have heard, in all the other news swirling about the events, that the FAA had suspended all domestic flights, but it didn't register. Instead, she was still spiraling inward, from the ceaseless coverage of the attacks—all other programming had been suspended—and the already cacophonous din for retaliation, revenge. The president's own vocabulary had shifted from a midday acknowledgement of the attacks, to an early evening call to arms, a veritable declaration of war. Against, exactly, whom? she wondered. "We face an invisible enemy…" he'd said. So how were they to fight a war? Between the repeated images of devastation on the tube, and the images of bombs dropping and strafing fighter planes in her mind, Marilyn would have indeed *loved* the completely empty skies just outside her bunkered house, if only she could have found a necessary perch of stability from which to appreciate it.

Scarlot was trolling for headlines. She had yielded to the blanket coverage, that had preempted the soaps, the talks shows, the local news and weather. It was the only game in town, she conceded. "Who's going to care about rabid nuns or human skull bowling balls today," she had mused at one point.

"Ah, here's one," she said, *Washington Under Siege: Car Bombs at the State House, Fires on the Mall.*

"This is insane!"

"It's a world gone crazy."

When Marilyn sat down to seek out some filler for the headline, she entered the line, "world gone crazy," as her search string. Her results were song lyrics. *Song* lyrics! By Glenn Campbell, Tears for Fears. "*Song* lyrics?" And this: "Dealing with a world gone crazy," where some anonymous writer was quoting scripture: Hebrews, Psalms, and John, ending the sermon with, "May God speedily hasten that day!"

"What day?" she wondered out loud, and allowed herself, her attention, to become fixed on that question, adsorbed by its implications, remembering—what seemed like so long ago now, like an entirely different time, an entirely different place, an epochal shift—Peter's insistence that there was a day, a specific day coming. "Of course," she muttered, what other day than this day, this day that had wrought so much unmitigated havoc, had opened gaping fissures in all things secure, or comfortable, familiar, or assumed. "What other day?" she said, closing the arch of the initial question with but another, rhetorical question, a Mobius, Platonic step, that she took, willingly enough, along a circuitous path blazed by Escher, Göedel, Bach, and Schrödinger, losing herself along the way, which was preferable, a better alternative than repeatedly bumping into herself, and all the attendant, confounding reality, but leaving Scarlot behind in the process, which was maybe not the best option; just the most immediate.

Scarlot, for her part, remained vigilant, plugged in, a fulcrum of connectedness, in the ensuing disorientation. She watched, and listened, and waited, waited for crazy Marilyn to land on her feet, or catch her own tail, however she'd characterize this current retreat, whether free-falling or running around in circles, it was all the same in the end: a journey through darkness and fear, past whispering crannies and cold, reaching fingers, presences looming but not identifying themselves, missed-steps, inverted promontories, beguiling opposites, weightlessness *and* gravity, helpless inertia and crushing import, all of it, all of it, fueled by fear, fear of the unknown, of the invisible enemies, nameless attackers, convinced of their mal-intent, oblivious to their methods.

Fear: She remembered *Him* telling her once, "You can't be afraid of everything."

"I can't?" As if that was an option. Because she was, pretty much, afraid of everything. Elevators, for instance. Suspended by a cable, rising higher and higher off the ground, that was nothing but frightening for her.

"Check the records," he told her. "These things *work*," he insisted, standing in the lobby of some building—hotels, typically—where, after begging, unsuccessfully, for a room on the ground floor, he would wait with her, passing up car after car to their lodging, luggage at his feet, while she worked up the courage to step through the sighing doors.

And when she did check the records, what she usually found was a report of where an elevator *did* fail, plummeting ten, twenty, thirty flights.

"Yes, yes, yes," he countered, "but for every one that falls, millions don't!"

Which didn't help either. For every one she got on, and survived, in Marilyn's mind, that only reduced the odds of survival.

"Oh, jeez," he would surrender. It's no wonder *He* left.

In Marilyn's mind, she was born too late, birthed, in 1956, into the age of color television, FM radio, at the starting line of the space race, where people hurtled themselves into the void, chasing danger and disaster. It was too much, too much to comprehend, and keep up with. She should've been born an earlier, easier time, a time when threats were immediate, recognizable, known. So she retreated to those times, researching events, eras, characters from the past.

For the moment, she was in 1933, a familiar destination, FDR's inaugural, "The only thing we have to fear, is fear itself!" Exactly! Marilyn felt. "Ex*act*ly."

"But," she said, the time was fraught with treachery, too, the very beginnings of treachery: construction began on the Golden Gate Bridge, Dachau opened, so many of the huge mega-dams were underway, the idea for nuclear chain reaction was conceived, "by a guy waiting at a damn traffic light!" And then, in October, the first, "The *first*," commercial airliner was sabotaged over Ohio, the Reichstag fire. "No, no," Marilyn said. Not there, don't go there. "Earlier…"

Scarlot listened, and waited. When Jack called from the road, she welcomed the distraction.

"Now where are you?" she answered, unaware of the passage of time, or the time of the day, caught in the grip of this latest episode.

"Kentucky," he said.

"Kentucky? Thought you were going to New York?"

"I was, but you can't get a flight anywhere."

"You mean *you* can't get a flight. We don't fly, remember?" Scarlot had still, *still*, failed to get Marilyn anywhere near an airplane, or an airport, for that matter.

"*No* one can get a flight. Everything's grounded."

"Really?"

"Really. What's happening there?"

"M's gone."

"Gone? Where?"

"Chasing shadows. Plato's cave, I think."

"Oh, Lord. Should I sing?" he asked, but before answered, crooned, "Dear Prudence…"

"Good God, no," Scarlot cut him off.

"Then take her outside in the morning. There're no sharks in the sky."

"It's night-time?" she asked.

"Lord," he said again. "I guess you would be locked up tight on a day like today. Whatever else you think about me Scarlot, I don't envy you."

"Of course you do," she said, "and I *know* it," then hung up.

He knew it, too. Driving eastward through the pitch of Kentucky night, he knew there was much about Scarlot to envy, by anyone's estimate. He envied her ability and willingness to say the truth, for one, that often no-nonsense, no qualms, no regrets, bad-ass stance she could assume at pivotal times and hold up a truth, even uncomfortable truths, the only weapon she needed at such moments.

She'd done just that a little over two years ago when she kicked him out of their house, for his own good, as she insisted: *that* truth. He'd been staying there intermittently, one of his bases spread around the country where he retreated from time to time in the midst of chasing pictures here or there, retreats that had lately turned into whining sessions, Jack decrying his lack of respect, lack of notoriety, too many people on the roads he traveled treating him like a common paparazzo, a sensation mongering parasite.

"Take pictures for us," Marilyn would offer from time to time.

"For you? Sorry, girls, but that's not the kind of exposure I'm looking for."

"I know what you mean," she said.

"Bullshit!" Scarlot thundered. "You two are pathetic. You actually think there're more legitimate, *truer* outlets out there? Nobody *cares*, Johnny, haven't you figured that out yet?"

"He's an *artist*, Scar."

"Oh, *meh*."

"What does *that* mean?"

"Don't take that tone with me: I'm going easy on you. It *means* I want to puke. Artist… What does *that* mean?"

"An artisan, one who practices one of the fine arts…"

"Oh, jeez, thank you, Ms. Webster. He's a leech."

"Photography's different."

"Right. You're a *special* leech."

"Must you be so crude?"

"You want crude? He's a *fucking* leech."

"Not photography. The fact is, all fine art *but* photography, is plagiarism, and all commercial art but photography is theft."

"That's *so* true," Marilyn said.

"That's so *not* true," Scarlot corrected, just like that. "Get *over* yourself."

Then, later, she said, "You should quit staying here. Get your own place."

"You kicking me out?"

"Yes."

"Why?"

"Because she's babying you," meaning Marilyn.

"You're serious?"

"As hell."

"What does Marilyn think?"

"Doesn't matter. You two share the same insecurities, which is the problem. So she doesn't get to vote."

"That hardly seems fair."

"Don't be such a baby."

"Scarlot?"

"Quiet! It's the *truth*, Johnny-boy, and you *know* it."

And he did, knew it the moment she uttered it, though that didn't necessarily lead to unquestioning acceptance, which is the usual way *he* dealt with truth, questioning it, shaping it, allowing it to shift, as he had over the intervening months, actually allowing himself to believe that at least *part* of the problem resided in his resemblance to Paul. Even though they'd started to lose some of their identicalness in recent years, Marilyn wouldn't have realized that, not having seen much of *Him* in those same years. Jack tried, even suggesting that part of his exaggerated mannerisms was his attempt to not remind Marilyn of *Him*.

Scarlot's response to that suggestion was always the same. "Bullshit."

That brought a grin to his face, a self-effacing, sad realization of a grin. That's what he did with truth, allowed it to slip out of the light and into shadows, a lot like his journey along I-40, eastbound, through Kentucky, bound for Virginia, DC, New York, during those frequent stretches where there was no other traffic, just him, in his metallic green, convertible Mustang, with the top down, and the high lamp posts, casting a yellow glow of illumination down upon him that he sped through, back into darkness, light, and darkness, marking his way, all his ways.

9.

POKING her head, only, out the door the next morning, kind of peering at an angle beyond the eaves, after Scarlot commanded, "Go *outside*, now!" Marilyn truly loved the emptiness above, loved it in her tentative way, but couldn't bring herself to trust it. It was too quiet. In a hub city that would normally be humming with air and ground and water traffic, having served as a gateway for the country for a couple of centuries, the Midwest's "Grand Central," there was nothing but silence, a collective, vigilant waiting. St. Louis was reduced to a stunned audience, waiting for what would come next. The whole world was on hold.

"Eerie, isn't it?" Scarlot said for her.

Which was enough for Marilyn to slip back inside, close and latch the door. "It's pregnant," she said, bracing her back to the door, barring whatever expectancy she imagined, which could have been anything.

"What do you know about pregnancy?" Scarlot muttered, without thinking.

The question stung, they both knew. Scarlot even offered a rare apology, "Sorry."

But the remark did have one desirable effect; it knocked Marilyn out of one phobic loop into another. "Did Jack say Kentucky?"

she asked, moving to the computer.

"Yeah. Why?"

"I just thought I saw," she said, searching, "Thought I saw a report of another plane going down in Kentucky…" She couldn't find the reference she'd seen earlier—when was that, exactly?—about another jet going down along the Ohio-Kentucky border, but still said, "Could you call him?"

"You think a plane fell on him?"

"Please?"

Beyond seizing up into a fit at the very thought of boarding a plane, Marilyn was convinced that they routinely, randomly, fell from the sky. She *knew* that was just bound to happen, and had long ago, back when she could more easily be coaxed outside, avoided any proximity to any airport, or any other potential flight path, any place the "sky sharks," as she called them, might be hovering, looming, lurking.

"Jack?" Scarlot shouted into the phone.

"What?"

"Has a plane fallen on you?"

"Say that again."

"What the hell is all that noise?"

"It's a parade."

"A *parade*?" Marilyn interrupted. "For *what*?"

"Fundamentalists. It's the bicentennial of their first ever camp-meeting."

"Oh my God," Marilyn said, dropping the phone.

"Jack?"

"What's the matter with her?"

"Gone again."

"Why?"

"Never mind that now. Where are you, exactly?"

"Near Lexington, a little place called Cane Ridge, Kentucky. It's actually just outside of Fort Knox," he started, then said, "I'll be damned."

"What is it?"

"An airplane."

"What kind of airplane?"

"Oh my God!" Marilyn cried.

"Strange," he said, "but it looks like some Arabic line."

"What can that mean?"

"I don't have a clue, honey, not one damn clue."

In the few days to follow, they would get answers to their questions, not that the furious sequence of events made any more sense, just that they were explained—from the identities of the hijackers to the group behind the attacks to the purpose of the plane Jack saw in Kentucky. They had the facts. But if bin Laden was the mastermind behind everything, why were his family members being whisked out of the country—at a time when the entirety of the contingent states was a no-fly zone. Didn't make sense. And there was seemingly no time to ponder the story as the country was hurtling toward war.

It was all completely too much for Marilyn. She retreated further, to the 17th century, repelled by the present as much as drawn by past parallels. She thought of the Pilgrims, fundamentalists who hated the Catholic Church, the Church of England's alignment with papist dictates, and, eventually, the monarchy itself. In mid-century they provided much of the militia muscle to overthrow Charles I in the British Civil Wars—their belief being that if they deposed Charles and toppled his government that would pave the way for the return of Jesus and his thousand-year reign.

They managed to defeat Charles and the monarchy was indeed dissolved by Cromwell, but Jesus was a no-show.

And then, as those things typically did, the monarchy cycled back around with the Restoration of Charles II. That was not good news for the Pilgrims. Jr.'s Prime Minister, Lord Clarendon, suspended *habeas corpus*, rounded up scores of them and exported them to off-shore detention centers. The message was pretty clear, prompting the "great migration" to Virginia, Carolina, and the Massachusetts Bay colonies, bringing their attitude with them.

"Why are you going there?" Scarlot finally interrupted.

"What if they had been *in* the palace instead of outside with pitch forks?"

"They weren't."

"They are now."

"Exactly. How many times have they tried this shit?"

Marilyn thought on it. An argument could be made "they" have been rallying the troops for the assured "second coming" since day one, or at least as early as 70 AD with the fall of Jerusalem, the Preterists claiming Caesar was the antichrist. From the earliest millennialists Joachim of Fiore and Hildegard of Bingen through the Reformation to the Pilgrims, the American Revolutionaries, the Confederates, to the allies for "good" in every war since. At almost any point in history you could find groups or individuals that took a look at what was going on around them and said, "This is it. This is the moment."

"And yet it never happened," Scarlot said.

"They've always been outside, though, on the fringe, afraid of events and needing an explanation," Marilyn told her. "They've never been *inside* before."

The numbers were staggering, for Marilyn. Religiosity, particularly fundamental religiosity was on the rise, dramatically, over the last seventy-five years, while most reasonable folks thought they'd overplayed their hand with the ridiculous Scopes trial and moved on to really important issues. To make matters worse, the mainline denominations, the more moderate, moderating, just plain privately spiritual folks, were dwindling. While the Catholics and the Methodists and the Presbyterians were losing their faithful in droves, the Baptists and Mormons and Pentecostals were absorbing *millions* into their ranks, multiplying membership by hundreds of percentages. Conservative estimates put one quarter of the nation now identifying and aligning themselves with the network of right-wing Protestant churches—fundamentalist, evangelical, holiness, or Pentecostal—advocating and adhering their unwavering hardcore notions from biblical inerrancy to the imminence of the end times.

"When the Attorney General of the United States anoints himself in cooking oil like he's some latter-day King David," Marilyn said, "that's cause for concern."

"But if it never happened—it has a one hundred percent failure rate!—despite however many times there've been people absolutely certain that it was going to, maybe it ain't *gonna* happen at all."

"That was Peter's point. They're not going to wait around for it to happen. They're *determined*."

"But Mare, think of what that says about their prophesy." If the whole impetus for that particular belief system rested on the blind faith that ultimately there was going to be some divine intervention in a world that otherwise doesn't make any sense to them, what happens to that faith when they have to take that prophesy into their own hands, they have to play god. "These are the same people that think God decides high school football games, for crying out loud, because that's enough to make their puny lives somehow better, enough to reinforce their Prophetic belief. You're worried about *them*?"

"They can still do a whole lot of damage, with their wars, their *crusades*, earthquakes and plagues, killing billions of people. If you don't think they're crazy enough and powerful enough to cause famines and disease epidemics, to concoct their own seven deadly vials—the only heavenly signs they need to start their wars—take a look around."

"Why do you concern yourself with all this shit?"

"Because He took my love away."

"A government job and fear of the big city did that."

"I blame Him."

"Still, maybe Jack's right. Maybe you shouldn't be reading all that stuff."

Jack would have been as surprised as anyone to hear Scarlot say such a thing. He was more used to near unanimous condemnation of everything from his lifestyle to his choice of profession to how he went about it, from family, friends, even strangers. All of which partially explained his preference for going it alone and without entanglement, his steadfast non-commitment, romantically or professionally. That being the case, what was he doing in DC instead of New York, looking for a bar, looking to meet someone?

He'd stopped in Hagerstown, Maryland, after a series of interstate switches in the daylong drive from Kentucky, to spend the night before Monday morning's jog on into the Big Apple. He happened to be in the hotel bar and caught the replay of a Rose Garden press conference earlier in the day, when the president called for a "crusade" against the perpetrators of the terrorist attacks, on national television.

While the rest of the bar cheered, Jack felt sick to his stomach, dizzy, even faint. "Is he out of his fucking mind?" he thought. "Does he even *know* what he's saying?" And then he thought of Peter, what little he'd listened to Marilyn and Scarlot say about his latest absorption, and decided—without really thinking about it too much—that he'd go to the capital and ask the one person he knew who might be able to tell him what the hell was *really* going on, his twin brother Paul.

Had he put much thought into it, he would have been hard pressed to follow through. He hadn't seen—or really spoken to—Paul in almost fifteen years, since his graduation from GW Law School back in the 80s. The rift was all Jack's doing, even if not his fault, he wanted to believe, though he'd never been able to convince anyone else of that fuzzy distinction, especially Paul, and wasn't absolutely sure he saw the difference anymore.

It had happened the night of Paul's graduation. Jack had flown in for the celebration. After a long evening of partying with his classmates and friends they had retired to the plush Washington Court, a hotel on New Jersey Avenue.

"It's the only hotel in the city with a view of the Capital," Paul had drunkenly told him, insisting they stay there, no matter the cost. "Can you feel the power?" Paul wanted his brother to experience the "juice" he was going to be plugged into now that he'd gotten his degree. And true enough, there was an aura, a sense of wonder looking out the window of their suite and seeing the seat of the most powerful deliberative body in the world.

They closed down the Federal City Bar in the lobby of the place—signing gallons of draught beer, red wine and tequila shots to their room tab—by collapsing together into the opulent waterfall cascading in the nearby atrium, laughing idiotically, squishing across the deep-piled carpeted lobby and puddling the elevator riding toward their room to the accompaniment of Yanni.

Once in the room they finished off a bottle of champagne while throwing open the floor length curtains and stripping off their sodden tuxedos. They donned the monogrammed bathrobes provided with the room and climbed into the two double beds, Paul in the one nearest the window so he could glimpse his future "office" when he woke in the morning. Sometime in the night, though, Jack had crawled over into that adjacent bed to snuggle his brother—though Paul accused him of groping. The morning ended badly, with Jack being evicted to fend for himself in the sleeping city and the two remaining mostly estranged ever since.

Jack had always maintained that he was moved by exaggerated, drunken filial love, which he would not apologize for. But the fact that he was moved at all, he understood, had cast a dark shadow that he was powerless to mitigate. And the more he'd thought about the episode over the years, to be honest, he no longer really knew, couldn't definitively say, exactly what aroused and provoked him. All he could say with any assurance was that it was completely innocent, though that was hardly any salve for the phobic. He'd never pressed the point, having already had plenty of experience being a pariah.

He'd always secretly hoped—"All right, not *that* secretly"— for just such an occasion, a neutral *entrée* back into Paul's life, because of his belief in an ultimate long view of history, and because he really did love and *really* missed his brother.

"You really are nothing but a girly-man," he said to himself, which reminded him of Scarlot, strength enough to continue.

He set off that morning toward I-70 a few miles away, which

would take him to Frederick, and then Glen Burnie, where he could jump on the BW Parkway toward Annapolis, Fort Meade and "The Building," headquarters of the National Security Agency. But as he approached the exit he thought the green directional sign said, then confirmed that it said, "NSA Employees Only." He pulled to the shoulder directly in front of it, studying the thing, trying to fathom its implications, though the message was quite clear: no visitors, no sightseers, no happy wanderers allowed. "Damn," he said. He'd never seen anything like it.

He eased back into the southbound traffic and ventured the thirty additional miles on into the district, found a hotel considerably cheaper than the Court, the Hotel Helix on Rhode Island Avenue. He seemed to remember there was a very good Italian restaurant down the street. He checked in and called his mother.

"Hey, Mom, it's Jack. Listen, do you have a number for Paul?"

"Johnny, where are you?"

"D.C."

"I thought you were going to New York."

"Yeah, I know. Decided to stop over here first."

"That's nice."

"So, you got a number?"

"Hold on, let me get it."

Jack smiled as he listened to her hum away in the background while she rifled through an address book. He knew her levity resulted from her belief that everything was well with her children, and they mostly let her believe that fiction. Never mind that no two of them ever visited her at the same time or that none of them had heard from Peter in months. In her world, the absence of bad news was comfort enough. That was often endearing for Jack, at other times downright envious.

He then called Paul, asked to meet.

"Why?"

Nonplussed, Jack said, "It's been a while. Besides, these are strange times."

"I'll say. All right. There's a bar right near you, the Post Pub. I get off in an hour. I'll meet you then."

Just like that. Strange, Jack thought, that he really felt no hesitance, no awkwardness, and just that token resistance from Paul. Couldn't say he wasn't relieved. Maybe he was just busy doing spy stuff. Or maybe in this skewed era where people knocked down skyscrapers with jetliners, nothing shocked anyone anymore.

Jack fiddled in his room for a while—unpacking his overnight bag, arranging his toiletries, not that it mattered that much, just to kill time. He went downstairs to the Helix bar, ordered a Bacardi on the rocks, directions to the Pub.

"Oh yeah, that's walkable," the bartender told him, diagramming his route on a bar napkin. "Ten minutes, tops."

Jack nursed his drink and studied the muted cable news shows still showing the scenes from lower Manhattan over and over again. He wanted to feel the outrage he saw in the faces of the commentators, the bystanders, but couldn't, or wouldn't. It *was* outrageous, to be sure, but it was also something much, much bigger than that. The whole world had changed in a matter of minutes, and he doubted there were too many people who had a very good idea of what it would look like next. So far as he could see, everyone—across the television dial, in any chance encounter he'd happened upon in the last few days—was fixated on the events of Tuesday morning—their thoughts, their comments, their existence, rooted in that hour and a half. He was pretty sure there was someone, somewhere, working pretty hard—for good or ill—to fill that void. If anything, he felt a little scared, and suddenly glad that he hadn't gone to New York, no matter what happened next. That would have only compounded what he was feeling, he knew.

At exactly an hour after their phone call Jack paid his tab and left the hotel. When he found the place at Vermont and L, it was a bleached out stumpy three-story building, "Post Pub" written down the exposed outside wall and along the black awning that stretched over *al fresco* tables fronting the place. He'd never been there before but he knew about the place, knew that because of its proximity to *The Washington Post* that was how it got its name and much of its notoriety. It was a storied lunch time stop for mid-town yeoman—reputed to have the best bar steak going—and the place where journalists brought their toughest nuts to soften them up over burgers and brew to try and get their scoop. He was actually a little pleased Paul had picked the place, taking that to mean at the very least that over the course of time he'd become comfortable enough with the idea of being seen with his gay brother in public.

"It's truly a brave new world," Jack said as he pushed on the door and entered the dim space. He took a moment for his sight to adjust in the smoky interior and then looked for a booth back in a corner or out of the way, just to be safe.

"Jack," he heard. "Over here."

He spied his brother at a booth mid-way down the far wall, facing the door, waving, with a mostly finished beer set before him.

"Paul," he said, warmly shaking hands, but surprised too. "How the hell did you get here so fast? You guys got secret tunnels or something?"

"What are you talking about, I work a couple of blocks from

here."

"But," Jack said, pointing over his shoulder without any idea how true to north it might be, "the NSA is at least half an hour up the road, near that Army base with your own 'NSA Employees Only' exit?"

He laughed, a hollow, edgy chuckle. "I don't work for *that* NSA," he said. "I work for the little nsa—the National Security Archives."

"You're not a spook?"

"Nope."

"Holy shit."

"More like a gopher. We process freedom of information requests."

Jack smiled. So, they both shared the feeling of letting someone think one thing while silently knowing the truth. "Oh," he tried. "Well, I'm sure that's exciting."

Paul tilted his head a little. "Oh yeah, it's a riot," he sneered. "What're you drinking?"

Turned out Paul hadn't spent as much time or nearly as many years in the corridors of government and power as he'd expected to. He'd gotten a position as congressional aide to Missouri Representative Norvell "Bill" Emerson out of law school, and for a year or so was angling to work his way up the food chain. But when Emerson checked into the Betty Ford Clinic in 1988 it was enough of a scandal in the highly politicized election year the entire office found itself in the headlights. And then when he voted against his party on the Gulf War authorization in 1991, it was bend over and kiss 'em time: no Senatorial advisor slot, no White House under-secretary of something-sump, no Ambassadorship, and no cushy lobbying job. Paul ended up back at GW working in the non-profit archives started up in 1985 as a final hedge against Nixon's brand of secrecy basically channeling requests and screening which of those FOIA requests could be made public.

"A fucking riot," he said again, as Jack's rum and coke arrived.

"Why'd you stay?"

"What else was I supposed to do, go back to St. Louis?"

Paul had always had only one ambition in life, crystallized in his mind with the 1980 ascension of Ronald Reagan. He wanted to be in politics, if not hands on the levers then at least the voice in the ear of whoever was driving. He *loved* being inside the Beltway, or at least used to.

"So, what are you doing in DC?"

"To talk to you."

"What about?"

"Is this a good place?" Jack asked, of the Pub's reputation.

"Sure, this is the last place hacks'll show up given a choice. They're all celebrities these days, unwilling to mingle with the masses. And their sources know it, expect more than bar chum for leaks."

"It's about Peter," Jack told him. "And Marilyn."

Paul flinched at that last, said, "What's up with Peter?"

"When's the last time you've talked to him?"

It had been a few years. When Peter became enlightened, Paul was the first one he contacted, because they held such similar views, on Christianity, the bible, homosexuality—or so Peter thought. Paul, still smarting from his own fall from grace, let Peter know in less-than-charitable terms that he never really gave a rat's ass about any of that shit. He was just riding with the fastest horses to the finish line. "Imagine, a *Christian*, calling me a hypocrite.

Haven't talked to him since."

"He's disappeared."

"*Again*?" Paul said.

"This may be different," Jack said. "He kind of predicted all this shit."

"All what shit?"

"New York, the Pentagon."

"9/11? Get out of here. *Nobody* predicted that shit."

Jack hunched a little lower over their table. "You're not *really* taking the administration's stance on this, are you?"

Leading up to his "crusade" comment, the president had also claimed "no one could have imagined" what had happened.

"Come on, Jack, tell me you haven't turned into one of those kooks. I have to deal with them every day."

"No, I'm not, really. But it's simply not true to say 'no one imagined.' People *did* imagine."

Paul squinted at him. He was getting those requests, too, for an August PDB, that *supposedly* warned of the attack.

"You honestly believe someone could have *imagined* these guys could successfully hijack four commercial airplanes, take them over and score a direct hit with three out of the four?"

"Maybe not, but that's a *real* good question, don't you think?"

Paul started to get up. "Why don't we just go look at the Pentagon, asshole? It's still smoldering."

"No, no, no," Jack said, pulling him back. "That's not my point. Pete was talking about something bigger than that."

"Bigger like how?"

"Well, why did he—the president—call it a 'crusade'?"

"How would I know that?" Paul said. Then, "He fucked up," he offered. "He does that all the time."

"Yeah, I heard that excuse too." Administration aides had hit the airwaves almost immediately after the press conference, explaining that all that was meant was that it wouldn't be a short effort, this "war on terrorism," that it should be a comprehensive, common cause. "What I can't help wondering, though," Jack said, "is whether it wasn't a moment of unintentional honesty."

MARILYN heard the call for a "crusade" remark too, which sent her reeling again, if she'd ever fully recovered. Where to start, where to start, Woodrow Wilson, Christopher Columbus, or Urban II? "Oh god," she moaned. What was this latest *crusade*, to make the world safe for democracy, find the new heaven and new earth, or rid the Holy Land of an alien race, rid the *world* of evil? What is the matter with these people that they keep trying this crap? Why don't they learn?

What did any of them learn, or, more often, *fail* to learn?

"Fuck, even *I* can answer that!" she said.

Alexius, for one, the godfather of the crusades, given a second chance, probably would have rethought his request of Urban for military aid back in 1095, had he known how itching the Pontiff was for a new *Pax Romana*—which wasn't *really* all that peaceful, unless you discount the sack of Jerusalem, the persecution of Christians and other conquests—only this time under the papacy—having lost much of his power and most of his influence amongst the barbarous warring secularists and the recent schism—though, to his credit, he figured it out easily enough when instead of the 300 special forces he'd asked for to ward off those pesky Turks, Urban sent 50,000 knights and serfs on a "just war" to retake the Holy Land using "justified violence"—whatever the hell that was supposed to mean, Gregory, though the world found out soon enough, thank you very much. Did the Byzantine Emperor say, "Thanks, but no thanks"? No, not really. He did lock the crusaders out of Constantinople and once they were hungry enough struck a deal: in exchange for food, any conquered lands would remain under Byzantine rule.

The Franks agreed, surprise, surprise. Of *course* they agreed. They were starving, for both gruel and blood—though they would, in pretty short order, combine those lusts at yet another starvation point in the campaign, feeding themselves with the blood of their own horses, and worse—they'd have agreed to *anything*!

A reasonable question might be how Urban motivated so many people not necessarily under his jurisdiction to march thousands of miles over the course of years and do such horrendous things? "Let's just say old Turdblossom would have been *very* proud."

For starters, he promised remission of their sins—past *and* future—a direct ticket to heaven, to take up arms against the blas-phemous infidels, that "alien" race that was defiling Christian al-tars, raping Christian women, "circumcising" Christian men, the horrors! "I, or rather the Lord, beseech you," he stirred the throng to the slaughter, in a momentarily revealing slip, "destroy that vile race!"

"*Deus vult! Deus vult!*"became the rallying cry. "God wills it!"

Did he not know the danger of that idea? Evidence shows he probably did. In a letter a month later, he wrote, "Let those who have been accustomed unjustly to wage private warfare against the faithful now go against the infidels and end with victory this war which should have been begun long ago. Let those who for a long time, have been robbers, now become knights. Let those who have been fighting against their brothers and relatives now fight in a proper way against the barbarians. Let those who have been serving as mercenaries for small pay now obtain the eternal reward. Let those who have been wearing themselves out in both body and soul now work for a double honor." Methinks he did, as those robber-knights marauded off to the east butchering Jews and pagans and anyone who even *looked* non-Christian along the way.

"Do we believe in reincarnation?" Marilyn asked in one of her fleeting cogent moments.

"Why would you ask that?"

"Occurred to me all of a sudden, that if you shaved his beard, Urban kind of looks like the current resident of the Naval Observatory, you know, which might explain some of his behavior."

"Careful, he's listening."

"He *is*?" Marilyn hesitated, looking around the room.

"Let's go back to life during wartime."

"Yes, yes, where were we?"

"Constantinople."

Precisely, Constantinople, crusading Franks, having made their deal with the Eastern devil—not to be confused with the Western devil, they're still a few hundred years off on the horizon—moved on to Antioch. That's where they were starved-out again because the Boy Scouts spent months trying to figure out how to breech the city's walls, unsuccessfully. Might have been the end of things except for the treachery of one of the tower guards who put out the welcome mat, to which the visitors responded by not just butchering the resident army but every single inhabitant inside, Jew, gentile, Muslim, all of them, and hoisting the king's severed head on a spear, a right "proper" way to fight.

"Crusaders win! Crusaders win!"

On to Jerusalem! But first, they feasted on Ma'arrat al-Numan—literally—a smallish Syrian town along the way, where, they promised, nothing would become of the inhabitants if they would only open the gates and allow for the plunder of their food stores—it being December, 1098, and all—but once inside commenced to slaughter all twenty thousand of the non-combatants, Jew, Christian, Muslim, old, young and indifferent and after it was discovered that there was not enough food inside to satisfy them, the army was "placed" in the "cruel necessity of feeding itself upon the bodies of the Saracens," according to one of the commanders. Said another chronicler, "In Ma-arra our troops boiled pagan adults in cooking pots; they impaled children on spits and devoured them grilled." That's right, they cannibalized the vanquished. Did anyone really wonder how that became the first step toward uniting a fractious Muslim community in whatever way necessary to evict those holy warriors—or, for that matter, whether there was any doubt left to the question of exactly who the barbarians in this picture were?

Later, apologetic historians suggested that the events at Ma'arrat weren't merely savage atrocities, but derived from the crusaders' "fanatical belief that the Muslims were even lower than the animals,"—offering this first-hand account as anecdote, "Not only did our troops not shrink from eating dead Turks and Saracens; they also ate dogs!"—as if that was supposed to mitigate the *human* tragedy somehow. Only the darkest, meanest, vilest of chicken-hawks could color that event as some kind of savvy battlefield tactic, one of the earliest examples of "shock and awe," as some have.

"Stupid, stupid, stupid son-of-a-bitches," Marilyn chanted, banging her head. "Stupid!"

Satiated, our heroes—though diminished by almost a third—

moved on to Jerusalem, even as the new, *moderate* Muslim leader there was asking for peace, arriving in June, 1099. Six weeks later—introducing another delightful battlefield term in the interim, "live ammunition," as the crusaders loaded captured Muslim soldiers into the nets of their catapults and hurled whole bodies or suitable pieces over the walls—the city fell, "Hep, hep, horray! Hep, hep," loosely translated, "Jerusalem has fallen."

And they all lived happily ever after.

"Oh wait, no they didn't." After conquering the city—a city, don't forget, which all three of the great monotheistic religions have some legitimate claim to, if you believe their stories, and which, for the most part, since the Romans that is, has had some success in accommodating all three—those rascally Franks killed everyone inside, *again*, of whatever denomination, ransacked both mosque *and* temple—who's defiling whom, Popey?—piled the dead bodies up outside the walls pyramid style—"Taller than houses," one of the participants said—and burned them. The Muslims, for one, were pissed; not to mention Alexius—remember him, remember their *agreement*? After the Catholic double-cross at Antioch, Edessa, Aleppo, Acre, etc., where not only did they *not* give the outposts back to the Byzantine, they established three more "crusader states" in the region, and the pope—not Urban, no, that bastard didn't live long enough to hear the chanting, "Hep, hep!"—exhorted *all* Western Christians to make yearly pilgrimages to the reclaimed holy sites, burgeoning the coffers of the border states—which, incidentally, probably paid for the Renaissance—and paving the pilgrimage routes with the bones of the faithful—necessitating yet another mercenary "army of the cross," the Knights Templar. Oh, and one more thing. This "Holy," "just" war of Urban's—which, some have rightly suggested, was nothing less "than a long act of intolerance in the name of God," to whit, it was the act that initiated the West's glorious tradition of organized violence against Jews in Europe—facilitated the "Saracens" dusting off and extracting from four hundred years of mothballs and putting it to new purpose that lovely little term, *jihad*.

That's right, *jihad* was the rallying cry for Saladin to marshal the Sunni and Shia who'd been infighting for half a millennia together toward a now common occupying enemy, not that it happened overnight. No, the animosities were so great it took ninety years to garner enough consensus to start pushing back against the Christians. Seems like that should have told us *something*, but no, once Saladin retook the city in 1187, the king himself, none other than Richard the Lion-hearted—a besotted, feckless, king in absentia, at best, certainly no Sean Connery—set off to defend the throne, defend God, defend something.

"Why?"

Because they were defiling Christian altars, raping Christian women, circumcising Christian men! Not actually. Unlike the previous inhabitants, Saladin, however he rose to his Sultanship—a lot of very powerful competitors conveniently died of mysterious means in the process—was a seemingly reasonable guy. He did *not* destroy the Church of the Holy Sepulcher—which informed part of the initial beef, having been destroyed in 1009, by the Romans, though, not the Muslims—and allowed Christians of varying sects access to worship there, even went so far as to negotiate a deal whereby a Muslim family would act as key-holders to the sacred place—a deal that's held up to this day—to keep the opposing adherents from bickering with each other, as those crazy Christians were wont to do.

Question is, how did he manage such restraint? Richard certainly didn't provide a very good example. He recaptured the port city of Acre in June, 1191, before Saladin could cover the sixty or so miles with reinforcements, taking twenty-seven hundred Muslim hostages in the process. Richard sought to strike a bargain, as he knew he didn't have nearly the forces necessary to take on the Sultan in open combat. He offered the prisoners for two-hundred thousand gold pieces and the "one true cross," a relic of the actual crucifixion vehicle which the former Christian protectorate had *carried into battle* against Saladin at Hadeen, certain the old piece of wood would grant them divinely inspired superiority, despite being outnumbered and outmaneuvered, after which the Sultan was able to take back Jerusalem peacefully.

Saladin stalled.

Richard then did something so heinous it's still talked about today. He beheaded every single one of the Muslim captives, complaining it was too much to feed and care for them.

Saladin went back to Jerusalem. Richard marched after him. They fought to a draw at Jaffa, halfway between. Saladin offered a truce. Keep the coastal cities, and he'd allow pilgrims into the Holy City. Richard still wanted the cross. He offered his Christian sister in marriage to the "infidel" for it, but she refused.

"I would have gone," Scarlot said.

"Seriously?"

"Are you kidding? Don't you know anything about life in a Sultan's harem?"

Marilyn considered it.

Saladin said, "Is that all you've got?"

Richard turned back for England, but not before vowing to take Jerusalem. Saladin said, "We'll be waiting." Richard never did get to Jerusalem, but was welcomed back as a hero.

"For *what*?"

"Being a little harsh, aren't you?" Scarlot asked her

"Harsh? In what way are facts harsh?"

"You know the answer to that, Mare; because they're *just* facts."

"But they're *important* facts, damnit, facts that *have* to be taken into account."

Marilyn knew what she was getting at, that there were other facts, broader facts, *relative* facts, that Islam had not necessarily always spread voluntarily to the willing or welcoming, that it had sometimes—maybe often—come with the kiss of a scimitar, that Christians flourished in Egypt before Islam and Iranians were Persian before Mohammed, that there haven't been any "official" Christian crusades since the Reformation, since the 15th and 16th centuries, that, by contrast, the Turks finally sacked Constantinople in 1453—could they *really* be blamed for that, though, considering the imported shit Alexius had brought down upon them—and *jihad* is as familiar around the world as is "Yankee go home," but what good does that kind of so-called "fair and balanced" treatment, what good has *any* such bankrupt relativism done anyone, where, in a very grown up world with real, serious, even existential issues to deal with, what purpose does it serve mankind to be able to middle-school your way through affairs by saying, "He hit me first," and what insight does it provide *anyone* to argue, "Can you *imagine* what the fallout would have been if FDR had treated Pearl Harbor as a criminal act," except insight into the speaker's blinkered demagogic intransigence, if you're not willing to pay attention to the facts, learn from the truth, accept that maybe, you know, *maybe* that crusade thing wasn't such a good idea.

Think about it: the absolute noblest impetus for the crusades, according to our man Urban, was to preserve the "sanctity of the Holy Land"—which hadn't been, in a long, long, *long* time, though allegedly—"must be in Christian possession so that prophesies about the end of the world could be fulfilled."

"*Voila!*" Marilyn shouted. "The first end-timer."

"I'll give you that one."

Prophesies which entail plague and pestilence, earthquakes and droughts, seas of blood and the wholesale slaughter of all non-believers, pagan, Jew, Muslim, and the unfaithful, all for the sake of what, exactly. Eternal salvation? And the people stirring this fetid stew whip armies of people into a froth and unleash them against the enemy *du jour* to act out these prophesies, pillaging, plundering, torturing and murdering in the name of *their* God, against some other supposedly unworthy God, or ungodly god, or godless people, and the witless sheep fall for it every single damn time, every single time through the centuries, because otherwise their oppressed lives have no meaning. Except all of them, the godly, godless and not-godly-enough all have their own versions, believe their own versions of the same scenario, the same *prophesies*, if you must. Daniel spurred the Jews into revolt against the Greeks, and St. John of Patmos was pissed about the Roman emperors. Hitler prophesized a Thousand Year Reich, and they believed him, though only because their lives so otherwise completely sucked.

They all believe the crap, so much so that every few years somebody else pops up and predicts when it'll all hit the fan. The Quakers calculated 1792, and William Miller predicted Christ's return between March 21, 1843, and March 21, 1844, but then revised his "prediction" to October 22, 1844. William Branham foretold rapture by 1977, Chuck Smith in 1981, Edgar Whisenant in 1989—or 1992, or 1995: stay tuned. A Korean mission pegged the date at October 28, 1992, and *everyone* thought tribulation would commence in 1993, in time for the Return of the Son in the year 2000. John Hinkle said, no, June 9, 1994. And Richard Schiller said 1997 (or 2009). Harold Camping changed his prediction to 2011, and even Sir Isaac Newton weighed in, saying Apocalypse couldn't happen any earlier than 2060. Yet they all, every single one (so far, to be fair), have been wrong.

Christopher Columbus lobbied for a "final crusade," though there's some question as to how much his stance was rooted in true belief, rather than politics. See, Ferdinand and Isabella didn't want to talk about any voyages of discovery until after they chased the last of the Moors from the Iberian Peninsula. And it was only in 1492, after they'd wiped out the remaining Muslims in Granada that they seemed to notice the pesky Italian hanging around the court. Only if enough of the world were converted to Christianity, he thought, would Jesus come back. He planned to do just that, and after he brought fame and fortune to the throne, surely they'd bankroll his "final" assault on Jerusalem. "God made me the messenger of the new heaven and the new earth of which he spoke in the Apocalypse of St. John after having spoken of it through the mouth of Isaiah," he wrote, "and he showed me the spot where to find it."

"Sounds like a plan," the royal couple said. "How much?"

And off he went—never mind that Columbus and God somehow got their maps mixed up—discovering new lands, converting new recruits, along with a healthy mix of piracy, looting, and helping to inaugurate the slave trade. Was that *really* God's plan? What if, Chris, God was pointing to a spot closer to home, say, Spain, where Christians and Jews and Muslims had been living side-by-

side, mostly peacefully, for the better part of a century, until *someone* decided there were just too many heretics—versus what, just
enough?—and launched an Inquisition, against the Jews, against
minor-league Christians (those, that is, not playing by papal rules)
and against Muslims. It had been a time of flourishing societies
all around, "golden" years by some estimates—hardly a "clash of
civilizations." We know that the Europeans sure liked the mathe-
matics and astronomy and medicine tips they picked up. What if
that *was* the "new earth" Chris?

No, no, no, the counterargument goes, it would have never
worked out, they were too un-accepting of each other—never
mind that "they" built houses of worship right down the block
from each other—"they" were exclusionary, hate-filled, mistrusting, militant—something that's always made Marilyn wonder,
if God is so good and Apocalypse so great, why does it have to
be so militantly defended or pursued?—and self-righteous. Who
knows? Not Marilyn, certainly, and probably not anyone. But the
one thing we do know, the one thing we should have learned, the
one absolutely unequivocal—and, you'd think, inviolate—lesson
we should have taken away from all that mess, maybe the *only*
thing to be taken from it is that it is stupidity, sheer, unadulterated
stupidity to ever, *ever* casually mention "crusade" when talking
about fighting any Muslims anywhere. It's asinine, unforgivably
asinine. Because what they hear is *Deus vult* and twenty-seven
hundred lopped off heads rolling around in the sand. When they
hear the president calling for a new kind of war for this "new kind
of enemy" and characterize it as a "crusade," they know it's the
same-old, same-old, even if the spoils have changed over the centuries. Ninety years ago "making the world safe for democracy"
meant pillaging the Middle East of its natural resources, witlessly

incensing the Islamic world yet again with the resultant puppet rulers and imperial behavior, giving rise to the radical Muslim Brotherhood much like Urban had resuscitated *jihad*, which spawned Qutb and now bin Laden—whom they've already fingered for the attacks, somehow. Now that the whole world understood that the region warehoused even more and precious resources than was projected back then, they get it, they most assuredly get it.

Equally asinine, his press secretary was out the day afterwards, trying to reassure—just whom, one wonders—in that smarmy way of his, that the president didn't intend to connote anything beyond a "broad cause."

"Right."

"Exactly. Bullshit. And we'd know it's bullshit if we knew our history. How many people know, for instance, that when Sir Edmund Allenby took Jerusalem in 1917 he said, 'Now the crusades have ended,' as if redeeming Richard seven hundred years later."

"Probably not many," Scarlot said tiredly.

"If enough did, don't you think they would have schlepped that little twerp off to the insane asylum where he belongs?"

"Not really."

"I JUST DON'T buy all that psychobabble claptrap," Paul said. "The guy's loose with the language, everyone knows that."

"Exactly," Jack told him. "But did you actually *hear* the comments."

"*Everyone's* heard those comments."

"Did you *hear* them though, the stammering?"

The president stuttered multiple times both before and after uttering the infamous word.

"It's like he was trying to find *any* word to say there other than 'crusade', but couldn't."

"So *what*, John?" Paul snapped.

"Something struck me about it is all, reminded me of," Jack started.

Paul sat there with a sudden bemused look on his face.

"What is it?"

"You remember when you first decided you wanted to be called Jack instead of John, when we were kids?"

"We weren't kids. We were in high school."

"I asked you why, and you said because it 'sounds so manly.'"

"And?"

"Am I the only one that didn't get that message?"

Jack sat back, studied his brother, shook his head slightly, said, "You should call Marilyn."

"Why?"

"To ask her about Peter," he said, finishing his drink.

"Why me?"

"Because you work for the *nsa*," Jack said, and left.

JACK checked out of the Helix the next morning and reversed his plans yet again. He woke up desperately wanting to wallow, but knew better. He set off for the best place he could think of at the moment to forget about himself, New York City, to be part of some larger pain, communal concern.

All the way up I-95 and then the Jersey Turnpike, that pain was seething through the airwaves—if not commentators screaming for swift and decisive vengeance then hysterical callers raving about anthrax attacks, Muslim infiltrators and World War III. It *was* a world gone crazy, still, but he couldn't turn it off, no one of a single mind but everyone at a signal emotional level.

And then he crossed through the Lincoln Tunnel into Manhattan and all the noise abated. It was Tuesday morning, a week later. The city was supposed to have come back to life and gone back to work a day earlier, but the Big Apple he found was still in muted shock. Whatever people were on the street moved around as though zombies in a trance, or worse, frightened kittens. Most visible was all the law enforcement and military presence. It sickened him to see the once indomitable spirit subdued, but he almost immediately understood why. US airspace had reopened the previous day, and though the volume was certainly reduced, each and every time he heard the distinctive drone of jet engines he shuddered with dread almost by rote, and he was just a visitor. He couldn't begin to imagine how traumatic the experience must be for a native New Yorker. It was easy to see why they might opt to stay off the streets bunkered down in a lightless, soundless cocoon.

As he moved through the canyon of lower Manhattan he was unceremoniously detoured from one thoroughfare after another—access to certain bridges and significant buildings locked down and protected by gun emplacements—traffic obligingly following these new patterns completely un-New York like, no blaring of horns, no shouting of colorful epithets, and he missed it. The closest he could get to "Ground Zero" was a couple of blocks away—close enough, though, for the ambient stench of destruction and decay to overtake him, pulverized dust still covering everything—and there, pulled to the side of an overpass, he got out of the car and took up his camera. Through the chain-link fencing he saw a familiar and oddly comforting scene, the same scene he'd witnessed in such dissimilar places as Bayou Canot, Alabama, in 1993, and Oklahoma City two years later. He saw the pile of smoking rubble swarming with workers like migrating Monarch butterflies bringing a bush to animated life. As he zoomed in on the scene he focused on the grey-filmed workers smudged free of any distinction, black, white, male, female, home-grown or itinerant, with nothing but the sacred task of recovery uniting them, and he felt better somehow, about himself, this world, even his stupid brother. How could he let such a snarky little comment get to him, he wondered, in the face of this unspeakable tragedy.

Joe Formichella

Part III

Joe Formichella

10.

"I WASN'T *there* in the beginning," Squat said. "A lot of what was going on was already in play."

"We've been over this, haven't we?" Settle said.

"Seems like," Bentley said. "What did Lisa tell you?"

"She's the one that said start at the beginning."

"*And?*" Settle asked.

"I told you, I wasn't there."

"Well, we don't mean to tell you how to write your book," Bentley started.

"He's already making excuses," Settle said.

"No I'm not."

"Sure you are. You *were* there in the beginning, just not out front. You were with him in Austin; you were on the campaign; you were probably clearing brush in Crawford."

Bentley asked, "How do you know all this?"

"But I wasn't *there* there," Montgomery protested. "I was just a deputy, until…"

"Aw, get out of here," Settle said. "He's wasting our time."

"Until?" Bentley urged.

"You know, the leak."

"The leak?"

"The CIA agent! Jesus," Settle said. "Don't you pay attention to anything?"

Bentley just shrugged.

"Right. That's when you took over. And what did you do?"

"I was *abused*."

"Oh whup."

"Whup?"

"That's right, big whup. You going to start whining and bawl-ing on us?" Settle asked Montgomery. "You lied."

"I was *lied* to."

"Whup."

"What does that mean, exactly?" Bentley asked.

Montgomery elevated to the main podium the day after Val-erie Plame's identity, a covert CIA op, was revealed in a column by the self-described "Prince of Darkness," Robert Novak, ruining her career, almost certainly costing lives, destroying undercover operations throughout the middle east and eastern Europe aimed at tracking nuclear proliferation, for the sole purpose of discred-iting her husband, Joe Wilson, who'd discovered that there was no truth to the fable that Saddam Hussein had tried to purchase uranium in Niger and therefore had to be removed. But then, we were already in Iraq, so it didn't make much difference, or so the administration calculated.

"You *knew* the pretense for going to war was *bullshit*, and yet you lied."

"I was just a spokesman."

"Oh, Squat, I gotta tell ya," Bentley said to him, "that's lame."

At one of his first press conferences, a reporter asked, "That column has now given rise to accusations that the administration deliberately blew the cover of an undercover CIA operative and, in so doing, violated a federal law that prohibits revealing the identity of undercover CIA operatives. Can you respond to that?"

He answered, "Thank you for bringing that up. That is not the way this president or this White House operates. And there is absolutely no information that has come to my attention or that I have seen that suggests that there is any truth to that suggestion. And certainly, no one in this White House would have been given authority to take such a step."

"No," Settle said, "*that's* lame."

Two months later the story was still gathering steam. "Joe Wilson now believes that the person who did this was Karl Rove," another reporter asked. "He's quoted from a speech last month as saying, 'At the end of the day, it's of keen interest to me to see whether or not we can get Karl Rove frog-marched out of the White House in handcuffs.'"

"I haven't heard that," the answer came. "That's just totally ridiculous. But we've already addressed this issue. If I could find out who anonymous people were, I would. I just said, it's totally ridiculous."

Settle grumbled, "*I'll* tell you what's ridiculous."

But still, later that month, he said on national television, "There's been no information that has been brought to our attention, beyond what we've seen in the media reports, to suggest White House involvement.

"It's public knowledge. I've said that it's not true. And I have spoken with Karl Rove. I'm not going to get into conversations that the President has with advisors or staff or anything of that nature. That's not my practice."

"No, you practice in bullshit."

"He *lied* to me!"

"You sound surprised?" Bentley said.

Two years after that when pretty much the whole world knew

he'd lied, knew what happened, and why, and the disastrous adventure that was Iraq—which *might* have been avoided had the truth of Wilson's findings been considered—was likewise apparent to all, he was asked, "You have said to the public, dating back to 2003, affirmatively, Karl Rove was not involved, and now we have evidence to the contrary. So how do you reconcile those two things? How does the President reconcile those two facts?"

"Again, if I were to get into discussing this, I would be getting into discussing an investigation that continues and could be prejudging the outcome of the investigation. I'm not going to do that from this podium."

"*That* couldn't have been easy," Bentley said.

"*That* was torture," Squat said to him.

"You pussy," Settle said, getting up from his chair and slamming it against his desk. "You didn't even have the balls to say it was wrong, investigation, politics, that's all bullshit. It was *wrong.*"

"Jim?"

"He couldn't even say that," Settle told his partner.

"But there's a difference between what's legal and what's right," another reporter asked. "Is what Karl Rove did right?"

"Well, I mean, you can state the obvious. I understand that, and I appreciate you all. I know you all want to get to the bottom of this. I want to get to the bottom of it. The President has said no one wants to get to the bottom of it more than he does. We want to see it come to a successful conclusion."

"At the very least, though," he was pressed, "could you say whether or not you stand by your statement—"

"John, I'll come back to you if I can."

"—of September 29th, 2003, that it's simply not true that Karl

Rove disclosed the identity of a CIA operative? Can you stand by that statement?"

"John, I look forward to talking about this at some point, but it's not the appropriate time to talk about those questions, while the investigation is continuing."

"You make me sick," Settle said.

"I was in a tough spot," he appealed to Bentley.

Bentley just stared at him

"I was *told* by the White House counsel's office that we could not comment on it, because it was an ongoing legal proceeding or ongoing investigation at that point. It's a terrible spot for a spokesman to be put into."

"Oh, please."

"He's got a point," Bentley said.

"Yeah, you try it!"

"I didn't take the job now did I?" Settle said to him.

"Easy, now."

"Was I supposed to know the job included passing along false information?"

"No, but once you figured it out, don't you think you had the responsibility to come clean?"

"I told you, the White House counsel—"

"Spare me," Settle said, sitting back down. "We all know 'I was just following orders' is no defense."

"There's no one on trial here," Bentley said.

"Maybe there should be."

"What?"

"For war crimes."

"War crimes? I had *nothing* to do with that war."

"Oh really?" Settle said, firing up his computer. "Let me read you a bit from Chris Hedges, *Times* reporter. "He says you were 'part of the smoke-and-mirrors machine that very consciously and deftly and shamelessly manipulated public opinion and lied to the press, you know, week after week after week to justify the invasion of Iraq.'"

"Is that true?"

Montgomery sat slumped in his chair.

"Of course it's true."

"Why?"

"That's why I want to write this book, to get to some of those answers."

"That'd be a good book, certainly," Bentley said to his partner.

"I don't trust him."

"Why not?"

"Haven't you been listening? He's a liar."

"But I want to come clean."

"Atonement?"

"Yes, yes."

"Sure you do," Settle said. "Why now?"

Montgomery looked puzzled. "*Now's* the appropriate time, don't you think?" he said.

"Better than never, as they say," Bentley said.

"How convenient."

"What do you mean?" Bentley asked.

"Ask him."

"What does he mean?"

"How would I know?"

"Richard Clarke."

"Oh, jeez…"

"What does that mean?"

"When Clarke's book came out, when was that Squat, 2004?"

"Yes."

"Our boy here said, from his podium, no less, said of his former colleague—this sound familiar Squat? I quote, 'all of a sudden he's raising these grave concerns that he claims he had. And I think you have to look at some of the facts. One, he is bringing this up in the heat of a presidential campaign. He has written a book, and he certainly wants to go out there and promote that book.'"

"Ouch."

"I apologized to Dick about that," Squat told them. "Those were just the talking points."

"See what I mean?"

"What would you have him do?"

"Tell the damn truth."

"Fair enough?" Bentley said to him.

"Sure."

"Then there it is."

Bentley and Settle returned to the tasks before them that Montgomery'd interrupted.

"But," Montgomery said, causing Settle to snap his pencil in half. "I still can't get a grasp on a beginning."

"Tell you what," Settle told him. "Take any one of your disasters—there are plenty to choose from—and tell us why, tell the American people why they had to go through these last eight years, tell them *all* of it, and maybe that'll scare the bejeezes out of enough people that it'll never happen again."

Squat sat there nodding.

"Sound like a plan?"

"That's all I want to do."

"Good," Settle told him. "Now get outa here."

"Better call Lisa," Bentley said, after Montgomery had retired to the adjacent office.

"She can't edit what he doesn't write," Settle answered. "Got any suggestions?"

He wanted to achieve a lasting legacy of greatness.
He wanted to be a great war-time president.
He wanted to beat his dad.
He wanted to punish his mom.

"Lord," Weaver said. "How *does* he start this thing?"

Hundreds of years ago the great Orang-Cina dynasty of the island nation of Negara Bersatu came to power by taking advantage of a natural disaster. There was a great and terrible **gempa**, according to legend, that shook and shook and shook throughout all the confederated islands of the country, dissolving mud huts, splitting cart paths, raining rock slides down upon the inland towns, but that wasn't the worst of it. A great wall of water, **ombak** after **ombak** after **ombak** crashed upon the shores and destroyed the coastal fishing villages. Not a community, not a family was spared, except for one, the Orang-Cina: none of their extended family was harmed, none of their dwellings were severely damaged, or so they said, over and over and over again to whoever would listen. Semak, the patriarch of the family convinced survivors that it was a sign from their almighty, **Dewa**, that they were **dipilih**, chosen, and that they both represented **Dewa** and could communicate directly with him. Therefore the Orang-Cina were to be venerated above all others, in control of all the country's affairs, if the people wanted similar protection and favor from **Dewa**, and so they were, which was no small feat for a nation of thousands of islands and almost as many languages. How did Semak pull it off? He insisted the family was **dipilih** by virtue of and through the facilitation of the **karang** they wore in their hair—live, carbonate, underwater sea formations—as combs or ornaments or tiaras. Once an object of ridicule—generations earlier a particularly challenged elder in the tribe, Gundu, had gotten it into his head that **karang** could be used as currency and/or accessory, oblivious, somehow, to the fact that once removed from water the creatures pretty quickly decayed, imbuing the holder with a profound odor, a swarm of insects and frequent infestations—Semak turned it into an empire. Gundu's enterprise never got off the ground, and the "habit" he'd insisted on for other family members pretty quickly faded into memory, though his antics survived in the lexicon: whenever someone was thought to have lost their mind, even in polite company, it was signified by pointing to your head, twirling your finger, and pronouncing, "Gundu." Semak was both heroic for the family, and brilliant, for having pulled it off at all. And on top of that, he suddenly found himself Raja Semak, **junjungan** of all!

But Semak was also a good-hearted man. He didn't abuse his new power. "It was reward enough," he liked to say privately, "to have restored the family name." Other than the fact that people bowed before him in public, were constantly seeking his advice and bestowing gifts on the family, he thought of himself as just a regular Joe, fond of fishing, weaving a net on occasion. The whole episode might have passed into obscurity had his wives not intervened. They loved the attention and the newfound celebrity. They took to wearing the most colorful clothing, commissioning elaborate palaces for themselves, and neglecting their children.

"People will get angry," Semak warned.

"Nonsense," they said. "Give them a pronouncement from **Dewa.**"

So he did, irregularly commenting on the rice harvest, the rainfall, and the tides, correctly, often enough, to maintain his stature—mostly because he really was brilliant.

Stupidity, and real abuse would wait until successive generations had passed. Instead of using information from **Dewa** as predictions or forecasts, they started handing down pronouncements from on high as retribution, retaliation, or divine consequence. After a few shipping disasters, Semak's son Rempah nationalized the trade industry, raking in tons of **uang** in the process, as Negara Bersatu was the principal supplier of **pala**, the world's most coveted spice.

His son Pejalan instituted a security force to protect the family's riches, and his son Menjala built up an army to ward off invasion. His son, Tekan, in turn, built a navy to expand the empire, and his son Jurang initiated steps to somehow maintain the family's grasp on power. First he outlawed multiple marriages, and then doled out betrothals of his own extended tribe as special favors for loyalty and service. Most significantly, he decreed water buffalo sacred—because it was a beast of both water and the land—and as such the Orang-Cina's lone, divinely restricted propriety. That might not seem like such a big deal, except that water buffalo, and only water buffalo, performed most of the yeoman work in the rice paddies, some three-quarters of the country's agriculture. For that reason, the **kerbau** could no longer be bought and sold, but only rented from the royal family, the cost of the lease being a portion of the harvest—in either cash or crop. That arrangement turned out to be so lucrative he created a secret service to both manage and enforce its tenets and manipulate the market so more and more rice was grown, and more and more return was garnered.

That kind of control was so seductive, his son, Apiun, used the service, the **Instansi**, throughout the empire in all sorts of malevolent ways, and even beyond the empire, to infiltrate and destabilize neighbors, sabotage other economies and plunder other resources. He also grew quite fond of using assassinations as his preferred method of dismissal, for increasingly venal offenses. If you don't think that's an absolute means of micromanaging, you ought not apply.

By the time of Apiun's generation, the family's wealth and power—and their penchant for inbreeding as a tactic for maintaining as much of it as they could—had spawned some notable, disturbing and self-destructive tendencies. The children, idle and spoiled, furnished with whatever their little hearts desired, waited on **tangan** and **kaki**, grew into libertine, lazy, often ruthless adults. Their mothers, absolved of any rearing responsibilities—any responsibilities at all, really—were for the most part cold, inattentive, even abusive, in their constant yearning for distraction or attention, one.

Apiun's—along with his Amazonian control-freak of a wife, Piarit—children could be viewed as prototypes for the principal demons that would soon populate the nascent science of psychoanalysis, especially the eldest, Ganda. He was, among other things, a textbook magical primitive, with a heaping helping of sadism thrown in. If Ganda's grandfather, who because of his habit of Moses-like handing down new commandments from on high, became known across the land as the **orang perintah**, Ganda envisioned himself the **penyelamet**, the savior, who could do no wrong, do anything he wanted, was culpable for nothing, with no thought for remorse or restraint. The closest he would ever come to accepting something like personal responsibility was to blame **Mata-Mata** for any heinous activity he happened to get caught engaging in. **Mata** was his evil imaginary friend developed very early in Ganda's life to occupy the darkest spaces in his psyche where he harbored plots of revenge and retaliation, the **algogo** of his fiendish grudges.

When his gargantuan mother spied young Ganda out in the back yard torturing and blowing up docile little **kodoks**, she asked the boy what he had against the native amphibians. "Mata-Mata doesn't like them," he answered.

Satisfied, her only reproach was, "Don't get any on your clothes."

Mata-Mata, unfortunately, didn't like anything, or anyone, for that matter.

As a young man Ganda liked to get tanked up on the **cairan** of the luscious **anggur** the family alone was permitted to grow, distill, and distribute, set out for town for a night of carousing revelry that often enough resulted in the wreckage of carriages or the ravishing of wenches, all because

Mata didn't "like" it or her. Townspeople, in an effort to either accommodate, to the point of enabling Ganda—truth was, he **could** be quite entertaining, until Mata took offense at something, anyway; no one ever paid for their own grog or gruel around him, for instance—or to forewarn anyone who might not know the danger of his company, took to calling him Ganda Anda, the "Double You."

Historians have never been of a consensus to explain why the nation put up so long with the antics of its royal family. Even psychologists, when they weighed in, couldn't quite agree whether it was classic example of "addict loyalty," where entire families, extended families, whole peoples will collectively walk on proverbial egg-shells around their afflicted one lest **their** behavior triggers another of his ruinous binges, or the complete "opiation of the masses," in their deep-seated, irreconcilable dependency on authoritarian governance. Whichever the case, Ganda continued his scorched earth approach to life with absolute impunity.

When he was of an age to oversee some of the family businesses, his management style was a mostly hands-off—to such an extent that he mostly crashed enterprise after enterprise, leaving it to his younger brothers to mature into reclamation positions—until, that is, Mata spotted or manufactured some grievance. As

Joe Formichella

chief vintner in the family winery, for example, he took to poisoning or at least fouling certain batches to be delivered to patrons in town who might have had the temerity to complain about his behavior at one time or another. Needless to say, that had a negative effect on sales.

From there he moved on to the rice mill, where itinerant hands might suddenly disappear in an avalanche of raw seed if Mata didn't like the accent of their dialect, or the particular hue of their skin. And at the **kerbau** ranch, just for fun, he'd show up on branding day and burn the family **jenis** into as many worker backsides as the beasts.

When he married his third cousin Kemenangan he settled down some. She brought him back into closer alignment with **Dewa**, which only meant he was a little less destructive, remaining every bit the unconscionable sadist, possibly even more so, with the now evangelically righteous tint to Mata's suggestions. Within the feeble mind of Ganda, it was no longer certain to those who witnessed his derangement, which voice he thought he was hearing, Mata's or **Dewa's**. And like always, he felt no particular need to sort it all out.

In point of fact, though, the general populace was never allowed to suspect any such thing, within the cloistered family circle there was growing concern about Ganda's fitness to rule.

"He's ruined **everything** he's touched," next in line Tusukan appealed to his parents.

"Not **everything**," the now doddering **Apiun** protested.

"It doesn't matter," his still obstinate wife told their second born.

"I don't want to be the one to have to clean up that big of a mess," Tusukan said.

"Then you **won't**," Piarit snapped, harshly intimating that she'd just as soon skip over him to Heran, their next eldest son, should it come to that.

That effectively muzzled Tusukan. Whatever other entanglements came with the package, they **all** lusted for their turn to power, **all** secretly schemed on how to enhance it, expand it, and further benefit from it. That, actually, was the family motto: **Kekuasaan untuk kepentingan kekuasaan**, Power for power's sake.

A modicum of alarm did eventually register with Piarit, though, when her wayward Ganda assumed directorate of the **Instansi**, and commenced utilizing his father's assassin squad against randomly selected—or so it seemed to everyone else—village elders throughout the country, all at the sole discretion of Mata-Mata, of course. The natives were getting restless. She tried to reason with Ganda that succession depended upon a male heir, and since he and Kemenangan had only sired two daughters, Akan and Pohon, it would pose a risk to the ascendancy were he to occupy the throne. Mata, it goes without saying, had an answer for that. Tusukan's eldest son, Tusukan Jr., disappeared.

"What have you done?" Piarit asked.

"I didn't do anything."

Equivocation about the line of succession ceased. The coronation was scheduled as soon as the case went cold.

SETTLE stopped reading. "What the fuck is this?"

"I told you he wouldn't like it," Lisa said.

Montgomery got up and circled around behind where he sat at his desk, looked at the pages in his hand, said, "It's an allegory."

"It's a *what*?"

"Allegory," Bentley said, "the representation of abstract ideas—"

"I *know* what allegory means," Settle barked. "I mean what the fuck is *this*," he repeated, tossing the pages into the air where they fluttered, turned in various directions and fell to the floor.

"Dad's a *realist*," Lisa said.

Squat set about retrieving them, picking up one, studying it, then trying to find the next in its sequence.

"Good, constructive criticism," Bentley said. "Nice."

"How do you criticize crap? Crap's crap."

"Surely, you can do better than that."

"All right, fine. It's not crap, it's nonsense."

"It's not nonsense," Bentley argued, uncharacteristically. "It's just non-specific, for your tastes."

"Exactly, it's irrelevant."

"He's got his reasons, I'm sure," Bentley said to Lisa.

"I tried to tell him."

"I just thought a fabled comparison would be the least offensive entry point," Montgomery said, still gathering pages.

"I thought we asked for the truth."

"It is."

"Then there's really such a place as—what did you call it—Negara Bersatu?"

"Of course not," Settle told him.

"It's a *representation*," Montgomery offered.

"You're still trying to hide."

"Hide from what?"

"Hide from them, hide from the truth."

"No I'm not, I'm just trying to tell it in a way that we don't all get killed before we can get it out there."

"I'm sorry," Bentley said. "Did you say 'killed'?"

"Pussy."

"Daddy?"

"You don't know these people."

"Neither does anyone else. That's why you have to tell the *truth* about them."

"That's what I'm *trying* to do," Squat pleaded, waving the pages in front of him.

"No you're not, you're talking about some crazy made-up island whackos, 'long ago and far away…'"

"I'm talking about abuses of power, serious psychopathic behavior, bad, *bad* advisors, and fraudulently engineered elections."

"I didn't see any elections in there," Settle said, gesturing toward the manuscript.

"It's an *allegory*."

"Why? Why bother the contortions?"

"Because so much of this story is so sensitive, legally."

"Truth is the only protection you need."

"You've lived your whole life out here in the sticks, haven't you?" Squat said.

"Pretty much," Lisa told him.

"Well," Settle said, "putting lies in your *fable* won't help you in any case."

"What lies?"

"Killing his nephew?"

"Metaphorically," Lisa told him.

"Oh, it's a metaphor now."

"And an allegory."

"And you can't be held liable for an allegory?" Bentley asked.

"Was Jesus liable for his parables?"

Bentley thought on that one. Seemed to him there was an argument out there that someone ought to be held accountable.

"That's not the point!" Settle said. "It doesn't make any sense."

"Oh, you don't think we're dealing with a dynasty?"

"That doesn't matter. How are you going to get the CIA, the unwarranted surveillance, sacking the judges, New Orleans and all that other shit in there?"

"It's a *long* story."

"Yeah, and how exactly does the whole Brownsville, Hands of Death thing come up?" Bentley asked.

"That comes later," Montgomery told him.

"Oh, like the sect infiltrates the *Instansi* or something?"

"Something like that. I haven't worked it all out yet."

"Oh, for crying out loud," Settle said. "You *can't* be serious?"

"I've seen worse plot twists," Bentley told him.

"True," Lisa said.

"God help me, I need a career change."

"Now?"

"He goes through these phases, every week or so," Bentley said.

"Could anyone *really* blame me?"

"Maybe you could remarry into wealth," Bentley suggested. "Are Akan or Pohon available?"

"Daddy, you wouldn't."

"Not really," Squat said, still reshuffling the un-numbered pages. "Pohon got married last year, and the rumor is—I didn't say this, don't have any idea if it's true, it's just what I heard—Akan's gay."

"Damn, the luck," Bentley said.

"Jesus Christ," Settle said, got up, grabbed his jacket, and moved for the door. "I need a drink. Anybody else?"

"What do you want me to do?" Montgomery asked.

"You?" Settle said, pausing at the threshold. "Keep writing."

11.

EVEN though someone with some sense of history must have gotten to him and said, "Don't *ever* mention the word 'crusade' again," what became the rallying cry in its stead, his "war on terrorism," worried Marilyn just as much. Did he really not know its historical ramifications either? Does he not know, or care that the British couldn't generate any traction with the phrase half a century earlier in their end game of the disastrous Palestinian Mandate? The world did not, would not, rise to its defense in its insistence that the Zionist and Arab attacks on its authority in the occupied lands constituted, called for, a "war on terrorism". Quite the contrary, the world's collective response was, "Get out!" Does he really think, do those around him really suppose that this time would be any different? What in the hell *is* a war on terrorism anyway?

"We've seen this movie," Scarlot said for her.

"No we *haven't*," she answered.

Within a week investigators had linked the hijackers to Osama bin Laden and his *jihadist* organization, Al Qaeda, the same group purportedly responsible for two African embassy bombings and the attack on the USS Cole. But because bin Laden and his gang were a state-less group of Arabs and Afghans the president was calling for a war on all terrorist organizations and anyone who aided them. "They will hand over the terrorists or they will share in their fate," he told Congress on the 20th. "Our war on terror begins with al Qaeda, but it does not end there."

"*What* war?" Marilyn agonized, begging her television screen for clarity.

"Afghanistan," Scarlot predicted.

"Afghanistan?" Marilyn cried again to the set. "Is he insane?"

She remained glued to the thing for weeks. She watched the announcement of the creation of a new federal department, of Homeland Security, and shuddered with historical reverberations, depositing her in 1933, again. "It's five minutes to twelve," she said to no one, "five minutes to twelve," referencing a speech given just days before the German parliament building's torching warning all the liberal organizations in country they had but one last chance to avoid certain devastation at the hands of the Nazis. The drums of war beat on, beat louder, everyone, seemingly, crying for the heads of these "terrorists," just like 1933.

Two weeks later their war commenced, with the serial bombing of Afghanistan.

"Every generation has its war," Scarlot deadpanned.

"Why?"

Ever since the war to end all wars there's been nothing *but* war. It's become big business, a profit center, a means versus an end.

"But the people supported it."

"No they didn't. Enough crazies believed in the slogan, thanks to H.G. Wells, because it sounded to them like the fulfillment of St. John's prophecy, the final battle between the legions of God and Satan, conveniently recast as England and Germany. The folks running the machine, hell, they didn't care where the support came from, so long as they got to wage their fight.

"Eisenhower was right," Scarlot said.

"Eisenhower was *wrong*." He may have been right at the end, when he could afford it, critical at a time when his criticism was toothless, but he was wrong, tragically wrong in all those dark days leading to that epiphany. We may have been laconically satisfied with our Maytag appliances and big-finned Buicks and color televisions during those sleepy times, while he, Eisenhower, as much as anyone else, *created* the monster we were now chasing thousands of miles away in the desolate "graveyard of empires."

"Except we're not there as an empire."

"Really? Then why *are* we there?"

"To get bin Laden," Scarlot mimicked. "Dead or alive."

Then *why*, Marilyn wondered, did we ignore the Taliban's proposal to try bin Laden in an Islamic court, and *why* one week into the bombing when the Taliban offered to turn him over to a third country for prosecution—provided we share our evidence—did we turn the offer down? "There's no need to discuss innocence or guilt," the president said. "We know he's guilty."

"Could it be they were going into Afghanistan no matter what, everything else was just pretense?"

"Pretense for what?"

"You tell me."

"All right, I'll tell you. For bin Laden. Dead or alive," Scarlot repeated. "You're either with us or against us," sounding appallingly too much like most of the rest of the country.

"That's how Ike felt, too," Marilyn said sadly.

It was Eisenhower's White House which funneled millions of dollars to the Saudi royal family to prop up the government and modernize the country, to build railroads and mosques, because Saudi Arabia had oil and Egypt did not—the stuff that feeds the war machine—and in our cold war stupidity we bank-rolled right-wing fundamentalists as a hedge against Arab nationalists—because to an otherwise ignorant Ike that smacked too much like communism—and poured money into the country in an attempt to buy their allegiance "with us" for fear of the vacuum created should they turn against us. That money wound up in the pockets of a dirt-scratcher from Yemen who turned it into the biggest, most profitable construction company in the Middle East, the bin Laden Group, unprecedented wealth that afforded his son the ability to buy an army of terrorists hell-bent on ridding the Holy Land, ridding the globe of the infidels who printed the money in the first place.

"It's madness," Marilyn said. "It's *always* been madness," as she watched press conference after press conference after interview of officials gleefully boasting about how swimmingly their war was going, except, "Where's bin Laden?"

Madness to have split up the Ottoman Empire into satellite protectorates, spawning vast swaths of instability and oceans of animosity imposing a new Jewish state on the region at the same time, promising one group Arab independence all the while promising the other Zionist return, madness to then turn our collective backs on the monumental consequences of such gerrymandering, action mindless of reaction all because we *could*, and only for oil. Madness to have set all those players in place, move them around like pawns in some grand imperial hegemonic game when we needed them, completely ignoring them when we didn't.

"You can't re-do history, Mare."

"No, but you can pay the fuck attention."

You can re-*member* that *all* the wars of the last hundred years have been about money or resources, making a profit, controlling the toys, *all* of them.

"Remember the Maine!" It was a complete fucking sham, an imperial scheme, a money maker.

It was the bankers who wanted to get into the "war to end all wars," not to fight, no, but to extend credit, fund the atrocities, profit off the death. "What if," a British finance minister asked a White House consultant, "the Germans sunk a luxury liner with American passengers on board? Would your country go to war then?" Certainly. Undoubtedly. Off goes the Lusitania, even after, even after the Germans warned us not to. Took out an advertisement in the *New York Times*, said, "by the way, that's a war zone." They sunk the boat, just like they said they would, and we were outraged, *outraged*!

"Don't *even* get me started on Pearl Harbor."

"You don't really think FDR was complicit in that?"

"Complicit? After he did everything in his power to provoke the Japanese—violating more than a couple of international rules of war in the process don't forget; after the Australians told him, 'They're coming'; what the fuck would you call it? You don't think Standard Oil and Union Banking, Rockefeller and Bush—who were oh so busy bankrolling Hitler—had any influence in the White House?"

"All those deaths."

"Each one an entry on a ledger sheet."

Vietnam was the classic case, and our last, viable, turning point. They couldn't get in, couldn't get in. Sure, Ike warned us, on his way out the door. And Kennedy resisted, but there was just too much money to be made.

"There's a reason they call JFK the last *real* American president."

"Who says that?"

"People who know."

"But what do *they* mean?"

"They mean he's the last one to stand up to Wall Street, not let them have their war."

"So *they* assassinated him?"

"Let's just say he wasn't around to stop them. The shadow government was in place."

"Shadow government?"

"You don't really think the Warren Commission spoke for the people, do you?"

"What are you *talking* about?"

"Arlen Spector's 'magic bullet'?"

"You really are insane."

"Look at the *facts*!"

Within a year they had their Tonkin "incident," and their war. Never mind that it was all a lie. McNamara himself generously called it a "mistake," the so-called naval attack on the Maddox. Didn't matter; LBJ got his resolution, his war, and Rockefeller was making too much money funding the Soviets so they could build the munitions that they then sold to the NVA. And just to make sure the gravy train didn't end any time too soon, the Pentagon instituted those ridiculous rules of engagement. It was never intended to be a winnable war.

"Maybe none of them have *ever* been about winning," Marilyn said.

"What about the Gulf War? We won that one."

"Oh, we did? We got a permanent base in Saudi Arabia. Don't know if you can call that a 'win' considering how well *that's* working out."

"You're losing it, kiddo."

"Me? *Afghanistan*? No one with any goddamn sense would *ever* invade Afghanistan. No one 'wins' in Afghanistan."

"So why are we there?"

"For the fucking *money*!"

"Oh Lord."

Marilyn's increasing belligerence was something of a twist. Her preference for history, for historical awareness, resulted from an almost desperate dependence on context. Her sometimes-jittery grasp on the present was often assuaged by that longer view. Abhorrent behavior or thoughts colored with precedent, viewed as part of a larger pattern, became a little less disturbing, signaled less of a need for correction. With a world slouching toward a-historical action and reaction—flying jetliners into skyscrapers, invading a country seven thousand miles away from the scene in retaliation, a newly passed Patriot Act, which, if we didn't learn the lessons of Hitler's Enabling Act, we didn't learn anything at all, a world where "war is peace," for God's sake—she had a comfortable reserve, which was good. It would serve her very well as she watched events unfold.

And that's when, and why, she turned off the tube, quit answering her phone.

"Johnny?"

"Hey, mom."

"Where are you honey?"

"Kabul. You should see it. It's glorious! This could actually work."

"Yes, but, your brother says that's not the story."

"My brother?"

"Paul."

"Sure seems like the story. The Taliban all but routed, the war all but over. Women shunning their burqas, little girls going to school. It's beautiful."

"Not according to your brother."

"Mom, what did he say?"

"He said something about Iraq, and the 'neo-cons'? I don't even know what that is."

"Iraq? Why?"

"Johnny? He doesn't sound like himself. Is he all right?"

"What makes you ask?"

"He sounded, I don't know; *mean*."

"That's a neo-con, mom."

They'd been gunning for just such a move for years—going into Iraq—all those folks newly ensconced in the Pentagon, the National Security Council and the White House, years. They'd been peddling their vision—of a "New World Order," a new era of "Enlightenment," brought about through imposing the "moral clarity and purpose" of "American exceptionalism" upon the world through forced military democratization—since the 90s. They aimed at nothing less than universal "American Empire," not just across the globe, but over space as well, a Wilsonian world made better, so long as it was remade the American way.

"They can't be serious," Jack said to his brother when he finally reached him.

"Serious as hell."

"Why?"

"Regime change over there has been the goal for a while."

"Yeah, but why now?"

"Part of the war on terrorism."

"Iraq has nothing to do with that."

"You watch."

That was the first step in the plan, ousting Hussein, for a lot of reasons, most of which couldn't be discussed publicly. But there was an answer for that. It's a rather ingenious caveat of their ideology, that truth is too hard for people to hear, too demoralizing, so it's necessary to tell lies to people about the nature of political reality. Tell them that Iraq's vast oil resources were mostly untapped, not even entirely explored; that Saddam was using his oil as a wedge to leverage Russia and China against the West; and that he was threatening to trade it in Euros, which would severely punish the dollar. But now there was a ready excuse, waiting to be exploited, something they started gaming almost immediately after 9/11.

"The real answer to your question: 'Permanent Revolution.'"

"What the hell is that?"

Part of the agenda, lifted from their granddaddy, Trotsky, and spelled out years ago, to transform the world in America's image. Their only concern was how to bring it about. They worried it would take too long to institute all the policy and position changes necessary, absent, quote, "some catastrophic and catalyzing event – like a new Pearl Harbor." Which is precisely how the Secretary of Defense initially referred to 9/11, within hours of the attacks, chief enabler of "remaking America's defense."

"How do you know all this?"

"It's all documented. They're not shy."

"And you have access to all these documents?"

"Jack, that's my job."

"What about Congress?"

"The Constitution? Don't be a simp."

"Paul, this is nuts. No one will go along with that."

"They've got a plan. Have had one for a while, is the word."

"Jesus. Why'd you want to tell me all this shit?"

"Thought you'd like to know your next stop."

"You're enjoying this, aren't you?"

"Why would you say that?"

"That whole town must be giddy."

"The fact is, we're the last superpower standing. We can't let ourselves be pushed around by fanatics or threatened by tyrants. We have an *obligation* to make the world safer."

"Can't believe I'm hearing this."

"It's just the truth, Jack."

"And you believe it?"

"It's the truth, pal. Another truth is, nobody can stop these guys."

"Is anybody *trying*?"

"Not really."

A thousand caustic comments raced through his mind. A boat-load of pent up venom ached to be spewed, but he held it all back, held against what he figured was certain futility. "You call Marilyn yet?"

"She won't talk to me."

"What does that mean?"

"She won't get on the phone with me."

"But she answers."

"Scarlot does."

"Close enough. I'll be back in a couple of weeks. I'll take care of it."

"Take care of what?"

"Marilyn."

"And Peter?"

"Right."

"You're as crazy as she is. You're going to miss the boat on this one, *John*."

"Fuck you."

"Yeah, you'd love—" Paul started before Jack cut him off. "Would have bet the family farm he'd come back with that," Jack said to himself, gazing around the downtown café, meetings—clandestine and otherwise—commerce buzzing all around him as the day gave way to evening. Bitter cold was forecast for the night, the front edge of a long, brutal winter. Maybe that accounted for how slow, and measured, deliberate, almost, life had become, a necessary acquiescence to the shorter days, the extra clothing. Maybe everything would heat up again with the spring thaw. He didn't think so. Something about sensing real, tangible hope in the air made him think otherwise. Whichever, he knew, such nostalgic leaning ruminations were the surest sign there was that it was time to leave.

WITHIN days of his return to country, it turned out, Jack listened to the president indict the so-called "axis of evil," Iraq, Iran, and North Korea, in his state of the union address.

"North Korea? How'd they get into this? They don't have any oil."

And Iran? He knew better. He'd been on the ground over there. Iran was helping us in Afghanistan. They hated the Taliban as much as anybody else.

And then he remembered what he'd said to Paul, what Marilyn had said to him. True, Syria had been omitted. That didn't necessarily mean Peter was wrong. Jack suspected just the opposite, in fact.

Still, though, what it all might mean, calling out this "axis of evil," he just couldn't know. That wasn't one of his strongest aspects, spinning out inferences toward their likely conclusions. His was a more immediate mind-set: recognize the picture before him, frame it, and capture it. He'd trained himself, damn near willed himself, to blot out anything peripheral. That suited his purposes, of course. But, time to time, he realized, it could be a handicap. That's one of the benefits he always found to his long, rambling talks with Marilyn. In the course of her rant, certain particulars would stand out in relief to his mind's eye, a sharper kind of contextual focus. If enough of those coalesced in any given diatribe, he could, in fact, begin to see a bigger picture, no matter how crazy it might have sounded at the outset. She really was quite clever, he thought, in her mad way, of course.

"Scarlot?"

"Jack?"

"Is Marilyn there?"

"It's me, Jack," she told him.

"Wow," Jack said. "It's been so long, I guess, I couldn't tell who's who."

"It's not just you, Jack. Things are changing."

"Changing? How do you mean?"

"Not now," she said. "Where are you?"

"DC."

"Are you with Him?"

"Paul? No. I don't know where he is. Don't really care. Talk about change, this place is in lock down."

Concrete barricades had sprung up everywhere, along with street closures, a lurking military presence around most federal buildings, and security checkpoints where you least expected them. Movement around the District had always been something you needed to approach with a situation room type of mentality—carefully planning departure, arrival and duration times, contingency routes, even potential way-stations, if you were going to evade the insatiable swarming traffic monster—these new restrictions discouraged any consideration of casual meandering. The ambient grip of the place was that if you were to make a wrong move, there would be dire consequences. That attitude carried over to the psyche of the place as well. Never exceedingly friendly, the default demeanor had become suspicion, even hostility, if not a suffocating paranoia.

"What do you mean 'don't really care'?"

"We had words."

"Jack, this is getting too weird for that."

"I know, trust me, I know."

"Will you try?"

"For you, honey, anything."

"Then what?"

"Then I'm going to get out of here. I'm coming to St. Louis."

Jack tried, but failed to raise his brother.

Paul had felt the same sense of desperate escape himself—though not from the perspective of an alarmed tourist, say, as Jack, as much as from a violated proprietor, indignant at the occupation of his turf—retreating deep into Virginia over the congressional break. He was back at work with a re-charged cell phone by the time Jack had reached Marilyn's and called.

"Tell Marilyn what's next."

"Put her on the phone."

"No, she'll only do it this way."

"What? Talk to me through you?"

"Right."

"But I already told you what's next."

"Come on, Paul, do it."

"All right. Iraq is next."

"Iraq is next," Jack repeated.

"Why?" she asked him.

"Why?" Jack said into his phone.

"Jesus Christ, I *heard* her," Paul lamented. "This is ridiculous."

"Paul?"

"I told you that, too. Permanent Revolution, *pax*-Americana, the new Anglo-American Empire, call it what you want. It's all part of the Project for a New American Century. Because we're the baddest cops around and they're evil."

"Evil?" Jack said.

"Evil?" Marilyn repeated. "Are you kidding me?"

"That's right, evil," Paul said.

"You guys don't even know what that word means anymore," she said.

"We know Saddam's a tyrant. We know he's a murderer. We know he's a threat to everyone in the region."

"We do?" Jack asked.

"He gassed his own people!"

"And where did he get the gas?" Marilyn asked.

"That doesn't matter."

"It very much *does* matter. The way you throw around that term as an excuse to do anything you want, if Saddam is evil for using weapons *we* gave him, what the *fuck* does that make us?"

"You getting all this?" Jack asked.

"More than I'd like."

"Here's the real question," Marilyn said. "Who benefits?"

"Benefits from what? Going in?"

"Right."

"I don't know. The Iraqis?"

"Oh come on."

"The neo-cons?"

"Right," Jack said. "And the Israelis."

"Not the Israelis," Marilyn told him. "The Zionists."

"What's the difference?" he asked.

"*Big* difference," she said.

They're a relatively new player in the game, the Zionists, but a particularly virulent and dangerous one. Austrian journalist Theodor Herzl wrote *Der Judenstaat* (*The Jewish State*) in 1896, calling for a large tract of land to be provided for the Jews. The next year he organized the first Zionist Congress in Basel, Switzerland, and it was at that conference that the WZO, the World Zionist Organization was formed. For the next twenty years they pandered their "ideal" reconciliation, the return of all Jews to their "promised" land, Palestine, and the rebuilding of the Jewish State, or at least that's what the world was led to believe. And it was the Zionists who convinced Milner and Balfour to double-cross Lawrence and the Arabs, a modern, "diplomatic" equivalent to Urban's crusade. But, some thought, that wasn't their only goal. Some suspected, given Herzl's tendencies, the real aim was establishing hegemony over the entire Middle East, even if that had to be achieved by force. Given the succession of wars, land grabs, the continuing settlements, "some" people are looking pretty prescient right about now.

Except, "*Except*," Marilyn said. "that agenda is in direct defiance of Tanakh law. They are compounding the very conditions of their exile in the first place."

"Tanakh law?" Jack said. "Sounds kinky."

"The *Torah*," Marilyn said to him.

"Their bible," Paul said into his other ear.

"I know, I know."

"You've never heard of the 'promised land'?" Paul asked.

"You've never heard of the 'promised land'?"

"Of course I've heard of it," she answered. "Everyone's heard of it. But do they also know there were conditions?"

"Conditions?"

"Leviticus, chapter 26, verses 40-42."

If they shall confess their iniquity, and the iniquity of their fathers, with their trespass which they trespassed against me, and that also they have walked contrary unto me;

And that I also have walked contrary unto them, and have brought them into the land of their enemies; if then their uncircumcised hearts be humbled, and they then accept of the punishment of their iniquity;

Then will I remember my covenant with Jacob, and also my covenant with Isaac, and also my covenant with Abraham will I remember; and I will remember the land.

"Uncircumcised hearts," Jack said, quizzically. "What might that mean?"

"Shut up, Jack," Paul said.

"Shut up, Jack," added Marilyn. "Means that Zionism is trying to bypass the very law that was given to the Jews in the first place, and establish their own kingdom in the Holy Land, probably for the purposes of some imagined super-Jewish-state ruling the Middle East and the world. What other reason could there be for such direct defiance of the authority of their God. According to their *book*," she said for Jack, "they are to remain in exile until the promised Messiah comes back to replant them. Zionism just wants to circumvent God and take on the world by themselves."

"Like I said," Paul jumped in. "The neo-cons."

"But wait," Jack said. "Not *all* the Jews feel this way, they don't all adhere to the whole promised land/right of return thing?"

"*No,*" Marilyn screamed. "Of course not. There are plenty of Jews, whole organizations, Jews Against Zionism, that understand, that know, Israel, Zionism, is for *anything* but peace."

"You think they *want* war in the region?" Paul asked.

"That's all they've been pursuing for half a century."

"Right. They want terrorism, want Hamas and Hezbollah lobbing rockets across the border?"

"Israel *created* Hamas!" Marilyn said.

"Really?" Jack asked.

"True."

All during the 70s and 80s Israel, the United States, the UK, supported, funded, trained, and armed fundamentalist groups like the Muslim Brotherhood and later Hamas, as a hedge against any nationalist movement—communists in the lexicon of the day—like Nassar or the PLO.

"We helped create Hamas. We single-handedly delivered Iran to the fanatics. And anyone with half a damn brain knew we were playing with fire. But we did it anyway."

"Why?" Jack asked.

"At the beginning," Paul said, "geo-political strategy. Iran was our bulkhead against the Soviets. Then it was for the oil. Now, Israel is the only stable democratic, westernized country in the region."

"And who's to blame for that?"

"Don't be simplistic," Paul said.

"What are you saying?" Jack asked Marilyn.

"I'm saying now it's the so-called Christians, the neo-cons and the Zionists all in bed with one another, all using the other for their own agenda, all determined to achieve their own version of the end of the world as we know it."

"Aw, Jesus Christ," Paul said. "I can't take any more."

"You can't, or you don't want to?"

"The 'end of the world as we know it'? Come on, Marilyn, you *got* to stop believing all that shit you read."

"And you need to get out of that DC bubble," she said, already loud enough not to need any relay from Jack. He'd taken to just holding the phone up for the two of them anyway. "You didn't use to be so blind."

"And you didn't use to be such a bitch."

"You just wait, Paul. You just wait," Marilyn hollered, as he hung up.

"Jesus," Jack said, holding the vacant cell phone. More than the fact that Paul had hung up on them, he was shocked to have heard her mention Paul's name. That hadn't happened in years. "Marilyn, honey, what's going on?"

She looked at him with a steadiness, a resolve he hadn't seen in her eyes in a long, *long* time either. "You got to trust me on this, Jack," she said. "We *need* to find Peter."

"I'll start digging around," he said. "See what leads are out there."

"We might not have a whole lot of time," she said, standing, pacing, like the Marilyn of old.

"Then what do we do?"

"Isn't there anyone that can help?"

"You mean like cops, PIs?"

"Higher up."

"Feds?"

"State Department, FBI; I don't guess we could get *Him* to help."

Jack smiled. "I'll see if I can broach it," he said, initially feeling like, That's my girl, but then wondered about the wisdom or prudence, the selfishness, of that. Better, he thought on a dime, to think more of her than himself.

"I'll get started on my end," she said, quit pacing suddenly, moved into what would have been a dining nook—before she'd had the walls taken out—and cleared off the table, replacing the centerpiece and single place mat with a handful of blank printing paper and a sampling of colored pencils.

"Marilyn, honey," Jack said. "Can I ask you a question?"

She looked over at him like she was surprised he was still there. "Sure."

"Where's Scarlot?"

"Oh," she said, half-laughing. "She's around here someplace. Don't worry."

He left her then, like that, busily starting into whatever the project was "on her end."

"I've got to piece all this together," Marilyn said to herself, in her empty house, at the table, scotch-taping together sheets of printing paper, until she had one single canvas that covered nearly the entire surface. Then she pulled the four chairs out from under it and away, and commenced circling her blank slate, colored pencils in hand.

She first drew a crude map of the Middle East in the center, different colored blobs for Turkey, Syria, Iraq, Iran, Afghanistan, and Pakistan. Below that Jordan, the spots of Israel, Lebanon and Kuwait, tuberculous Saudi Arabia and hapless Yemen. She shaded in with powder blue the eastern nub of the Mediterranean Sea, the slashing finger of the Red Sea, and the colic of the Persian Gulf. She then drew a bull's eye on Afghanistan and Iraq, marked the US military presence on Saudi territory, Kuwaiti, and Turkish, and drew a big red question mark across Iran.

"It's no wonder the dispensationalists are excited," she said, stepping back from her map for a moment. "Armies are supposed to amass from the north, and the east, for the final battle here," she said, drawing green arrows, one down from Turkey, the other from as far away as China, "hell, North Korea, for all we know," meeting at an approximate Arum Megiddo. "All of it orchestrated by the Anti-Christ operating out of a rebuilt Babylon," marking a brown dot on the east-west axis very near Baghdad. "No wonder at all, thank you very much, John Nelson Darby."

It was Darby, nineteenth century Brit, who puzzled together a miscellany of prophesy that resulted in most American notions about End Times, the Anti-Christ, Rapture, and Dispensationalism. His message was clear, and calculated: You can escape the tribulations, provided you get right with Jesus beforehand, promulgating an entire industry of dire predictions, offers of salvation—at a nominal fee, or course—and soon enough, Zionist drum-beating, because none of it happens without the restoration of Israel, the re-budding of the fig tree. After which, the DP's say, not a generation shall pass before the fulfillment of prophecy, though they fail to add that there are as many prophecies as there are gods, as many apocalyptic texts as there are prophets, none of which, obviously, are in anything like agreement with each other. Still, every couple of decades, like clockwork, at least over the last hundred and fifty years, since the days of the crazy Millerites, *cum*, even crazier Seventh Day Adventists, a new date certain for end times pops up and crazies get whipped into a froth, babbling in tongues, proselytizing doom and gloom and making hefty donations in an attempt to purchase salvation, capitalizing, literally, on real fears, about modernity, about war, about economic ruin. They were certain, *certain*, in May of 1948, for instance, with the UN mandated recreation of an Israeli state, that the fig tree had blossomed. They were *certain*, then, that end-time would happen in May of 1988, a generation later, and rapture would occur *exactly* May 14, 1981. When nothing happened that year but Reagan's tax cuts for the rich and breaking PATCO, they just went back to the drawing board. No, the new rationale went, the fig tree didn't bloom in 1948, rather, 1967 when Israel recaptured Jerusalem, which then meant end-times in 2007, and rapture with the millennium. Perfect! Except…

Clearly, the Zionists, the neo-cons, the fundamentalists, were tired of waiting on God. So what was the new prediction? Marilyn wondered. "What's their deadline?" she asked, looking at the circles and arrows drawn on the map. She figured that if there was a consensus date for their "final battle," she could work backwards from there and surmise what they'll have to achieve, maneuver, and manipulate leading up to it.

She was amazed to find cross-denominational, such as it was—between Christians, Muslims, and Mayans, for crying out loud—coalescence around December, 2012.

"Maybe there's something to all this hocus," she said out loud. "Nah…"

There was enough chatter out there, though, that the date was her best next threshold. She wrote "December, 2012," in the top right hand corner of her canvas, then drew a line back toward center-top, to a point which would represent the anticipated rapture, "December, 2005,"—passing through "June, 2009," which a fair number of crazies, the "mid-trib" crazies, believe rapture will happen, leaving the left half for all those things that have to happen before the rapture can occur.

Jack, meanwhile, back at his place, made a couple of exploratory calls. Paul wasn't answering his phone, which didn't surprise him. He tried a couple of his own contacts, a McClatchy station chief, an AP stringer, neither of which were too interested in helping him. He didn't know if the reason was the departure from their normal relations—usually he was the one giving them something, satisfying an assignment, not asking questions—or what he was asking about—Peter's whereabouts—just sounded so absurd.

"What're you asking me for? I don't find people."

"Do you know who could?"

"Cops?"

"Which cops?"

"Cops where he is."

"I don't *know* where he is."

It *was* absurd, when he thought about it.

He called Marilyn the next day, told her, "I'm not getting anywhere."

"He won't help?"

"He's not answering my calls yet."

"Typical," she said, which struck Jack as more than a little ironic. "Any ideas?"

"I hardly ever have good ideas cooped up here," he said, too tempted by rum and movie reruns. "I need to get back on the road."

"Where to?"

"Wherever the action is."

"Don't you ever get tired of that?"

"Tired?"

"Yeah, you know, don't you ever think about settling down?"

"Get me a honey," he laughed. "Get domesticated?"

"Something like that."

"Who the hell am I talking to, anyway?"

"Relax, Johnny, I'm just fucking with you."

"Thought so."

12.

B<small>UT</small> he couldn't shake the feeling that he was *supposed* to think just that, all the while he was packing his gear, that there were some mechanizations going on in the house across town he wasn't yet meant to be privy to. "Why not," he said, loading his last lenses and filters. "Fits right in with the rest of this crazy fucking world."

His first inclination was to go back to the war zone, back to Afghanistan. He'd left country not long after the botched Tora Bora offensive, with the Marines hopping mad. He wanted to get a look at how they'd channeled their anger in the last month or so.

He was in a Metro station in Atlanta when he heard about the Daniel Pearl murder. Much like the rest of the civilized world, the story shocked him, and momentarily chilled his headlong rush back into theater. He didn't know Pearl, really, though they'd crossed paths. But then, all journalists crossed paths, one way or another, sooner or later. It was in those paths, the network, the fabric of the *gestalt* of the trade where he felt the tear, and it hurt. War correspondents—or WCs—especially, trod the same muck, suffered the same gruel, and ground out the same military protocol of hurry up and wait, hurry up and wait, look out, watch your ass. It all granted them the same level of frustrations, the same gallows humor, the same laundry list of complaints with only an occasionally fresh story about some particular commander or mission to liven up the conversations. In such a common existence, you didn't really need to know someone personally. You knew plenty enough about their lives to feel the tear when one of them went down, especially the way Pearl had.

Jack remembered a true acquaintance within the trade, a forty year veteran of battlefields all over the world, one of the pioneers, really, the great Joe Galloway, warned him against plugging into that comfort zone, of dissatisfied guests on an adventure, somehow. "If you ever fail to think of yourself as anything than just another grunt, you'll fail to do your job, which is to tell *their* story," he told him over beers in some smoky dive somewhere, Bangkok or Mogadishu, he didn't remember that part. "Worse, you'll probably end up getting your dick shot off," he added, laughing a boisterous, scratchy, heartfelt, honest and direct laugh. Jack shook his head at the memory, as he gathered his things and moved forward on the platform, the airport train screeching into position, wishing he had a glass to raise at the thought of the great Joe Galloway and Daniel Pearl.

Marilyn had picked up on the Pearl story almost as soon as it broke, not long after the January 23rd kidnapping. She signed on to a handful of news-feeds, AP, CNN, etc., getting email notifications any time they posted a new story. She saw as soon as anyone the early administration promises to "find Danny Pearl and bring him back safely." She saw the venomous responses from readers like herself, and the outrage of the pundits. She wondered about that last, not whether the act was outrageously shocking behavior—capturing an innocent bystander, with a pregnant wife, no less, *and* Jewish, holding him hostage for the return of brethren criminal combatants—but by how unconvincingly startled that it had happened at all. Who did they think we were dealing with? What did they *suppose* would happen? With the public's insatiable appetite for comic strip, tabloid-like dispatches from the front and the administration's never-ending need to maintain this "war" effort with constant declarations that the good guys were winning, the "evildoers" were on the run, what else *could* happen.

She feared for Pearl, for all journalists, at once, caught in the crosshairs of this "war on terrorism," that had no precedent, no protocol, no guidelines, no rules, and probably no justification, beyond the messianic ambitions of a handful of "leaders" of men. She was surer and surer of that with each passing day. Why should *anyone* die for that?

She caught a BBC interview with the regional director of security in Karachi, who'd met Pearl just the day before he was kidnapped. "As a matter of fact," he told his audience, "there've been several kidnappings in the last few weeks, and we've managed to get them all back within 24 hours."

Never mind that he was speaking four days into the ordeal.

"Our fear is that Danny was lured outside of the city," beyond their security dragnet.

"Why would he do that?" Marilyn said, nearly echoing the sergeant-major.

Five days later the headlines blared, "Pearl is Dead!" Beheaded. The scimitar's arc reached all the way to St. Louis and pierced her psyche. Curiously, she didn't react in her customary way, did not retreat from the world, reality. She knew two things. She had to find Peter, which meant she had to get in touch with Jack. But he was somewhere—lord knows where—without cell reception. "Please don't let it be Afghanistan," she said.

And it wasn't. He was at The Hague, for the opening of the war crimes trial of Slobodan Milosevic, three long years after his indictment for "crimes against humanity" in Kosovo. Security was air tight—including jamming all cellular signals—as they prepared to bring the former Serbian president into the light of day for the first time in a long time, to face his accusers and answer for his crimes. Jack knew full well that he'd used the trial as an excuse to delay returning to the hotter environs of central Asia—even rationalizing the decision by telling himself there were plenty of others in that part of the world. But he'd also been to the mass graves around Belgrade. He'd been to the Trepca Mines, where hundreds upon hundreds of massacred Albanians had been disposed of by fire. He wanted one clear capture of the cold-blooded murderer's self-satisfied smirk, a picture that would tell people, *this* bastard tried to justify genocide as "anti-terrorism" too.

"Right and noble intentions Jack old boy," he found himself saying some weeks later. "But how do you explain *this*?" He was in London, for the Queen's funeral. But the answer was really very simple: money.

That's what he said to Marilyn when she finally caught up to him once he was back in a "civilized" part of the world.

"What the hell are you doing in London?"

As surprised as she may have been, she was also relieved. She'd been afraid that he'd been sucked back into the Middle East, after the Passover Massacre, the suicide bombing at Netanya, a most portentous event, at least in the matrix of historical implications running around in her brain. Its reverberations amplified directly with the whole Pearl assassination, which, because of the proximity of the occurrences, validated her fixation. Netanya had been the site of the infamous Sergeants Affair back in 1947, near the end of the Palestinian Mandate, where two British soldiers had been kidnapped and hung, in retaliation for the military's execution of three militant Jewish underground Irguns as "terrorists." The two bodies were "displayed" as "strange fruit" in a eucalyptus grove outside of town with IEDs placed beneath them in an attempt to spread and perpetuate the violence, which seemed to Marilyn to *always* be the case. Instead of unraveling the causes, the sources, the effects of violence, it was always met with more—both in quality and quantity—violence. What was outrageous, really, was the stupidity of the people—of the men, honestly—who kept turning that cycle.

But then the militants connected to the Passover bombing sought refuge in the Church of the Nativity in Bethlehem, and Marilyn feared that couldn't be anything *but* a powder keg ready to blow. One of the oldest churches in the world, supposedly built over the birthplace of Jesus, it was a sacred place in both Islam as well as Christianity. When Israeli forces set siege to the place and the tensions mounted over the course of the five-week standoff, of *course* Jack would be drawn to the scene. She was indeed thankful that he hadn't—how did *anyone* escape collateral damage in those situations—but still, London?

"Because it's easy money, deary," he told her. "People eat this royalty shit up."

"Yuck," she said, which didn't nearly articulate his visceral reaction to the circus he was witnessing.

The episode was a disgusting display of what *noblesse oblige* had come to mean in the 21st century—that the "responsibilities" of nobility boiled down to allowing commoners to participate in the royal ceremonies. Two hundred thousand camellias were draped on the Queen Mother's coffin over the three days it lay in state at Winchester. A million people lined the twenty-three mile route from central London to Windsor Castle, standing behind barriers bundled up against the dreary cold, snapping pictures of the flag-draped coffin rolling by on its carriage, escorted by the stoic Queen's Guard, resplendent in their red jackets and black plumes. Nothing, Jack thought, spoke so directly to the anachronism of empire and royalty as a grizzled old war veteran amputee saluting the passing of a woman whose legacy beyond being the longest-lived member of the royal family in British history—an "achievement" that lasted little more than a year—rested on her viciously sarcastic wit. Upon hearing that Edwina Mountbatten was buried at sea, for instance, she quipped, "Dear Edwina, she always liked to make a splash."

"Yuckier than yuck," Jack said, keeping the shot of the vet and his salutary prosthetic as viewed from the opposite side of the caisson for himself, "But it supports the habit."

"Never mind all that," she told him. There were more alarming developments. "Have you talked to Paul yet?"

He hadn't. "Why, what's up?"

Two relatively recent pronouncements from the administration had convinced her that Peter's conspiracy rant was no longer a theory. One a casual, off-the-cuff, off-script response at a press conference that the president was no longer concerned with bin Laden's whereabouts, that he didn't spend that much time on the question—this just six months after 9/11—and the other an official speech before the United Nations.

"You didn't hear Bolton?"

Of course not.

The ambassador had given a speech that first week of May, "Beyond the Axis of Evil," adding Libya, Syria and Cuba to their list of "state sponsors of terrorism that are pursuing or who have the potential to pursue weapons of mass destruction or have the capability to do so in violation of their treaty obligations."

"Cuba?"

"Goddamnit, Jack, that's not the point. *Syria's* the point, just like Peter said."

"But Cuba? That has to be a mistake. You sure you got your information right?"

She did. The State Department confirmed it all ten days later, issuing its own report on state sponsors of terror adding yet another country, the Sudan, to the list, which had prompted a return to her map for more shading, more arrows, for a much bleaker overall picture.

"Of *course* I got it right," she said. "But get this, they were planning on going into Afghanistan *before* 9/11!"

"No shit?"

"No shit."

A Presidential Directive was released to the press earlier in the month, which had been submitted in its final form two days before the attacks, detailing almost exactly what would be the blueprint for the invasion.

Jack made a concerted effort to contact his brother after that revelation.

"So what," Paul answered. "They had plans to get al Qaeda, finally. Word is they leaked that to hose down all those 9/11 Truther crazies."

"But Paul, invading the country?"

"Cheney's not known for pussy-footing around."

"Then no one sees this 'war on terrorism' as dubious?"

"Hell no, baby. The talk of the town is WMDs!"

"WMDs?"

"Going after Saddam."

However much he was starting to share Marilyn's sense of urgency, Jack didn't try to enlist Paul's help in finding their brother. He really did sound like he was drowning in that DC bubble. So Jack decided to return state-side as soon as possible to take up that effort himself.

That return was hampered considerably—logistically and professionally—by the massive flooding that ravaged Europe that summer.

Marilyn, meanwhile, was riding a roller coaster of emotion. She was deeply saddened by the bombing of the consulate in Karachi, retaliation, no doubt, for the arrests of Pearl's abductors—but proof, once again, of the insanity of it all—and then somewhat heartened to see just two weeks later the establishment of an International Criminal Court, claiming jurisdiction over all genocide, all crimes against humanity, all war crimes.

"Maybe there's hope," she wistfully murmured, but then another of her voices added, "So long as they've got teeth." As easy as she was finding it to silence those other voices lately, any real hope she harbored was likewise soon muted.

By that fall the WMD mantra was indeed all anyone heard out of official Washington, in its myriad panic-lathered variations. Marilyn didn't see opposing viewpoints offered too forcibly or too often. After the Labor Day recess the president looked certain to get his war resolution out of congress, and the only game in town was who would vote *against* it, further handicapping opposition, effectively, as those few voices were castigated as unpatriotic, or soft on terror, completely missing the larger implications, completely skewing the dialogue.

"Why *shouldn't* we take him out?" Paul asked in the week before the vote.

"Because we don't *do* that," Jack said.

"At least not officially," Marilyn added.

"Maybe it's time we did," Paul snapped. "Maybe it's long past time we did!"

"Jesus," Jack said, in the wake of another truncated phone call.

The next time they heard from Paul, just days later, he was even more combative. "You want to negotiate with terrorists now, you son-of-a-bitch?"

"What are you talking about?"

"Thought you followed the news, asshole."

He hadn't been, actually, being so focused on Peter, but the story of what they were calling the "Beltway sniper"—just a day old and all but obliterating the actual congressional vote—was just disseminating across the country at large. Jack turned on his television and it was everywhere: a gunman, or gunmen, seemingly shooting random targets in and around the DC area. Four different people in four different locations were gunned down the morning of October 3rd, with a fifth that evening. DC was in a panic, kids being pulled from schools, people avoiding gas stations, parking lots, open fields.

"They think it's another terror attack?"

"What do you think it is?"

"I don't know, but Paul, according to the report I'm watching, they killed a landscaper, a taxi driver, a babysitter—doesn't seem like very high profile targets."

"That's why everyone's so scared."

"I get that, but terrorism?"

Silly question, and to be fair, the authorities weren't calling it that, and they resisted all entreaties otherwise, as the killings lingered over three long weeks, albeit, at a slower pace. There was an authentic terrorist attack in the midst of the ordeal, though—two nightclubs in Bali were blown up, killing hundreds of people—fostering renewed demands on Western nations to go on the offensive in clamping down on radical groups.

And then, the same day the snipers were finally arrested—not terrorists at all, but one disgruntled and estranged man with his young mentally-challenged sidekick—Paul Wellstone, one of the loudest voices against war with Iraq—both past and pending—died in a plane crash in Minnesota. That was enough to render Marilyn nearly catatonic.

"What is it?" Jack asked when he found her like that, curled up in her chair. "What does it mean?"

"Means they're going in," she said. "They're going to get their Armageddon."

She'd been tracking other indicators. She checked off the things that had been happening—slipping beneath the radar of most rational people—that the fundamentalists in *this* country would view as signifying the nearness of their precious end-times. She heard the president's double-coded references in his calls for military response, to Revelation—"wrath of the lamb"—and Isaiah—"evildoers." She feared, as Peter had warned, the increasingly vast number of people who would hear those references and view concurrent events—the dot.com bubble collapse, the attack on the internet—through their filter of prophetic certainty.

"There can't be *that* many of them."

"There're more all the time."

"Why?"

"Because end-times, the second coming, Armageddon, all of that is the only tangible proof that their god even exists."

"But that's crazy."

"Of course it is. It always has been. But now they see their chance to make it real."

A volcano erupts near Sicily in December: check.

The Columbia disintegrates over Texas in February: check.

Then the Secretary of State gives a damning—and dubious—report to a reluctant United Nations: check.

"What do you mean, 'check'?" Jack asked her.

"Have you ever *read* Revelations?" she asked him.

"Well, no."

"Tell you what, don't bother. That's just a screed on revenge. Read something more contemporary, read any of Lahaye's books—he's sold like a jillion of them, *that's* how many crazies are out there. You hear WMD, mushroom cloud, war on terror. They hear good versus evil, the illegitimacy of the UN, French fecklessness, the anti-Christ rebuilding Babylon, check, check, check."

In March, the WHO issued a global alert about the SARS pandemic: "Like right out of one of the seven vials!"

That week's *Newsweek* broke a story about the president's daily "immersion" in a book of evangelical sermons by the Scottish Baptist, Oswald Chambers.

"Who the hell is that?"

"He's the lunatic who proselytized to the soldiers massed in Egypt in 1917 before their planned invasion of Palestine and re-capture of Jerusalem."

"That doesn't mean anything."

"Oh no?"

"He's a spiritual, *born again* guy."

"Really?"

If that were *really* true, wouldn't he have had a serious dialogue with the various church councils who were speaking out against his war plans? Wouldn't he have listened to those same councils—and others—who questioned the constitutionality of the Patriot Act or anti-gay marriage legislation? Even the National Association of Evangelicals appealed to him for policies promoting health care, decent housing and income for the poor. He gave tax cuts to the rich.

"He's pandering to the crazies."

"You're saying he's an end-timer?"

"I don't know *what* he is. I'm saying whether zealotry or deceit, it's dangerous."

But then, Marilyn saw a report in *Nature*, about the discovery of 350,000-year-old upright-walking human footprints in Italy.

"All right," she said. "That's it," to anyone, everyone. She seemed to have arrived at some crossroads, though exactly what, and how it would manifest itself, remained a mystery, suffused by current events yet again. The invasion of Iraq had begun.

Marilyn watched, horrified by the carnage. She didn't feel safer. She didn't feel special. She watched the giddy journalists in their flak jackets and helmets, talking about "shock and awe"—evermore biblical double coding—and bringing peace, liberty, and democracy to the Middle East.

"Bullshit," she answered.

"Saddam *is* a bad guy," Jack countered.

"Maybe, but he doesn't have anything to do with the 'war on terror'."

"Well, we're going to find out if that's true or not soon enough."

"Not you?" she said. "You're not going over there, are you?"

He'd thought about it, but resisted. In his typical passive-aggressive way, he told himself that he'd let the deadline for military clearance lapse, and as such he'd forfeited any chance that he *could* go. But from the reports he was getting, everybody and their brother was already over there. Three days before the "get out of town" deadline, there were already thousands of journalists and crews "in theater," as they so glibly put it. More than that, though, were his concerns about journalistic integrity. He was already hearing stories from friends that once the action started, those reporters embedded with military units were effectively muzzled, channeled away from the real story, and then briefed by official liaisons. All it took was one look at a Pentagon news conference for him to know the news coming out of those briefings was sterile, at best.

Watching one together, they heard this from the Secretary of Defense: "Mr. Secretary, what evidence do you have that it's actually working, that there are actually Iraqis who are heeding this call to—"

"We have evidence."

"And what sort of evidence is that?"

"Good evidence."

"What the fuck is that?" Jack asked.

"Why should it be any different now," Marilyn answered. "Nobody talked about the real costs, the real consequences, leading up the war. Why would any of them be an honest broker now?" Indeed, the talk was all about liberation, how easily, and cheaply that would be achieved, how oppressed Iraqis would welcome the "coalition" forces with flowers and candy. No domestic news organization saw fit to cover UN and humanitarian services estimates of 10 million people needing food assistance, half the population without potable water, a million or more refugees, thirty percent of Iraqi children at risk of death from malnutrition, half a million civilians requiring direct medical treatment, another half million susceptible to disease in the aftermath. No, the focus remained an insistence that Iraq posed some new half-baked imminent threat and that invading the country was "justified," the rest of world opinion be damned. "They've got half the country believing Hussein had something to do with 9/11. They don't need the truth."

"They ought to answer the question, at least."

"I'm just waiting for someone to ask him about the WMDs."

As the days ground on and public opinion started to sour, more and more people were waiting for the same revelation, as more and more excuses were offered instead.

A convicted felon from the Reagan administration, now a war "correspondent," claimed the French were destroying evidence of WMDs.

"Check."

His "network" quickly retracted the story.

"He must have smuggled them across the border into Syria," one apologist line went.

"Jesus, just how badly do they want to get in *there*."

Still, the breathless, toy-soldier reporting persisted. A week in, CNN devoted hours of live coverage to a camera crew embedded with a Marine unit in southern Iraq. The troops had taken fire from a nearby building and stopped along the road to retaliate. Missiles were fired at a house. "This is historic footage," the reporter deadpanned. "This is real-time battle you're seeing."

"Why are you watching that?" Marilyn asked.

"It's what's going on, right now," Jack said.

"Really? You actually believe that?"

"I *saw* it: A tank firing on a house, the place destroyed."

"That's *not* what's going on," she said. "Come here, watch this."

She logged on to Al-Jazeera, catching a stream of an hysterical family wailing about the destruction of their home, the deaths of their relatives—a 12-year-old child with half her head blown off—vehemently promising revenge.

"*That's* what's going on over there."

Jack stared at the images.

Asked about the prudence of broadcasting such footage—that, and earlier depictions of dead or imprisoned American soldiers, something the White House had the unmitigated temerity to condemn—the reporter answered, "It is only the truth," which was a far cry, obviously, from what any Americans were getting, or offering.

The White House press secretary told the nation, "There is no question we have evidence and information that Iraq has weapons of mass destruction."

The top general of the war expressed "no doubt" they'd be found, followed two days later by another Reagan sycophant who likewise expressed "no doubt."

The always trustworthy Secretary of Defense insisted, "we have seen intelligence" indicating the presence of said weapons, but when pressed about the possible whereabouts that intell might lead to—since no one had been able to find anything over the course of the first two weeks—responded confidently, laughably, that they were "east, west, south and north of Baghdad, somewhat."

"What?"

Two weeks later troops seized a trailer at a military checkpoint and the official message immediately became they'd captured a mobile biological weapons laboratory.

"Who knew such a thing existed?"

"Why would you want to be handling that kind of stuff while moving?"

"Makes as much sense as anything else."

Despite reasoned skepticism, the administration version never varied, as member after member, from top brass all the way down to deputy deputy spokesperson declared that they had in fact found the fabled WMDs. But it just wasn't true, no matter how many times they said it.

"Got to give them credit for staying on message," Jack tried.

"They're *lying*!"

So certain was she, she tried to go back to Al-Jazeera. It was shut down.

"What the fuck?" Jack said. "Try the BBC."

She did, as well as other foreign services, but all the chatter at the moment was about a US tank strike on the Palestine Hotel.

"The Palestine? That's where all the journalists are housed."

The footage showed bodies being carried through the lobby.

"They're lying and they're making sure no one else gets the true story out."

But then, somehow, someone within the administration strayed off the reservation, privately telling a reporter that they'd "be amazed" if any of the vaunted weapons were ever found. No harm, though, as that was after the ridiculously staged toppling of Saddam's statue in Baghdad and the equally vaudevillian landing on the Abraham Lincoln where the president declared, "Mission accomplished."

"What mission?"

"What accomplished?"

That's when Paul, of all people, decided to call them and gloat. "Told you so."

"He's kidding, right," Marilyn said.

"I don't think so," Jack told her, covering the mouthpiece.

"Mission accomplished, baby!"

"Ask him about the WMDs."

"Absence of evidence is not evidence of absence," Paul answered.

"He says evidence of absence," Jack started. "Wait, what was that?"

"Oh, please," Marilyn said.

"It's true!"

"It's *not* true," she shouted. "It's all lies."

"How would *she* know?"

"Ask him about the Presidential Records Act."

The 1974 Presidential Recordings and Materials Preservation Act, passed in the wake of Nixon's shenanigans, was supposed to limit executive secrecy, spread a little disinfecting sunshine around. Reagan era records were due to be released that fall of 2001. But in the hysteria following 9/11, the act was repealed by the White House. Fine time for some shade, burying everything from 1980's "October surprise" up to and including Iran-Contra. It went all but unnoticed until recently. Only someone at Archives would have really been aware of the move at the time.

"Paul?"

"I stand by what I said: Absence of evidence is not evidence of absence."

"Jesus Christ, you don't *really* believe that, do you?" Jack said to his brother.

"I do until you prove otherwise," Paul said.

Proof quickly ceased to be a commodity with any value though. All that seemed to matter was who said what often enough and the loudest. Truth became subjective, belief a guiding principle—that is, believe first, without question, rejecting all evidence to the contrary—and faith a virtue, if only because being wrong would be too politically painful. Even when someone does manage to rise above the cacophony, a formerly independent, formerly respected, an ambassador, for crying out loud—as if that word, too, no longer had any meaning—and proclaims, "What I didn't find in Niger,"—that is, virtually no evidence of one of the more incendiary pre-war claims—the official response is *not*, "Oops, our bad," but to attack his wife, a CIA operative, who'd been toiling in anonymity for *years* in a successful effort to do the very thing they went to war over.

No matter.

No matter that at about the same time one of the main architects of the war was saying that weapons of mass destruction wasn't the "core reason" for the invasion, a ringer for the administration at *The New York Times* was claiming that the failure to find any was the Pentagon's fault. No matter.

No matter that the argument became exactly how many antiquities were looted in the chaos that ensued in Baghdad—was it 33, as stated by one of the more regenerate neo-conservative cheerleaders for the misguided adventure, or closer to the 170,000 as evidenced by anyone with cable television watching the bedlam— and not the fact that the cradle of civilization was being looted at all. No, no matter. "Stuff happens," the recalcitrant Secretary of Defense explained.

No matter that the press secretary, when asked if there was any remorse in the administration about going to war under false pretenses that have resulted in thousands of innocent civilian deaths, answered, "I think that part of the world is breathing a sigh of relief," a sigh that "at long last" they have a chance "to build a future that is based on freedom and opportunity and not on tyranny."

"Try shoveling that manure to the Ivory Coast."

"What?"

"We blocked a UN plan to send peacekeepers there to enforce a truce in their civil war."

"Why?" Jack asked.

"Officially? 'It cost too much.' But they're lying, as usual. The unofficial reason is to get back at the French."

"We were not lying," another administration official told reporters about the threat of Saddam.

"Of course not."

"It was just a matter of emphasis," after *The Independent* reported that "they ignored intelligence assessments which said Iraq was not a threat."

"And the sun revolves around the earth," Jack said.

"Exactly," Marilyn said. "Exactly."

It was as if the world had retarded a couple of centuries and the same species of inerrant bible thumpers were now running the foreign policy of the most powerful nation on the planet and a goddamn Attorney General who thinks the establishment clause is "a wall of religious oppression."

"God's got to go," she said.

"What?"

"God's got to go. Face it, Jack, belief in God only, eventually, leads us to kill one another, because every one of those believers are also certain that their God wrote a book, and that book, necessarily, is infallible, which makes the competing Gods incompatible, which can only lead to conflict."

"But not everyone is such a literalist."

"Ah, the so-called 'moderate' believers?"

"Right."

"There's no such thing."

"Of course there is."

"They're cowards. They're failed believers and failed secularists, failing both reason *and* faith."

"But they're not bomb-throwing fundamentalists."

"No, they just enable the crazies."

"So what would you have them do, get *more* religious?"

"I would have them use their fucking intelligence and challenge their dogmas."

"And move *beyond* God?"

"He's *got* to go."

"Good luck with that one."

"Think about it. Let's say we could find the most educated Christian from the fourteenth century and bring him to today. He'd be regarded as a blithering idiot in all matters *except* faith. His education taught him that the earth was flat, the sun *did* revolve around the earth, and to cure epilepsy you drilled a hole in the patient's head to let the demons out. In every other field of study—medicine, geography, engineering, astronomy, agriculture, metallurgy, economics, all of them—we'd laugh him out of the room. But he would know as much or more than anyone alive today about God. How is that possible?"

"Because religious thought was handed down in already perfect form?"

"Come on, Jack."

"For the sake of argument."

"To the exclusion of every other pursuit of knowledge? Really?"

"I get it, I do. But most people are going to say if I die tomorrow, I'll take my chances with God."

"Exactly. How about this one: if you were to wake up tomorrow and all your knowledge was erased, gone."

"That's nuts."

"Nuttier than God?"

"Check."

"What would you want to relearn first, how to pray or, oh, I don't know, how to grow corn maybe?"

"*And* mate. Still, tough sale."

"Why? That's where your cherished 'moderates' come from, from the implicit fact that even the dumbest person alive today knows eons more than anyone did a thousand years ago—without even thinking about it we *know* disease doesn't result from sin or demonic possession or the preposterous supposition that the earth and everything on it was created in a week six thousand years ago is ridiculous—and it's that knowledge that's incompatible with scripture. So they fake it, just for a hedge against death. Time to call them out."

"What about the crazies who *do* believe dinosaurs and human beings lived together?"

"They have to be stopped."

"Whoa, how are you going to do that?"

"We *need* to find Peter."

"Still drawing a blank there, sweetie."

"What if," she said. "Do you think you could get me a list of good reporters *not* on the war beat?"

"Why?"

"Well, I figure if they're not playing toy soldier, maybe they've got some integrity left."

"Enough to help you find Peter?"

"In a way."

"I don't get it."

"Neither do I, totally," she told him, and shrugged. "It just popped into my head."

"That's a scary thought," Jack said, got up, kissed her on the forehead. "I'm on the job, honey."

Marilyn's declaration of apostasy was not nearly so spontaneous or reckless as those who knew her might have first thought. It had been developing over the summer. She read in the Israeli newspaper *Haaretz* in late June that the president told top Palestinian officials weeks earlier that, "I'm driven with a mission from God. God would tell me, 'go and fight those terrorists in Afghanistan.' And I did, and then God would tell me, 'go and end the tyranny in Iraq...' And I did. And now again, I feel God's words coming to me, 'Go and get the Palestinians their state and get the Israelis their security in the Middle East.' And by God, I'm gonna do it." There was no White House rebuttal in the story and the American press let it go altogether, which needn't have surprised her. At the beginning of the same month, the FCC, chaired by the son of the Secretary of State, abolished all rules against broadcast and print media consolidation. There would be, in short order, a handful of multinational conglomerates who would control the flow of information so vital to any society and critical to a democratic one, and that message would become WAR IS PEACE, ISLAM IS EVIL, GREED IS GOOD, by which they mean the margins that can be realized in a perpetual 'war on terrorism.'

All thought and all debate had been reduced to that simple binary, good and evil, in a move straight out of *1984*, straight out of Goebbels.

"Did you know Joey started as a journalist?" Jack once asked her.

"Like his friend Adolph?"

"That's right. He was also a novelist and a playwright."

"Really? What did he write?"

"We'll never know. All of his manuscripts were rejected."

"Small wonder. He only had one plot line."

"Kill everyone else."

"Exactly."

Which is all great and good for the Christians, and the enablers of war—not the generals, not the soldiers, but those cowards who start them, perpetuate them, profit off them, never have and never intend to participate in them. And so long as the Christians are riled up with a great and good cause, in the name of *Jesus*—the executive administrator of the National Association of Evangelicals said of the invasion, "Iraq will become the center for spreading the gospel of Jesus Christ to Iran, Libya and throughout the Middle East," even as those enablers, our *leaders*, the neocons, were encouraging the radical Islamists to reach for power as they toppled or destabilized secular governments in the region in the astonishing belief that the world would be better off with the fundamentalists, in accordance to their theory of "Lebanonizing" the region, reducing the artificial states created by the post-World War I gamesmen "into a chaos of squabbling, feuding, fighting sects, tribes, regions and parties," reducing the threat to their Israeli sponsors, they never *intended* to foster democracy in Iraq, but to flatten it and remove it as a regional threat—they'll get their wars. That was why, "God has *got* to go."

As September, October—with Israel's bombing raid inside Syria—and November wound on and the war got nastier and nastier, and more and more experts came out and said there was no pre-war evidence of WMDs and sure enough none were ever found, though plenty of people were still dying by the day, and Osama bin Laden was no longer much of a concern of the administration, and troops started complaining about unarmored vehicles and shortages of water and extensions of tours, from six months to nine months to twelve months or more, the propaganda and cheerleading and "primitive patriotism" reached a new pitch—where anyone questioning the motives, the strategy, the conduct or the results of the unprecedented imperial adventurism was branded as not supporting the troops, and therefore not supporting the nation; where criticism of America's behavior was criticism of America itself and criticism of the country was faithlessness of the country's Christian foundation, as near to heretical blasphemy as you could get in those godforsaken vegged-out times, and had to be singled out, shouted down and punished. Enter the FBI, with newfound powers to keep tabs on your library loans, Internet visits, and subversive associations—everything from the Pennsylvania Dutch Quakers to Fresno For Peace.

"God has got to go."

And then, in the middle of December, Saddam was captured. Paul called with the news before many of the major outlets were breaking the story, as if he'd moved into the real live situation room.

"We got him!"

"So fucking what."

"Scarlot?"

"Scarlot's not here."

"Not there? Where is she?"

"Not *here*."

"All right, all right. Jesus, what's gotten into you?"

"Maybe I've changed. Of all people, you should know things change."

"What things?"

"You don't intimidate me anymore Paul. I know what you're doing, I know how you're doing it, and I know why."

"What am I supposedly *doing*?"

"Why did you call?"

"To tell you we got him."

"Him, Saddam," she said, repeating, "So fucking what."

"What do mean so fucking what?"

"I mean, *so* fucking what: was it worth the 500 American deaths, the 20,000 Iraqi deaths?"

Silence.

"Of course you can't answer that you fucking coward, because there's only one answer and you can't afford to acknowledge it, just like you can't allow anyone to see the military caskets coming home or the *collateral* damage over there to women and children and can't even permit other organizations to cover that carnage, and do you know why? I'll tell you why, it's not because of dead American boys and girls, it's not about destroyed Iraqi mothers and babies, it's because if you showed the *real* picture of this fucking 'war on terrorism' of yours, you might lose the support of your idiotic Christian base, that's why."

"Marilyn, I'm not—"

"Of *course* you are, you chickenshit. If you support any part of this scam you're as guilty as Rumsfeld and Cheney and Wolfowitz and Ledeen and Kristol and Condi and Colin, you're fucking guilty Paul, and you've got blood on your hands."

"I didn't have anything to do—"

"BLOOD ON YOUR HANDS!" she screamed.

Her volcanic anger had been brewing for the better part of two decades, and it had far less to do with his leaving her as it did with her being duped by the man she thought she loved. During the interim she'd kept it capped by either mistrusting her instincts and arguing that she must be wrong about him, or in softer moments persuading herself that he wasn't really the "Reagan democrat" he was pretending to be and would, surely, at some point, come around. On this day, though, she didn't hold back. She let loose with a full-throated, scathing disembowelment of what he'd become.

"You've had blood on your hands since 1980! You rode in on the coattails of that *actor* who had to get in bed with Islamic fundamentalists to get elected, and participated in the ruination of this country, from union busting to his disastrous voodoo economics, raiding the Social Security Trust to pay for his Star Wars so they can then turn around and say 'Social Security doesn't work', destroying the social contract; privatizing the commons, privatizing the government, privatizing *democracy*, Paul, throwing the doors open to the forces of greed, selfishness, inequity, unfairness, arrogance, intolerance, racism, religious bigotry, hypocrisy, false pride, nationalism, and militarism, all under the bogus mantra of 'enlightened self-interest' and the 'invisible hand' of 'free markets,' so that now you get outfits like Blackwater."

"What's Blackwater?"

"No, you wouldn't know about them. It's a private, no-bid, fundamentalist army over in Iraq. You just watch the shit they stir up."

"What's all that got to do with me?"

"You were in on it. When your man went into rehab in that ridiculously religious election of 1988, you used faith to get him re-elected; you courted the co-mingling of government and religion."

"What's wrong with that?"

"You get wars, Paul. You get wars. The fundamentalists come out of the woodwork in times of crisis, whether it's real or not. In the 90s you jackasses convinced them that there was a moral crisis in this country and you spawned a war on the presidency, a war on drugs, a war on Christmas, and now you've convinced them there's a crisis of civilizations and you've got two hot wars, looking for a third."

"Who's looking for a third?"

"Haven't you been listening to those crazies?"

"It's more than just the fundamentalists supporting the president."

"Oh, bullshit, Paul. They're the loudest, the craziest, and they're all over that administration. Everyone knows they can be whipped up into a froth and mobilized by screaming their way of life is endangered."

"Maybe it is."

"Nonsense. You *know* that's nonsense. You're using those people because you can, and you can only because of *God*, the way they've *always* been used, manipulated, by people speaking for their *God*. And because there will always be people like you taking advantage of that, it's time for God to go."

"What?"

"It's time for God to go."

"You're nuts," he said. "Call me when the aliens land," and

hung up.

"Maybe," she answered no one. "But I'm right."

And then the world went and proved how right she was. The day after Christmas an Indian Ocean earthquake—the second strongest ever recorded and longest lasting—unleashed a monstrous tsunami that washed away thousands of lives across a dozen nations. At one and the same time the worldwide response showed just how much human beings *could* do—as aid poured in from hundreds of countries around the globe, from the poorest countries on Earth sending five hundred dollars and a case of powdered milk, to the richest pledging scores of volunteers and hundreds of millions of dollars—and what "men of God" *will* do in such situations: blame the disaster on the native island inhabitants, proclaiming that an angry deity had triggered the tidal wave as punishment for their heathen, idolatrous ways. Even though everyone knows, the Christian deity told Noah, "No more water, fire next time…"

"Yeah," Marilyn said, covering the aftermath, both weeping at the devastation and the outpouring of humanitarian assistance, and seething that those pompous, pampered blowhards should have any kind of platform to make such vile, hate-filled pronouncements. "How's that God thing working out for you now?"

13.

"YOU said *what*?" Jack asked her.

"I called him a chickenshit."

"Damn."

"I'm sick and tired of him sitting there and watching like it doesn't affect him or there's nothing he could do about it."

"What do you want him to do?"

"*Some*thing," though even as she said it she knew how hollow it sounded.

What was there to do? With this White House, "honeycombed with prayer groups and bible study cells," as one reporter put it last year, a president who really and truly seems to *believe* he has "God on his side," willing to act unilaterally and illegally, what is there that *anyone* could do? Even exposing it didn't seem to have any effect.

"Where are you?" she asked Jack.

"Madrid."

"Spain?"

"Yeah, the train bombings," he said. "It's awful."

"What about the CIA?"

"I'm sure they're here somewhere."

"No, their admission, that there was no WMD threat."

"I'm shocked."

"Jesus," she said tiredly. "Keep in touch."

Joe Formichella

Nobody cared.

Just like nobody cared a week later when the president mocked the search for WMD in front of a ballroom full of correspondents, mocking the CIA, making a mockery of his "war on terrorism," from the troops to the innocent collateral to all the subsequent victims *of* terror.

"Why isn't he in jail?" Marilyn asked as she watched the clip over and over again.

And nobody *really* cared when the atrocities at Abu Ghraib were finally exposed a month after that. How else to explain the collective acceptance of the Secretary's laughable excuse that the behavior was the result of the misdeeds of "a few bad apples," when there were mountains of evidence dictating otherwise? Nobody cared and nobody had any reason to ask, "Why do they hate us?" ever again. Tell me again how evil *they* are, she thought.

"What is *wrong* with this country?"

She got her answer when Jack next called.

"Where are you now?"

"Cal-e-*forn*ya," he said, imitating the state's new governor.

"Vomit. Why?"

"You're not going to like it."

"Why?"

"Reagan's funeral."

"Ah, Jesus, Jack."

"Sorry."

"You're helping lionize the guy who got us in most of this trouble in the first place."

"I'm just trying to make my nut."

"That's disgusting."

"It's a *circus* phrase."

"I know, I know. It's still disgusting. You got any names for me?"

"A couple."

"At least you're good for something."

"Chill, honey. This'll all be over in five months."

"No it won't."

"What are you talking about? Not even Kerry could lose this election."

"I think you're wrong, Jack, and it's scaring me to death."

"And I was having such a good time out here."

"I'm sure you were."

She'd been watching the signs, the indicators. She read of the incumbent out campaigning telling people, "I trust God speaks through me," and cringed, both at the audacity of such a statement and at how well it played with the crazies.

"You can't keep calling them crazies."

"Why not? They believe in something unproven and improvable, they live, kill, and die on the basis of that belief. If that's not crazy, what is?"

She watched them shift the color-coded threat alert up and down in almost exact synchronization with political liability or opportunity, like puppet strings on the electorate. She listened as white, conservative, evangelical church leaders blatantly positioned themselves as organizational cheerleaders for the Republican party. What was worse, leaked headquarter emails documented the strategy to enlist churches around the country in distributing political information and registering voters. In Pennsylvania alone, the campaign sought to identify hundreds of friendly congregations that might meet regularly to disseminate their message. One sane reverend was quoted as saying, "I never thought that anyone could so attempt to meld a political party with a network of religious organizations."

One right-wing think tank advised forty-five *thousand* churches that "short of endorsing a candidate by name from the pulpit, they were free to do almost anything."

They appointed fifty thousand Catholic "team leaders" to propagandize for them and asked the Pope to push American bishops to be more aggressive politically on family and life issues.

No, not only did she not hold out any hope in the election, she feared the situation getting far worse, by quantum measurements, and sure enough, within minutes of the polls closing, they started ratcheting up the vitriol against *another* Middle Eastern country, Iran.

"These people are murderously *crazy*," she said. She had to find Peter.

But it was Paul who called a week after the election.

"I'll bet you're just tickled pink," she said to him.

"No, Mare, I'm not, not at all," he told her.

His voice was strained, and shaky.

"I didn't want to believe you, but you might be right."

"About what?"

"About these *lunatics*," he whispered.

"What they're saying about Iran?"

"No, what their overall motivation is. I mean, I was sickened about Abu Ghraib, sickened, as were a lot of people, especially the way they sat on the story for months, let the abuse continue. But this..." he started.

"What?" she asked.

"Listen, they've somehow kept this out of the press so far, but the word is that when he was trying to get France to go along with the Iraq invasion, the president told Chirac that 'Gog and Magog are at work in the Middle East.' You know who they are, right?"

"Revelations."

"Right. He said, 'The biblical prophecies are being fulfilled,' that the war was 'willed by God' who wanted to 'use this conflict to erase his people's enemies before a New Age begins.'"

"*Peter* was right," she said. "How are they keeping reporters off that?"

"You know how the news is put together. They just call it crazy talk and everyone believes them. I *believed* them. But then," he paused, as if checking his surroundings, "then," he said, in a still lower voice, "I started hearing rumors that Arafat's death might not have been natural."

"What?"

"Polonium."

Marilyn thought a moment. She culled from reserves she didn't think she still had, marshaled a determination and directive she thought she'd lost, a determination and directive rooted in fear, driven by necessity. "Are you at work?"

"No. Home."

"On a land line?"

"Yeah."

"Go get a cell, a disposable one, and call me back."

But he didn't. Days went by, then weeks. By then she was *really* scared, unplugged her phone and ordered a pre-paid cell off the internet, too afraid to even go out to the corner pharmacy.

She waited, while Seymour Hersh reported on "The Coming Wars," how military commandos had been in Iran for months mapping targets. Emboldened by the election, administration officials refused to rule out military options.

"Rule out?" she said. "That's all they ever wanted."

At one and the same time—comically, or tragically—the White House *finally* acknowledged they weren't even looking for WMD anymore, the worthless press secretary telling everyone that, "Based on what we know today, the president would have taken the same action because this is about protecting the American people," and the stenographers assembled dutifully copied it all down without challenge.

"You *idiots!*" Marilyn screamed, and waited, and paced.

Weeks later, thoroughly convinced that something not good had happened to Paul—though as much as she wracked her brain, she could not light on as convincing a reason why that might be the case, something that heightened her fears—she found Jack out of the country again. He wouldn't tell her exactly where at first.

"Not now," he dodged her inquiries. "What's going on with Paul?"

"He's vanished."

"Vanished?"

"Vanished. He was supposed to call me, but I haven't heard a peep. And his other phones are dead."

"Maybe he's just pouting."

"I don't think so. When we talked, right after the election, he seemed," she started, and then stopped. "When are you coming back?"

"Couple of days."

"Where are you?"

"Why do you want to ask that?"

"Jack?"

"Don't make me do this."

"Jack?"

"The Vatican."

"Aw, hell, Jack. What is it with you and these funerals?"

"I'm a whore."

The buzz in the industry has always been that such celebrity shots brought fame—at least it was viewed as the quickest route to fame—fame brought access, with access came prestige, and with prestige came deals, for books, exclusives, you name it.

Marilyn laughed. "At least you're honest." Then she thought about it a moment. "And you may have just hit on an answer."

"How's that?"

"That's the man we need, someone who's not a whore, *and* honest. Someone completely unlike you, and like you."

"I can give you that name right now."

She listened, then asked, "Why him?"

"He's pissed off *everyone*."

"And he's good?"

"Shit, honey, he's good enough to marry."

"Marry who?"

"Why, me, of course."

"That's why I love you, Jack."

"Let's not start the orgy just yet. He probably won't answer his phone."

"Then I'll go to him," she said, trying to sound convincing.

"No you won't, and we both know it."

Which was true enough. In the quiet of her house, she quickly realized that even if she could, even if she *did*, she had no idea of what she'd say to him. What could she possibly say to cause him to give a damn about Peter, much less Paul. After years of freely holding solitary conversations out loud, she'd grown more than a little dependent on that process for making any decisions—even if those decisions were often suspect. If there was any hope of anything working—she couldn't even define "working"; what would that be: finding Peter? Finding out what he knew?—she had to somehow relearn—if she ever really knew—how to work out a rational, rationalized strategy. She devoted the entirety of a weekend to the effort.

There was just so much to unravel though. What did she know about Peter's disappearance?

"That it'd happened before, for one."

True, but this was different. Before, he'd always been pursuing something, whether mystical enlightenment or missionary fulfillment. This time he seemed bent on avoiding, or escaping something. But what? The machinations of some theoretical apocalyptic conspiracy: He wouldn't have been eliminated for that. He would have been laughed at.

"Crazy talk, just like Paul said."

If that's true, then Paul's account of the conversation with Chirac wouldn't have posed a threat either. They were already dealing with that.

"But if Paul was right about the war being billed as the opening battle of Armageddon, that would mean Peter was right about the conspiracy. Right?"

Her head was starting to hurt.

The only other possible causality was Arafat. But how would his death—natural or not—fit in with the plan and what about it would be so sensitive to necessitate nabbing Paul?

She started pacing at that point and would continue pacing all through that Saturday night, occasionally circulating by and around the table where her map of the Middle East lay, along with a separate spreadsheet where she'd detailed what she called an "algorithm to Apocalypse."

She paused over the three different colored diagrams, one each for pre-, mid-, and post-trib. She traced the lines to the point where they all intersected.

"They can't do *anything* without the third temple."

How would Arafat's death affect that? It would damn sure rile up the Palestinians. Was that a desirable result? If agitated enough, she reasoned, it could lead to all out conflict, maybe, *maybe* even enough to orchestrate destruction of the mosque, she thought, resting a finger on a sketch of the complex. There'd been an attempt for years to negotiate the relocation of the mosque—to Mecca, or some such. If that effort had finally been abandoned, plan B could be to escalate the violence.

"They'd have to be awfully pissed," she said.

Naturally, there'd be the suspicion of foul play. "Was suspicion enough?" What would confirmation do? Tip off the rest of the world? Would that be enough to scuttle that plan?

"Possibly."

And what would the reaction be in that kind of scenario? Marilyn went back to her notes for examples. The Wilson/Plame case was the readiest parallel. But that was too public, too high profile to retaliate directly.

"Didn't keep them from breaking some very serious laws, though."

She dug further into the pile of notes. "What was his name?" she kept asking, peeling down page after page into the stack. A third of the way in she started to see a slightly different style of handwriting. A wave of recognition and foreignness coursed through her, all at once. She recognized the writing, but the idea that those two sources could have co-existed so easily on one page seemed as foreign as anything else at the moment. "But that explains it." Why she couldn't remember the name. And then she found it. "Hatfield."

All at once she had an answer, and a plan. There were two options. They could try to find Paul, but that undoubtedly involved dealing with some heavy hitters. Or they could continue looking for Peter in the faint hope that his information might unravel the whole scheme, maybe even shaking Paul from their web, if he was still alive. She had to focus on Peter. And if she was going to get Jack's mark interested in that endeavor, she had to walk him through some hoops, had to create the impression of direction and discovery, all at the same time. It would take time, she knew. But it was the only way. In the end, come what may, with any kind of success, it'd be worth it. It would begin with Jack.

He got back to town later in the week. By then she'd already started putting the pieces in play, with more ease than she thought, if she could just keep it together long enough.

"He's out of our reach, Jack," she said to him, to keep him from going directly to DC.

"You don't know that."

"We both know that, Jack. Come on."

"Who?" was all Jack wanted to know at that point.

"Think about it, Jack. If he disappeared because of that phone call, the FBI's likely involved, probably the Pentagon too."

"Son of a bitch," he answered.

"I'm sorry," she said, hugging him.

"We've got to do *something*," he said into her hair.

"Peter's the important thing at this point," she whispered very close to his ear. "What *you* should do is keep up normal appearances, keep chasing your disaster scenes and celebrity funerals.

We can use it."

"Oh, sure, use me," he said, collapsing into a chair. "Any immediate suggestions?"

"Yes, as a matter of fact. Can you conjure a reason to go to LA?"

"There's always something to shoot in LA."

"Very funny."

"You know what I mean," Jack said, even though secretly he would've preferred to confirm whether it was indeed funny or not. He'd always believed that the only way out of all this—without even knowing fully exactly what it was—was through humor.

"Whatever. I need you to find an address and mail this to it," she said, handing over a sealed manila envelope.

Jack studied it, looked at her, said, "Where'd you find this kind of moxie, darling?"

"Desperate times," she said. "And I mean to hang on to it for a while," trying to maintain the façade.

While Marilyn struggled to do just that, the world seemed to be coming completely off its bearings—which, in an odd way, made her task somewhat easier. The horrific London Underground bombings shattered a dreary summer morning, killing scores and escalating the police presence in transit systems all over the world. Two weeks later more bomb blasts in Egypt—on the heels of the British jihadists promising such explosive behavior day after day in retaliation for Western and Israeli policies—had people everywhere conducting their mundane day-to-day activities as if each was a trip through a minefield.

Meanwhile, within a week, the IRA finally laid down its arms after decades of terrorizing Northern Ireland. The cessation of the conflict had only happened after years of negotiations and diplomacy, and the irony of the juxtaposition couldn't have struck Marilyn with any more bitterness and clarity, though few other accounts she happened upon even bothered to mention the dissonance.

It was, to her, a crystalline instance where adults finally interceded and convinced enough of the participants that it was in everyone's better interest—even Protestants *and* Catholics, by this point, for crying out loud, in 2005—to work out their differences in a peaceful, Parliamentarian, *reasonable* manner. Put down your books and come to the table. It was the only hope. So long as leaders saw themselves as men of "faith," behaving and deciding in accordance to their faith, there was little hope.

"It's so *fucking* simple," she said, but instantly chided herself. She could not come off as reactionary, not now, not until...

And then, as if by miracle—but a miracle of secular intervention—it was announced that Sharon had finagled Israeli disengagement from the occupied territories in the West Bank and Gaza. She, along with most other casual observers in the West, didn't think that day was possible.

"He's not going to make many friends doing that," she said.

She scanned and scanned the sites for news of the blowback that was surely coming, but all news stopped less than forty-eight hours later when a monstrous hurricane occupied the Gulf of Mexico, and the whole world watched its inevitable advance on New Orleans.

She watched, day one, day two, after the levees broke, couldn't take it anymore, and made the phone call, even if it was a little too soon.

"I *SAW* him," Jack said breathlessly into the phone.

"Saw who?" Marilyn asked.

"Peter!" he said.

"You're kidding."

He told her how he'd been in New Orleans, overwhelmed by the destruction of Katrina, furious at the government's non-response. He said he'd ended up helping out, wherever, however he could, more than taking pictures. Within hours of hitting the Crescent City, he didn't even *want* to subject those poor people to the permanence of film.

"Plenty of people took up that slack. You don't have to worry about that," she told him.

When the feds finally did arrive mid-week, they pushed most of the civilian volunteers aside, leaving it all to "faith-based" organizations and Blackwater.

"Of course."

He decided to head east, trace the trail of devastation along the Mississippi coast.

"Whole towns, Mare, *entire* towns—Waveland, Bay St. Louis, Pass Christian, Long Beach—are just wiped off the map. People there told me there were buildings that had survived Carmen that were destroyed," antebellum mansions that had withstood a direct hit from the category 5 storm some forty years earlier.

"And then I heard there were shrimp boats in the trees over in Alabama. I *had* to see that."

"Have a heart, Jack."

"I do, I do, but come on: Shrimp boats, in the *trees*! Wait till you see them."

He pushed further into Alabama, from Bayou La Batre to Dauphin Island—a barrier island that had its west end amputated by the storm—to Mobile, where high water marks stained downtown buildings twelve feet above the ground. Out on the Causeway that crosses Mobile Bay he found the eastern terminus of the storm damage, a distinct dividing line splitting the roadway, where on one side a gas station was destroyed, on the other a restaurant was open for business.

"It picked up and moved a goddamn *battleship*, Mare, can you believe that?" the USS Alabama, that had been retired in the bay, serving as the center piece of a whole complex of former instruments of war put on display, *and* as a storm shelter, though not the most reliable one this time.

He went on into Baldwin County, on the eastern shore of the bay, and aside from a general littering of pine straw and the occasional downed limb, the little towns up and down the coast were virtually untouched. In one of those towns, Fairhope, chock full of the typical tourist trappings, the place was just buzzing with people. He took in the scene and wondered, for the longest time, How can you people live here under the threat of such chaos?

"And then I saw him. He rode by me on this little red scooter. It was the damnest thing."

"Perfect," she said, checking the ID on another incoming call. "See if you can find out where he's living, but discreetly. Don't do anything until you hear from me."

"You got it boss lady."

"I got a call I've been waiting on. Be careful."

"You're good at this, you know that?"

"Just don't tell anyone."

"Who would I tell?" he wondered, but she was gone.

14.

Ganda Anda was maybe the worst ruler Negara Bersatu could have ever had. No one will ever know, of course, since he managed to ruin the country long before they could get rid of him. But he possessed the worst aspects of the worst manifestations of human nature, and he had a raspy villainous cheerleading voice inside his head egging him on. He operated under purely personal, vindictive motivations. He wanted a lasting legacy. He most certainly got it, though **Mata-Mata** might have done him the favor of saying, "Careful what you wish for."

He wanted to beat his dad **Apiun** and punish his mother **Piarit.** Once he ascended to the throne, that's **all** he did.

And he wanted to be a wartime ruler. That was the easiest part. He simply modified a page out of the old family playbook. He convinced his fellow Bersatans that the world—the world as they knew it, that is, which for most of them extended not much past the horizon—was after their wealth, their most cherished resource, their **karang**. It was a shrewd enough scheme to put together, once **Mata-Mata** deposited the seed notion into his feeble brain, "Use **Dewa**."

The propaganda went like this: Since so many neighboring nations were failing, comparatively—for which he never offered any evidence, to which, **Mata-Mata** advised, "Just keep repeating it"—they would naturally deduce that their deity had abandoned them. They were jealous of **Dewa** and plotting to wrestle the good graces of the "great and powerful **Maha-kuasa**" from Bersatu. In order to placate **Dewa** and attract his attention, or so went the family lore, they would need **karang**—plus the blood of ritually sacrificed Bersatan baby girls, a provision **Mata-Mata** made up and added in for good measure. It worked perfectly, on a few fronts.

It was then easy enough to convince the people to harvest all the **karang** they could and deposit it for safekeeping in the royal palace. It mattered little to Ganda that this fostered, first, considerable illegal siphoning off of portions of the haul by private, petty thieves, and secondly a burgeoning black market for the stuff. For one, **Mata-Mata** reasoned, that would limit the public supply and dramatically increase the value, which would only perpetuate the myth. "And," he said, provide logical justification for beefing up the **Instansi** for an internal "war on vice."

Externally, he sent his great navy, the vaunted **laut**, casting about off the shores of other island nations poaching their foreign **ka-rang**, provoking war-like gestures against the marauding pirates, allowing Ganda to angrily proclaim, "We're under attack! They hate our ships, our way of life, they're coming to get you!" It was easy enough then to build up a massive **tentara,** conscripting any and all able-bodied men and boys as foot soldiers in defense of the "**tanah air!**"—which was a bit confusing for some Bersatans, actually: translated one way, the phrase meant "ground water," which had many of them staring down at the sodden earth beneath their feet wondering why they should have to defend such a thing, and exactly how would one **do** that. Translated another, of course, it meant "Fatherland."

"That's **perfect**," said **Mata-Mata.** "Confusion is **good**."

The formula of confusion, perpetual war and fear was, in fact, just about perfect. It was more than enough to consolidate power and pursue antagonisms against friend and foe alike. Ganda had his mother committed to a state asylum, his father to bed. His brother Tusukan disappeared, under circumstances that were never less than suspicious, but no one was about to challenge the **tertinggi** Ganda Anda, especially with the nation quaking beneath threat level **merah**.

But all of Ganda's machinations weren't

enough to fend off a force greater even than **Dewa**. Nature, it seemed, was intent on recovering all of the looted **karang**. It unleashed a millennial **umbak**, sixty-foot waves, dwarfing even the tallest of structures, swamping entire islands, leaving little if anything in its wake. Turns out that the **karang** reefs, apart from all their other purported decorative or mystical qualities, had once served as a pretty effective wave break, busting off most rogue walls of water at their knees, significantly limiting damage. After years and years of wholesale harvest and hoarding, the Bersatans were left completely defenseless.

Those few, lucky islanders who managed to survive with their lives, the barest of abodes, and a modicum of drenched possessions, took those possessions—either shreds of cloth, pieces of glass, even the brightly colored and now completely useless **karang**—and used them to spell out pleas for help, "**MEMBANTU**," on what was left of their huts or any other flat, dry surface, beseeching their precious **Dewa**, presumably, since no one else was likely to come to their aid. "HELP US."

"WHAT the fuck is this?"

"Al? I *just* emailed those pages," Jerry said, looking at his computer, as if for explanation.

"I *know*," Al said. "What the fuck is it?"

"It's more of a synopsis than anything else," Jerry started. "The idea just came to me, you know, with everything that's going on."

"You sure you want to do this?"

"Why not, too pointed?"

"Not pointed enough, actually," Al told him. "But you sure you want to make fun of religion?"

"I'm not making fun of religion. I'm making fun of faith."

"What's religion without faith?"

"Depends on the faith. Some of it's pretty silly."

"*All* of it's silly, Weave. Are you *sure* you want to do this?"

"Some of it's sillier than others."

"As silly as this?"

"Are you kidding? Take a look at fourteenth century France."

In the midst of the plague, King Philip asked University medical professors for an explanation. They duly reported that "a disturbance in the skies"—code, that is, for an "angry God"—had caused the overheating of Eastern oceans, loosing noxious vapors that brought about the pestilence. Not to worry, though, there was a fix. Broth, for one, if seasoned with pepper, ginger, and cloves, was a good starter. Meat was bad, olive oil deadly, as was bathing, though enemas might be helpful. Chastity, above all else, was a life saver.

When that didn't work, the King issued an edict against blasphemy to try and assuage God. Anyone caught taking the Lord's name in vain would have their lip cut off. A second offense cost the other lip, and a third, the tongue.

Further laws prohibited the tolling of bells, wearing black clothing, gatherings of more than two people at a funeral, and any display of grief in public. All work after noon on Saturday was banned, as was gambling and swearing in general, and anyone living in sin had to get married immediately. That was good for the hitching business, bad for the dice makers. They started making rosaries instead, astute businessmen that they were, recognizing a wave of opportunity when they saw one.

"When they would have been much better off, and maybe even *really* saved, by eating a little moldy bread," Jerry said.

"I get it," Al said. "What next?"

"Not sure yet. Figure I'll watch some more news. These clowns are pretty dependable for ideas."

"—DOESN'T care about black people."

The look on Myers' face was priceless. He stood there in near panic, casting nervously about for an off-camera rescue and finally just said, "Please call," before they cut to commercial.

"Fucking A," Jerry said, muted the noise again, and dialed.

"Congratulations."

"Excuse me?" Jerry said, to the oddly familiar voice.

"Congratulations," she said again. "You solved the riddle."

"Coyote?"

"Ding, ding, ding."

"What the…"

"Not important now," she said. "I need you to do something."

"What?"

"Go to Alabama."

"Alabama? Why would I want to do that?"

"Why wouldn't you?"

"It's *Alabama*."

"I know, I know," she said. "But listen." She told him about Peter, his disappearance, what he'd been on to before disappearing.

"And you think they're really trying to force end times?"

"All the signs are there."

"Then why'd you send me on that goose chase about unraveling the dynasty?"

"Because he's the one that tipped the balance between fundamentalist GOP and secular liberals, toward theocracy. Have you read any of that insane dominionist shit?"

"You know, I heard a funny line about that. Something like, other presidents petitioned for blessings and guidance, but he positions himself as a prophet, speaking *for* God."

"*That's* why I sent you after him."

"Okay, so what's next?"

"Alabama. Talk to Peter, find out what spooked him, what he knows."

"What makes you think he'll talk to me if he's so spooked?"

"His brother Jack will be with you. He's there now, waiting for you."

"It'd help if I had some idea where this is supposed to go."

"Right. Look, all I can tell you is what I suspect. In all the various apocalyptic schemes, there's one general commonality. They've *got* to rebuild the temple."

"On the Mount."

"Right. Antichrists and false prophets come and go, earthquakes, volcanoes, who can ever tell if all that's prophecy or not. Hell, they think credit cards and bar codes are the 'mark of the beast.' The one thing that absolutely has to happen is rebuilding that temple."

"And you think that can be stopped?"

"I have no idea. But I know what'll happen if it isn't."

That much was indisputable. Controlled by Israel since 1967 but managed by the Muslim Waqf, for non-Muslims to even set foot on the Mount is enough—has been enough—to spark violence in the region. They don't even like archeological excavations of the site—which supposedly contains the "Foundation Rock," from which the rest of the known world sprung—its regarded as that sacred, protected that fiercely.

"I thought you wanted me to write a book?"

"I wanted you to get to the truth."

"I *always* get to the truth."

"Yeah, I know, reporters *always* say that. But you're not the gatekeepers of the truth. Your owners are."

"Nobody owns me."

Why is it, Jerry wondered, every time I talk to this woman she annoys me. And why, then, another part of him asked, do I keep talking to her?

"Which is why I called you."

"So how was a book supposed to stop anything?"

"It wasn't. And frankly, we'd be better off with a lot less books."

"That's encouraging."

"It's a theory."

"You know who you're dealing with, right?"

"Yes, I do. The question is, do you?"

"Fanatics."

"Worse. Those nineteen guys that flew planes into buildings, why'd they do it?"

"They certainly weren't cowards," as the conservative media repeatedly referred to the hijackers, and then browbeat anyone who disagreed with them as unpatriotic.

"No, they were men of perfect faith. They believed, word for word, their *book*." And they weren't crazy, was the notion she'd lately been formulating. That was the thing about faith, especially *perfect* faith. It allowed otherwise normal human beings to do insane, horrific things, and consider them holy, justified, even required, all because of some ancient, preposterous, *absurd* literature.

"So what chance do the rest of us have?"

"Not much at all, unless they're called out."

"That, I can do," Jerry said, unsure until that very moment how much of this he was going to go along with. It seemed, suddenly, that if anything in this world ought to be unraveled, this was it. And, he had to admit, he'd *love* to have a hand in that.

"Good," Marilyn said. "Call me back when you've got travel plans. And Jerry," she said, the first time she'd ever used his name, "be careful with the phone. Jack's other brother, Paul, has gone missing."

"Fuck," Jerry said after hanging up. "Playing with the big boys." It was at one and the same time an adrenalizing and a sobering thought. He didn't know whether to get good and drunk, or buy a flak jacket.

He didn't do either, mostly. He did manage to get a little tipsy as he set about gathering the things he might need for this trip he knew no other dimensions of—how long he'd be gone, whether he'd return at all. He vacillated between taking everything he could, to taking nothing at all.

It was a curious dilemma—like going off to war, or readying to meet your maker, whatever that might mean. Some choices were easy, rote—toiletries, extra socks, good shoes. Others not so much: Books? Suntan lotion? Baseball glove?

It all really hit home when he went to make his plane reservation. Even the on-line service was complicit, defaulting the options to "round trip." The irony of deliberately switching that to "one way," tickled the shit out of him and snuffed out any residual, flickering sense of caution. "What's the worst that could happen?" he said.

He called Coyote back and relayed his itinerary—leaving LAX in the morning, Mobile by noon.

"Good," she said. "Jack will be waiting."

"Got any tips with Peter?" he asked.

"Ask him about the temple."

"Duh," he said, laughing. "Hey, can I ask you a question?"

"Sure."

"How come you're not going to Alabama?"

"How do you know I'm not already there?"

"Lucky guess. That, and the area code."

He would not be dissuaded. It's not like the question hadn't occurred to her, or she didn't think it would come up. It was obvious, had always been obvious, but she had yet to steel herself enough to confront it. She thought about her answer, then, a long minute, and another. It was time, she knew, for brutal honesty, in this desperate quest for truth. He waited.

"Because I *am* a coward," she finally said.

"You know," Jerry told her, "up until this moment I was never really sure if I liked you or not."

"And?"

"You're all right."

"Well, at least I've got that going for me."

"Wish me luck."

"You've got to be good to be lucky."

"And there it is."

15.

"THIS guy's nuts," Jerry said into the pre-paid he'd bought on the way from the airport in west Mobile.

"Aren't we all," she laughed. "Aren't we all."

"No, I mean *really* nuts."

He'd been there three days already, three days of following the guy around aimlessly, hoping against hope he'd meander onto a subject, any subject, of interest. Once they were allowed on the premises, that is.

"Halt!" they'd been greeted at the head of the drive—well, not really a drive, as much as parallel ruts grooved into the rough grass.

Jack ducked for cover in the driver's seat, banging his forehead on the lip of the steering wheel, "What the fuck."

"It's a BB gun," Jerry told him, pulling him back up by the shoulder. "Is that your brother?"

Jack straightened, one hand on his head, one eye squinted, said, "Yeah, that's Peter."

"What say we go meet him?" Jerry said.

They got out of the sedan, hands raised in surrender.

"Peter, it's me, Jack."

Nobody moved.

"You sure that's your bother?" Jerry asked, after several seconds of the standoff.

Jack looked over at him quizzically, took a few steps forward, said again, "Peter?"

Still no recognition.

"Are you Peter Pardew?" Jerry tried, taking a few tentative steps forward himself. That resulted in the BB gun being swung in his direction.

"Who the fuck are you?"

"I'm Jack, your brother."

"My brother, huh." He shifted the weapon back onto its original target. "What kind of dog did you get for Christmas when you were five years old?"

Jack looked over at Jerry. "Puppy?" he tried.

"I never got any dog," Jack answered. "Mom was allergic to pets."

Peter put down the gun, said, "Can't take any chances these days."

"Jesus, Peter," Jack said. "Can't take any chances of what?"

But he'd turned his back, ascended the three short porch steps and disappeared into the house.

"You *sure* that's your brother?" Jerry asked again.

They traced the path onto the porch, found the kitchen door there locked. Jack called through the partially opened window-panes into the darkened room, "Peter, we just want to talk to you."

Silence.

"Really, Peter. We just want to talk."

"Talk to me?" a voice came back from somewhere inside. "How do you propose to do that when you can't even address me properly?"

They stared at each other.

"How are we supposed to address you?" Jerry asked.

"As Mr. Mayor, numb nuts."

Jerry shook his head. "Mr. Mayor, we'd like to talk to you."

"Why didn't you say so?" he asked, appearing at the door suddenly.

"Mayor of what?" Jerry asked, stepping into the kitchen behind Jack.

He didn't answer Jerry, looked at Jack instead, said, "You're the gay one, right?"

Jack cocked his head, asked, "The gay what?"

"It's all right, we don't hold that against you here."

"What's 'here'?" Jerry tried again.

"Waterhole Branch."

Jerry almost wished he hadn't asked.

"We'll have to talk on the move," the Mayor told them. "Lots of work to do," and sauntered out of the kitchen, through an interior room, and onto another porch on the other side of the house.

They followed, past an extremely dangerous looking homemade spiral staircase that disappeared into the ceiling, walls, furniture, the floor, even, littered with books and album jackets, and found him out on the porch standing before a primed canvas, paint brush clutched in a knurled left hand, holding that elbow with his right hand down in front of himself, looking pensively off into the distance.

"Mr. Mayor?"

"Something's missing," he answered, without breaking the pose or otherwise acknowledging their existence.

After a few more frozen seconds, he said, "Music," and vanished inside once more.

Moments later Sam Cooke's raspy voice was blaring from speakers big and little suspended everywhere, crooning "A

Change is Gonna Come." The Mayor reappeared, briefly, slipped the paintbrush into a breast pocket, walked past the easel out into the bright sunshine, picked up a shovel and started digging into the turf of his lawn.

"Mr. Mayor?" Jerry said again.

"What's on your mind?" he answered, without breaking stride, poking the shovel face into the ground, stepping on the back lip and then leveraging a dark clod out of place.

"What are you doing, Peter?" Jack asked.

When he didn't respond, Jerry prompted Jack with a shrug.

"What are you doing, Mr. Mayor?"

He stopped, looked at him. "What are you, stupid? I'm digging a moat."

"A moat?" Jerry asked.

"Yes, a moat. You know, a ditch, filled with water, maybe an alligator or two, for protection. You saw how easily you two infiltrated the compound."

"The compound?"

But he was gone, leaving the shovel stuck in the ground. He'd moved on to a wheelbarrow, filled with assorted short lengths of lumber, and was pushing down the slope of the lawn toward a river bank, sixty yards away.

For three days it went like that. The information they'd gathered over the course of that time could have been gleaned from a five-minute conversation with any normal person. The compound, Waterhole Branch, was seven-and-a-half acres of land the Mayor owned abutting a tributary of Fish River, in southeast Alabama, thirty minutes from the Gulf of Mexico, light years from sanity. It was accessible only via a quarter-mile twisting dirt road that peeled off paved County Road 24 and ended at the Branch, or by a short-draft boat likewise winding a quarter-mile westward from the main river. The land itself was pockmarked with stout live oak trees, each one draping lush, ghostly shrouds of Spanish moss from several thick limbs, as well as the Mayor's assorted projects. Beside the mote, there was a larger hole carved out of the flattest part of the property farthest from the river. What was at one time, they were told, going to be a swimming pool, was now the presumably final resting place for a dilapidated vintage wooden Boston Whaler, for reasons they didn't even bother to ask.

Flanking the pool was a twenty-foot high pile, or "monument," the Mayor called it, of abandoned appliances, and ladders, and fencing, skeletons of metal chairs, pieces of shelving. There was a naked shower nozzle attached to a utility pole, an outhouse constructed of empty beer cans, a massive fire pit from which the aroma of a recent blaze still wafted, surrounded by what he called his "outdoor living room," an over-stuffed armchair, a recliner, a wooden bench, a church pew and three bar stools. On the sharpest slope of the yard leading to the water two wooden doors lay on the grass, the "entrance," he said, to his bomb shelter. But when Jerry reached for one of the knobs and lifted it there was nothing underneath but grass that had been covered up long enough to start turning brown.

The pieces of timber in the wheelbarrow, they were told, were to reinforce a cobbled together fifteen-foot tall wooden scaffolding down at the water's edge, his "guard tower." A ladder-back kitchen chair set at its peak, nailed into place, with a yellow and green umbrella shading the seat.

The lot was dotted with various vehicles of questionable utility—everything from a burly Suburban SUV to the little red scooter—but the only driving he did while they were there was aboard his big orange Kubota tractor accessorized with a green 3210 brush hog that he rode around in for hours at a time, not cutting grass, not doing anything, it seemed, beyond patrolling the perimeter.

"They're going to have a hell of a time getting me out of here," he said to them one night over a plate of red beans and rice, their second night there, their fourth consecutive meal of beans and rice.

"Who?" Jerry asked.

"I got everything I need," he said. "Plenty of beans, plenty of water." He'd showed them where he kept nearly an entire bay of what in normal environs would have been a garage stacked with cases of bottled water and fifty-pound bags of dried beans and rice, under lock and key.

"It's gonna take all seven angels and all their vials and trumpets to get me to budge, I'm telling you."

"What about the temple?" Jerry tried, out of the blue, which seemed perfectly appropriate, considering.

"Your body's your temple, son," the Mayor told him, then went off on a rant about trans-fat and corn sugar. "You look like you could use some more roughage," he said, reached into the refrigerator and pulled out half a head of cabbage and set it on the table.

He woke them the next morning by proclaiming, "You know they're going to get their Armageddon," he said, "just as soon as they grow that crimson calf, so you'd better be ready," silhouetting the doorway to the room they were staying in. "Now, who's up for a dump run?"

"ALL RIGHT, all right, so he's nuts. Did he tell you anything?"

"He said something about a crimson calf."

"Crimson calf?"

"Armageddon, seven angels, once they get the cow," Jerry continued.

"That's *it*," she said. "The red heifer."

"I'm beginning to think all you people are nuts."

"No, it makes perfect sense. Listen."

Simply rebuilding the temple won't do anyone any good unless they can enter it and perform the necessary rituals. And for that they need the ashes of a pure, three-year-old red heifer.

"Says who?"

"Says God, supposedly."

Numbers: "Speak to the people of Israel, that they bring you a red heifer without spot, which has no blemish, and upon which never came yoke." The perfect red heifer, then, is burnt—"its skin, and its flesh, and its blood, with its dung"—its ashes mixed with spring water, and only in that manner can the priests be ritually purified to the specifications necessary to enter the Temple.

"*That's* nuts."

"Yeah, that's what Solomon said."

"Solomon?"

"You know, Jewish King, three-thousand years ago, built the first Temple. Smartest guy around, allegedly, but even he couldn't figure it out."

"So they're waiting around for a red bull."

"Heifer," she said.

"Wow, tough audience."

"This is serious, Jerry. He's right, once they get their cow, there's nothing else to stop them. But they're not that easy to come by. Hasn't been one in two thousand years, since the last Temple.

It has to be perfect, without a single off-color hair. They thought they had one in 1997, just in time for millennial end-times, and again a couple of years ago, but they both turned."

And each time news of the births brought immediate, vehement responses, from all parties concerned. Zealots, of course, took it as a sign from God, that Christ's return was imminent, and fringe groups actually put plans in play to storm the Temple Mount and destroy it, in preparation for the rebuilding of the Jewish Temple. Muslims, needless to say, went ballistic, rioting, taking up arms. So-called moderate Jews, predictably, recognized the events for their explosively destabilizing potential, but called merely for the destruction of the cows, otherwise leaving the fundamentalists—Jewish, Muslim, *and* Christian, who were *so* helpful, in *so* many ways, from funds, to breeding assistance, to cheerleading: the siege, conquest and destruction of the Jewish state—not to mention the slaughter of non-converting Jews themselves—as an essential component of New Testament end-times prophecy—to their own devices.

"Tell me *exactly* what he said."

"He said something like 'you know they're going to get their Armageddon, just as soon as they grow that crimson calf.'"

"They who?"

"Who knows with this guy?"

"We've got to find out."

"Do you know what it's like trying to communicate with this fruitcake?"

"Yes, yes."

They found him out on the farthest reaches of his property, clearing away weeds and tall grass with a small chain saw, sweeping it horizontally like a scythe.

"Mr. Mayor," Jerry tried, over the tubercular two-stroke engine. "Can I ask you a question?"

His response was lost in the noise.

"What?" Jack yelled.

He cut the engine, said, "I already know the answer."

"The answer to what?" Jack asked.

"The answer to the question."

"You don't even know the question," Jerry said.

"Doesn't matter," he said, starting up the tool again. "The answer is nine. The answer is always nine," he said, returning to work.

Jerry threw his hands up, turned, and stomped off.

Later, back down by the riverbank, the Mayor was threading lengths of rope through eyelets screwed into three-foot planks of wood.

"What's that?" they asked.

"A bridge."

"A bridge?" they both asked, incredulously. "A bridge for what?"

"For there," he said, pointing across ten feet of placid water to an overgrown copse of land supporting maybe half a dozen trees the river had split around and appeared to swallow at regular intervals, from the mildewed sogginess of the place. "Last Chance Atoll."

They stared at him blankly.

"You know there's a monument in Helena, Montana, built in 1916, commemorating the Confederates of Last Chance Gulch."

"You talk to him," Jerry said, walking off again.

That evening, after another serving of rice and beans, once everyone had retired, Jerry asked into the darkness, "Anything?"

"Not really," Jack said. Then, "Maybe. It's kind of hard to tell."

"I know what you mean."

"He didn't used to be like this."

"Really, how did he used to be?"

"Well, he used to be," Jack thought. "Cogent."

"Those were the days."

"He said we had a cousin, Steve, in Down Land, Texas."

"What the fuck does that mean?"

"I have no idea," Jack said. "And I checked an old atlas he had lying around. I couldn't find any Down Land, Texas."

"Figures."

In what had become a regular feature of the start to their day, the Mayor announced the next morning, "It's the supralapsarianists," turning from the doorway, calling, "Remember to eliminate your debt!"

"THERE *is* no Down Land, Texas," she said.

"I told you that."

She'd thought she'd have more luck locating the place online, versus the dated Rand-McNally they were limited to.

"He must be confused."

"Confused would be a blessing."

"And what was the other thing?"

"Eliminate your debt."

"Not that. The *other* thing."

"Supra, something," Jerry said. "Lapsarian, maybe. Christ, I don't know."

It took her a while, but she figured it out, kind of. The second clue was actually the better of the two. Once she put the word back together she traced it to the Calvinist belief that once predestined, God's elect people could do no wrong. Those seemed like exactly the flavor of people that would feel no compunction whatsoever about hastening the apocalypse. "Justified sinners," they called themselves, sounding an awfully lot like and acting on the same twisted impulses as their *jihadist* brethren.

After that, she just needed a little luck, matching Calvin to some physical location in Texas. There was, in fact, a Calvin, Texas, thirty miles southeast of Austin, though she couldn't for the life of her figure why he'd refer to it as Down Land. There was a Geneva, Texas, near San Augustine, sixty miles north of Port Arthur, but there again, no matter how many languages she translated it through she couldn't come up with anything hinting at a connection.

She looked at the history of Calvinism, from the beginnings in Strasbourg, to his being an early signatory of Luther's Augsburg Confessions, but came up empty with those. She traced its spread from Concord to Scotland to England to the Netherlands, and came up with only one hit there, Scotland, Texas, way the hell on the other side of Dallas.

That's when the luck kicked in. She remembered, for some reason, that Netherlands in Dutch is actually Nederland, and sure enough, it both translated to English as Down Land, *and* there was a Nederland, Texas, outside of Port Arthur.

"I got four possibilities for you," she told Jerry.

"That's all."

"Yeah, and the first, the closest one, is the most likely."

"What, exactly, am I looking for?"

"A cattle ranch, of course," she told him.

"I'm sure there aren't that many of those in Texas."

"Run by fundamentalists."

"That supposed to make me feel better?"

But he actually welcomed the seemingly hopeless quest, for the ranch, the uber-right ranchers, and their herd of crimson cattle—almost anything to get away from the Mayor, lest he kill himself, or someone else. They discussed leaving Jack behind at Waterhole Branch—and Jerry felt truly sorry for that—in case the Mayor was forthcoming with any more information.

"You're going to leave me here?" he shouted over Jerry's shoulder when he heard his half of the negotiations.

"Tell him it's his brother."

"It's your brother."

"So? He's trying to kill me. If I eat any more beans I'll explode."

"He's got a point there," Jerry said into the phone.

"Tell him to grow a pair."

"I'll leave that to you," Jerry said, hanging up.

"Leave what to her?"

"Advice."

"Bitch."

"You don't *really* want to go to Texas, do you?" Jerry asked him.

"Hell no," Jack answered. "But I don't *really* want to stay here, either."

"Shouldn't be long," Jerry told him, and started gathering up his things.

"You actually think you're going to find this guy, this place?"

Jerry stared back at him for several moments. "Not really." He expected to find a sleepy little Texas town, probably some brash talkers, possibly some disgruntled libertines—how far was Nederland from Waco?—but little else. He couldn't quite make himself believe that an oil-busted coastal Texas town could tilt the world one way or another. But he'd go. He didn't know what he'd do when he got there, didn't know what cover he'd use, but he'd go.

16.

"You *found* him?" Marilyn said, as surprised as anyone else.

"I got a lead on him."

"How'd you do that?"

"Hang around long enough, you can usually find out anything."

"And no one wondered why you were hanging around?"

"Told them I was interested in high-school football."

"That always works."

"Nothing gets them talking quicker."

He drove the four hundred miles from Waterhole Branch in a straight shot, checked into the Villa Motel on Nederland Avenue. The next morning he roamed around the town, just to get its pulse. The other main drag, Boston Avenue, two blocks over, had been the commercial center since its founding, a hundred-some years earlier. It was the usual mix of dry goods, florists, pet stores, fast food, banks, churches, the Chamber of Commerce. It was an easily imagined place, full of older white people coursing the aged routines of their day, serviced and waited on by young immigrants. Jerry figured there was a black section of town, probably along the railroad tracks or pushed up against refinery row by the river.

He found a café downtown and spent his mornings headquartered there, sitting at the counter with a constant cup of coffee, letting whatever conversations would come to him, which wasn't difficult, given he was tagged as an outsider immediately. And *everyone* liked to talk about local football.

The second morning he found what he was looking for, what every town has at least one of, a café regular and amateur historian named Sam, gruff old guy who sported flannel shirts and denim overalls, spoke with authority about anything he chose, in a folksy, homegrown style.

"Ya know this is the oldest continuously running business in Nederland?"

"The café?"

"Usta be a pharmacy, but yup, right here in the Wagner Building."

He'd prattle on without any prompting, which was fine, occasionally including other regulars in the tales.

"Hey, Petey, you remember the old Rat Theater?" he'd call out.

"Oh, yeah, the Reo."

"Rat theater?"

"Usta be when the light first flashed on the screen, big ol' rat shadow running along the board," he said, imitating the creature across the counter, Jerry's forearm, laughing a big, boisterous laugh.

He told further tales about Boston Avenue businesses—the three saloons that "usta" be in one block alone, but were shut down in 1909 after the town's first murder occurred in one of them. "Town stayed dry for thirty years," before three honky-tonks sprung up during the war years, but were soon likewise put out of business, "By arsonists," Sam said.

"Alleged arsonists," someone tried to correct him.

"They never caught nobody," he told Jerry. "But everone

knows what happened."

Other times he'd launch a question to the general gathering, "What's the *only* Texas town that's ever been Dutch-English bi-linguated?"

"Nederland," the answer came.

When he offered to take Jerry on a tour of the town, the high-school football stadium, the old Mashed-O ranch, and Jerry happily accepted, Sam passed a pint bottle of Evan Williams beneath the counter for Jerry to "jazz up" his coffee, Jerry knew he'd scored a friend.

Jerry tried to cement it by responding, "Sam, you know where I can get some of that?" he said, gesturing to where Sam had pocketed the bottle. "I've been looking for a liquor store."

"Oh, yeah," he said. "There's one out on 347. We can go there directly. Just finish that up," he said, raising his own cup.

It was while they were out on the road, in between stories—"That ranch rightere," he said, pointing to empty pastureland, "25,000 cows died in 1935 after a three-day sleet storm, froze to death, just standing at the fence. Put a lot of people to work skinning hides, though."—that he finally asked, "Why Nederland?"

Jerry told him he had a distant cousin, Steve, who was from around those parts, remembered him talking about the football, "And the ghost stories."

"Aw, hell, boy, none a them stories is true," Sam said, but then proceeded to catalogue the various sightings and pointing out the supposed sites, the secondary school, the mustachioed man at Smith's Bluff, the woman with a sword sticking out of her head at Adam's Park, and the hooded woman at Anderson Gully.

He also allowed as how he thought he knew a Steve Pardew,

seemed to recall he worked at the Ag Center, out by the airport.

"The Ag Center?" Marilyn said. "Sounds promising."

"Yeah, it does," Jerry said. "I'm going to check it out in the morning."

"You got a plan?"

"That's what I'm calling you about. What is it you want to accomplish?"

"Well," she said, careful about the words she chose, lest any of them get snared in a Boolean net. "Expose it, of course. If you could get any scoop on the breadth of the network, that'd be good."

"How do you know there's a network?"

"There're organizations that've been prepping for this for years."

"Anything else?"

"If they've got a red one, if it went away would be best."

"How much of this is legal?"

"We're talking about people that want to bring back Deutero-nomic governance, *and* the end of the world," she said. "And you think we should be concerned with legalities?"

"Good point."

"Damn right good point."

"Am I ever going to get to meet you?" Jerry asked.

"Let's hope we make it that far," she said, even as she felt a reflexive cringe at anything hinting at social interaction.

"Fair enough," he said. "I'm ditching this phone. I'll be in touch."

Then she waited.

Jerry immediately worried over exactly how he was going to get far enough into the plant to find anything out. He could go all "Sneakers" on them, setting up sophisticated surveillance equipment, spying for weak spots, exploitable routines.

"People always say I kind of favor Redford," he said, something he never failed to not argue with.

Given that thought, he wondered if he shouldn't just try to pick up some woman, "Or guy," leaving work in the afternoon, try to get them to offer up info. Charm the story out of them.

"Right," he said.

Neither plan—if you could call them that—seemed particularly interesting, or affordable, or doable, to say the least. And then he remembered what Coyote had said about the hijackers, that they were men of "perfect faith."

If that was true, he thought, it came with an abundance of absolute certainty, a blind self-righteousness. They wouldn't then, of necessity, think they were doing anything wrong, wouldn't perhaps, be attuned to anyone snooping around in their midst, if that someone had indeed been accepted into their midst. Seemed simple enough: He'd apply for a job.

He decided to spend the next morning just checking out the physical layout of the plant, and then the weekend at the Assembly of God church, studying the men in the congregation for a believable costume.

Monday morning he showed up at the Human Resources Department with his hair slicked down, sporting the dullest and weakest solid-framed reading glasses off the rack, and the gayest polo shirt he could find at the mall. He applied for a Maintenance Technician's job, after reading the postings tacked to the glassed-in bulletin board inside. According to the description it required only a high school diploma, came with minimal supervision and was part time. He would roam around the plant completing "work orders," tweaking shit here, swapping out there, hauling stuff out of the way. Perfect.

The other thing he picked up over the weekend was that you simply could not go wrong in the fundamentalist world by praising God. You could not overdo it. He'd tested. Asked, in the vestibule after service Sunday evening, standing there with his "Visitor" sticker in place, how he had come to land in Nederland, he answered brightly, "God steered me here." They ate it up.

So he was ready in the interview for the inevitable, "What made you choose us?"

Jerry answered, "God told me to seek a higher calling."

He got the job.

"Who knew?"

TWO months later, Marilyn got an email from the Beaumont Public Library. In the body of the message was only a link, to an article in the *Beaumont Enterprise*. "Designer Apocalypse, Texas Style," by special correspondent to the *Enterprise*, Jerry Weaver.

"He did it," she said to Jack.

Jack'd made his way back from Alabama some weeks earlier, bearing a gift. When he showed up at her place, banging on the door repeatedly as she tried to ignore him, hollering, "God*damn* it, Marilyn, open the door! This thing is heavy," she opened the door to find him standing there holding it.

"What's that?" she asked, after hugging him.

"A wind chime," he said. "Courtesy of the Mayor."

Peter hadn't allowed Jack to leave before it was completed. From a vicious looking giant fishing hook he'd strung pretzel bent heavy-duty wire and from the bends in the wire he'd used fishing line to hang warped utensils, pieces of colored glass, telephone parts, crucifixes, old Zippos: junk.

Joe Formichella

"Be careful with that thing," Marilyn said as he tried to push it on her.

"I've been carrying this thing for 700 miles," Jack said. "I ain't carrying it no more."

"What does it mean?" she asked, handling it gingerly.

"Means, like Jerry said, he's *nuts*."

"And he calls himself the Mayor."

"Right."

"Mayor of what?"

"Waterhole Branch," Jack said, already knowing that any attempt to make any kind of sense out of what had become of his brother, for himself or anyone else, would only drive him crazy as well. He wasn't even going to tell his mother he'd seen him.

"But what *is* that, Waterhole Branch."

Jack closed his eyes against the ensuing headache. "It's an Art Commune."

"And there are other artists there?"

"He said there were, said there was a painter, a sculptor, several writers, a whole rock-and-roll band, the requisite groupies, a playwright, a couple of actors, and a mime."

"A mime?"

"That's right," Jack said, slowly nodding his head. "A mime."

"And?"

"And, a 'hula-hoop artist.'"

"A what?"

Jack stared at her. Then he said, "We never saw any evidence of any other human being on the place. Just a couple of fat old lazy dogs who slept in the yard all day and farted all night—their diet consisting of rice and beans, too. But we did see a hula-hoop."

"Really," she answered. "That's kind of scary."

"Tell me about it!"

"He's gone nuts."

"*Thank* you."

They scanned the article together. In it, Jerry introduced the world to the group behind the effort, CUFTIT—"Rather unfortunate acronym," Jack said—Christians United For The Israeli Temple, and their work to bioengineer a suitable red heifer that could be donated to the WWTF—"Another unfortunate acronym"—Worldwide Temple Foundation, the folks spearheading the push to rebuild the Temple Mount. They were using stem cell advancements, chemical polymerization, *in vitro* insemination, all in the rush to deliver the elusive *Parah Adumah*.

"You won't find any of that shit in Numbers," Marilyn grumbled.

"It's kind of exciting," one plant worker said for the record, "like a global competition, to be the first to grow one," and then provided a list of other groups after the same goal.

"He really fucking did it," Marilyn said, bouncing up and down in her seat, jiggling the screen.

"We're just trying to hurry God up," one engineer told Jerry.

"Do you *believe* this shit?"

He'd gotten quoted reactions, too, and none of them good. Ministers, rabbis, priests, and especially mullahs all over southeast Texas condemned the program, demanded it be shut down.

"These people are playing with *very* serious fire," one said.

"This is *not* God's work."

"Allah will *not* be merciful."

"See, there're good people," Jack said. "Even in Texas."

"I guess."

"Even good religious people."

"I'm not ready to go that far."

"Then God's still got to go."

"I'm working on it."

Epilogue

Two days after that she had another email from the Beaumont Public Library, with another link to the *Enterprise*'s on-line page. She opened it, saw right away it was their obituary page, said to Jack, "You read it," getting up and pacing back and forth in front of him.

He sat with the laptop perched on his knees, scrolled down the page until he saw a familiar face. "Aw, shit," he said.

"What?"

"Jerry Weaver, award-winning investigative journalist was found dead last night in his room at the Beaumont Red Carpet Inn."

"Of what?" she demanded.

"It doesn't say, Mare. It's just an obit piece."

"Find a news article."

Jack searched, and after a little bit, said, "Here we go. Jerry Weaver, blah, blah, blah," he said, skimming. "Authorities have ruled it a suicide."

"Damn it," she said, stomping her foot, feeling the tears forming. "How?" she said again.

Jack kept reading. "Gunshot wound to the head."

"He didn't have a gun, did he?"

"Not that I know of," Jack said. "Oh, but get this: it says *two* gunshot wounds to the head."

"I *knew* it."

"This is weird."

"What?"

"It says there was a message written in blood on the carpet next to his body."

"Message?"

"Ganda Anda burned alive."

"What the hell does that mean?"

"Search me."

As they both pondered the message, Jack went back to the original email, asking, "Who sent you this?"

"How should I know."

"Fuck!" Jack said, when it dawned on him what that meant, jumping up from the chair, dropping the computer onto its cushion and backing away from it as if the thing was ticking. "How did they find you?"

"I don't care."

"You don't *care*?"

"I don't care. Who's the next name on your list?"

"*List*? What list?"

"List of reporters, snoops, someone willing to go after these guys."

"Go after them? Do you know who you're fucking with?"

"Yes I do. And so do you. And a whole lot of other people *ought* to know. Because you know what, Jack," she said, agitated now, more than saddened, or frightened, "they sure as hell aren't going to have any 'come to Jesus' moment and stop all on their own, now, are they," she said, throwing her arms up at her sides.

Jack just smiled at her.

"What?"

"Now I know what he meant."

"Who?"

"Jerry. Last thing he said to me, as he was leaving for Texas, he said, 'What's the worst that can happen?'"

Joe Formichella

End

"JERRY?"

"Al?"

"Are you all right?"

"Sure. Why do you ask?

"This, this," he stammered, unsure of what to call it.

"The book?"

"Yeah, I guess. The book."

"What about it?"

"It's, it's," Al said, again stymied by exactness.

"Different?"

"What does it mean?"

"Doesn't mean anything. I made it all up."

"All of it?"

"Al, it's fiction."

"All of it?" he asked again.

"What don't you understand about fiction?"

"Coyote?"

"Fiction."

"Marilyn?"

"Fiction."

"The phone calls?"

"Al, nobody's interested in the truth these days. They prefer a good lie. That's all this is, a good lie."

"The Mayor?"

"Sounds like you got into it."

"No, Jerry, you *put* me into it."

"We never had those conversations."

"But *I'm* real!"

"I thought you'd be pleased."

"Fatally pleased, more than likely."

"Then you think it'll fly?"

"If by that you mean will people react, are you kidding?"

"That's good. Because it's all true."

"But you just said…"

"I said the story's fiction. The facts are true."

"Goddamn it, Jerry, which is it? Tell me the truth."

"I *did*."

"Which?"

"All of them."

"The red heifer?"

"True."

"The president?"

"True."

"Arafat?"

"Jerry?"

"Jerry?"

The guy responsible for all this.